THE
DAY-DREAMING LADY

THE DAY-DREAMING LADY

=== Jacqueline Diamond ===

Walker and Company
New York

First published in the United States of America
in 1985 by the Walker Publishing Company, Inc.

Published simultaneously in Canada by John Wiley & Sons
Canada, Limited, Rexdale, Ontario.

Library of Congress Cataloging in Publication Data

Diamond, Jacqueline.
  The day-dreaming lady.
    I. Title.
PS3554.I24D3   1985   813'.54   84-17284
ISBN 0-8027-0805-6

Printed in the United States of America

10 9 8 7 6 5 4 3 2 1

For Fannie

=1=

THE MATCHMAKING BEGAN the moment it was learned that Captain Kenneth Link, so recently lacking a feather to fly with, had—as a result of one carriage accident, one drowning, and one death from fever in India—unexpectedly inherited the title of Marquess of Broadmoor.

As well, of course, as a fortune.

Captain Link's accession to the title formerly held by his father's eldest brother became the talk of the assembly rooms at Almack's as well as of dozens of London drawing rooms, parlours, and sitting rooms, in which eager mamas mulled this new entry on the social scene. For he was not only wealthy, handsome, and personable but, at the age of thirty-two, remarkably unmarried.

Servants were sent scurrying from household to household to learn the latest titbits.

At least fifty ladies were informed the moment Broadmoor removed from the family seat outside Camelford to the handsome townhouse in Grosvenor Square.

Nor did the gossip-mongers spare themselves any details concerning the elegant breeches, coats, trousers, waistcoats, shirts, and neckcloths he ordered in Bond Street, with his boots, of course, from Hoby's.

And there were many to admire, before it was even delivered, his choice of a black and gold high-perch phaeton with brushed-brass hardware to add to the already extensive collection of carriages belonging to his estates.

It all pointed, everyone said, to one indisputable conclusion: The new marquess, casting off the grime of the battlefield where he had heroically acquitted himself the previous year under Wellington's command, intended to join the merry life of London's beau monde. And to what other end, the matrons demanded of themselves, than to find himself a wife? And who better suited than one's own daughter?

Nor were the young ladies themselves insensible of this new attraction in their narrow world. Although he had not yet presented himself among the *ton*, the very mention of Broadmoor's name added spice to the card parties, balls, Venetian breakfasts, and excursions to Vauxhall Gardens at which they pursued their careers of finding husbands.

As a topic of conversation, the new-made marquess rivaled even the departure of the scandalous Lord Byron from England. It was generally agreed that whatever lady should win the position of his marchioness would be unquestioningly acclaimed the Incomparable of the spring of 1816.

As for the man himself, details of his escapades at Cambridge, of his exemplary military service, and of his upbringing in the wild country of northwest Cornwall were pried and bribed from sons and nephews who had known him in his younger days.

However, the piece of gossip most cherished by the ladies concerned an earlier affair of the heart with Lady Sarah Rowdon, the pretty but shy daughter of the Earl of Rowdon. The cruelest thing said of her was that she lacked conversation; the cruelest thing said of her father, and unfortunately true, was that he had gambled away the family fortune.

The rumour spread that the marquess would make his first public appearance one Wednesday night at the exclusive weekly subscription ball at Almack's. It was finally confirmed by that arbiter of fashion, Lady Sally Jersey.

This was certain to be one of the most important social occasions of the year—eclipsed only, perhaps, by the wedding of Princess Charlotte to Prince Leopold of Saxe-Coburg—and a peek into chambers across London before the commencement of the ball would have revealed a flurry of activity.

The principals in the drama, everyone anticipated, were to be his lordship and the subject of his former *tendre*, Lady Sarah, along with her present suitor, Sir Lindsay Manx. But a number of other ladies were also determined, as they donned their ball-gowns and public faces, that they should be chosen to become the envy of their sex.

One might have expected Lady Estelle Mansfield to wear black for the occasion, her late husband—the Baron Mansfield—having gone to his Maker a mere ten months before. Black, however, did not flatter her pale blonde looks.

Yet white or pink, so well suited to girls in their first season, could only serve to remind an onlooker that Lady Mansfield had reached the less than exalted age of twenty-eight.

"Pale blue, I should think," suggested Mrs. Patience Buxton, Lady Mansfield's elderly cousin and companion. "Twas what I wore when I began going out again after Mr. Buxton died. And so fine with your grey eyes, my dear."

Lady Mansfield turned about in astonishment, her slender, rigidly erect figure framed by the wardrobe door. "I do believe you're right," she said, her amazement deriving from the fact that since Mrs. Buxton had come to live with her six months ago, that lady had not until now offered a single suggestion of any merit whatsoever.

"No one will take it as disrespectful." Mrs. Buxton nodded to herself, her cheeks flushed from the heat of the fire before which she sat toasting her feet in Lady Mansfield's dressing room. "Such a love match, you and dear Mansfield. Like two turtle doves, you were. Such a shame there weren't any children."

"Yes. Such a shame," said Stella, who had only tolerated her late, gouty husband despite her considerable respect for his fortune. "But no jewels tonight, I shouldn't think, save for a simple strand of pearls."

She tugged at the bell-pull and her maid, Timms, appeared and quickly removed the chosen dress to be pressed.

Lady Mansfield seated herself before her mirror. Other women across London might even now be scheming to win the marquess for themselves, but I, she told her proud, high-boned reflexion, have them all at the disadvantage.

"Timms made reference to some matter or other concerning tonight," Mrs. Buxton rambled on, taking up a nondescript piece of knitting. "Link, wasn't it? Kenneth Link. I remember his father. Now what was it about Link? Oh yes, he's going to marry Lady Sarah Rowdon, ain't he?"

"*What?*" cried Stella, her involuntary gesture sending pots of powders and creams clattering onto the floor. "Marry Lady Sarah? Timms!"

The dresser reappeared. "My lady?"

"What have you been telling Mrs. Buxton about the Marquess of Broadmoor?"

Timms's plain, sturdy face contorted itself with the effort of searching her memory. "Only that he's to be at Almack's tonight, my lady."

"And what of Lady Sarah?" Stella demanded.

"He's offered for her," repeated her cousin. "'Twasn't Timms who told me, though, now I think on it. I had the story from Lady Jersey."

"Oh, cousin!" An exasperated Lady Mansfield thumped one fist down upon her much-abused dressing table. "You've not seen Sally Jersey for years! This is old news you give me."

"Perhaps so," agreed Mrs. Buxton mildly. "Now I recollect, I believe that was some time ago. Must have two, three children by now."

"He offered for her—though heaven knows why; she appears to spend most of her time wool-gathering—but she refused him," said Stella. "Can you not keep from mixing things up so?"

"It is a fault of my age, and not of any want of character," her companion reproved mildly. "I shall endeavour to sort the past from the present for your sake, my dear, but I am not entirely convinced the distinction much signifies."

"It does in this case," snapped Stella. "The marquess is not going to marry Lady Sarah, he is going to marry me!"

Realising at once that she had spoken out of turn, she added, "And not a word of this to anyone, either of you."

"As you wish," said Mrs. Buxton, resuming work on her shapeless knitted garment. She had been labouring at it for as many years as Stella could recall, without ever finishing, and on occasion had identified it variously as a scarf, a pair of socks, a cap, and a shawl. "But please accept my felicitations. When is the wedding to be?"

"That depends upon when he comes up to scratch." Stella waited impatiently as Timms gathered the fallen pots before she could set to powdering her fair skin.

"Then he's not asked you yet?" said her cousin. "Ah, me. How times do change. When I was a girl, one didn't announce one's engagement until one had at least consulted the groom."

Timms departed silently to finish pressing the dress.

He will ask me to marry him soon enough, thought Lady Mansfield, frowning as she noticed a brown spot on the back of her hand. She must remember to apply cucumber water.

Six years ago Kenneth Link—then a mere lieutenant—had been among those who worshipped Stella through the ballrooms and gardens of London, quite ignoring the come-out that year of the timid Lady Sarah.

Although his lack of prospects, as the second son of a younger brother, offered no inducement to matrimony, she had bestowed upon the dashing young man more than his share of waltzes and gavottes and quadrilles at the season's balls.

Then his duty to his country called him away, and by the time he returned she was married to the baron. A few months later she heard he had developed a *tendre* for the insipid Lady Sarah that culminated, after weeks of courtship, in her refusing his hand and his returning to his military duties.

Now he would rediscover the original object of his admiration, Lady Mansfield told herself as Timms returned and assisted her into the high-necked blue dress with its dark blue underskirt. Surely her reserved manner and costume would contrast favourably with the airs and excesses of younger rivals.

Quite unaware that their enthusiasms and low necklines would be considered "airs and excesses" by her ladyship, two optimistic young rivals were at that very moment making themselves ready for the ball.

"I can't wait to see if he gives Lady Sarah the cut direct," Miss Mary Elizabeth Williams was saying as she and her cousin, Miss Catherine Williams, allowed their abigails to dress them. Piles of rejected gowns and jewellery scattered across Mary Beth's room testified to the seriousness with which they had made their choices, there not having been time to order new clothes for the occasion. "How bitterly she must rue her foolishness in refusing him!"

"It's all that toplofty mother of hers," Kitty sniffed, then interrupted herself to cast her pink ribbons to the floor, stamp on them, and shout at her maid, "Oh, Liza, you know I loathe this colour! Do find my cherry ribbons, and be quick about it!"

The abigail scurried away and Kitty resumed her commentary to her cousin. "Lady Rowdon thought he wasn't good enough for her daughter, I suppose. Well, they've come down in the world since then, haven't they? It's said Lady Sarah must make over last year's gowns. Can you imagine?"

"She must be all of three-and-twenty." Mary Beth examined her reflexion in the glass and admired her peaches-and-cream complexion, evidence of that first bloom of youth that can never be recaptured. "Practically an ape-leader. She'll count herself lucky to marry a tradesman if he's wealthy enough to suit her papa, I'd warrant."

"Milk-and-water thing, anyway," agreed Kitty as the abigail returned with the cherry ribbons and wove them through her stylish hair, piled atop her head *à la Méduse*. "Always walking about staring into the air as if she weren't quite sure where she was."

The two cousins primped in silence for a moment, each occupied with her own thoughts as she gazed into the mirror.

Said Mary Beth to herself, studying her light brown hair, blue eyes, and heart-shaped face: There's no reason on earth he shouldn't choose *me*.

What a master stroke that would be, to win the greatest prize in England, and during her first season! For she was barely eighteen, a year younger than her cousin, with whose family she lived.

She had the additional advantage of being the sole heiress to her deceased parents' estate. And, she told herself with one last flirtatious glance in the looking-glass, wealth does like to marry wealth!

Kitty, as it happened, was musing along similar lines, although her fancies featured a different heroine.

I doubt he would have offered for Lady Sarah had I been out at the time, she thought. That was, what, four years ago? Can't imagine what he saw in her; true, her family still had money then, but she's such a meek little thing. Hasn't the least notion where to shop and never knows the latest *on-dits*.

Kitty tried to view herself with some objectivity. The jaw might be termed a trifle narrow, but the auburn hair was the inspiration of much poetry during her first season, and her brown eyes had been described as vivid. They had also been described as sharp and calculating, but only by jealous young ladies.

Not for naught had she refused her hand to several inferior suitors. She awaited precisely such a man as the Marquess of Broadmoor, and even though she had never clapped eyes upon him, she knew beyond a glimmer of a doubt that they should deal well together.

Mary Beth, not unaware of her cousin's train of thought, smiled to herself. If only Kitty could see what a quiz she was, such a pointy-featured thing, and everyone knew she was hanging out for a title.

Poor Mary Beth, Kitty was thinking. Her first season, and not a whisker of town polish on her yet. She's a sweet thing, of course, but she has no style.

Both finding themselves in a jovial mood, the two cousins linked arms and went downstairs chattering happily together.

It would have greatly surprised them to learn that there were those in London who, although planning to attend Almack's that night, spared scarcely a thought for the man lately known as Kenneth Link.

Among these were three men dining at Watier's, which, in addition to providing the gambling and good company any gentleman required of his club, reigned supreme in the area of the table as well, having been founded by a chef.

Two of the three would have stirred much interest, had they shown themselves in a place frequented by such female leaders of the *ton* as Lady Jersey and the Countess Lieven. Prime among them was Sir Lindsay Manx, Lady Sarah's suitor.

There was also the Viscount Vincent Quires, a connoisseur of gossip who could be counted on to have the very latest information through his manservant Finley, a chap fleet of foot and generous with coins to loosen the tongues of other people's servants.

The only unremarkable member of the trio was their friend, Mr. Franklin Lenham, who, although of unobjectionable family and character, possessed neither money nor notoriety.

"Going to ask her tonight, are you?" Mr. Lenham was asking his friend, the baronet Lindsay Manx.

"Already spoken to her father, and he's given his consent." His little finger raised delicately away from the fork, Sir Lindsay nibbled a morsel of quail.

"Given his consent? Begged you to marry her at once, 'less I miss my guess," chuckled Mr. Lenham, who was young enough to find the matter fascinating but well bred enough to keep his voice too low to be heard by diners at other tables. "Badly dipped, is Rowdon. I hear his debts top thirty thousand, and he's mortgaged everything but his title."

"Old news." The third member of their party, the beefy but richly dressed Viscount Vincent Quires, appeared to dismiss the subject as he savoured a glass of French claret, now legally imported again since Wellington's victory. "Superb," he murmured. "So tired of those horrible Madeiras."

"Indeed," said Sir Lindsay. "Worth whipping Boney for, weren't it?" He shifted in his chair, taking care not to tip any wine onto his yellow coat or the green and gold striped swanskin waistcoat that sprawled across his extensive belly.

"You hardly seem excited, for a man on the verge of getting himself leg-shackled!" exclaimed Mr. Lenham, who was at four-and-twenty considerably the youngest of the three.

"My dear friend, I am not marrying for excitement. Quite the opposite." Sir Lindsay signalled a waiter to bring the dessert. "Lady Sarah is a mild sort of miss, and that's what I have a mind to. Want a wife I can tuck away in the country and breed children with, not someone eternally interfering in my affairs."

"She's well enough born," agreed Lord Quires, selecting a cherry torte from the dessert tray. "Bit of a strange duck, always walking about lost in her own thoughts. How well do you know her, Manx? I paid her court once or twice myself, before Rowdon lost all his blunt, you know. Thought I saw a flash of spirit in her eye a time or two, though heaven knows she hides it well enough."

"Flash of spirit in her eye?" snorted the baronet, finishing a peach torte and starting on one of apples and cinnamon. "Sounds as if she were feverish, Quires, or you were a trifle foxed."

His companion shrugged. "I suppose you know best. Only giving you a word of warning."

Had the baronet possessed the social swordsmanship of a Lady Jersey or a Countess Lieven, he might have taken more stock in the viscount's warning, but he lacked their appreciation of his friend's talent for accuracy. Now Lord Quires asked with seeming blandness, "She'll agree to the match, will she?"

Sir Lindsay raised his shoulders eloquently. "Her father says she will, and that's good enough for me."

"You're not going to Almack's tonight, then?" asked Mr. Lenham. "All the world will be there, you know."

"Indeed I am, for that is where I am to encounter Lady Sarah," said Sir Lindsay. "And you'd best go yourself. You'll never have a better chance of snaring an heiress, for they'll all be there tonight, casting their caps at Broadmoor. Nay, don't look darts at me, friend. It's no shame to marry for money, when you've no other choice but the clergy."

All three men observed a moment of silence in contemplating the misery that awaited Mr. Lenham, should he fail in his quest. Life in a country parsonage might have its compensations, but none of them, used as they were to unending entertainments, rich clothing, and sumptuous food, could guess at what those compensations might be.

"Too bad we can't all have Broadmoor's good fortune," sighed Mr. Lenham.

"Buck up, lad." Sir Lindsay, in a jovial mood due to his own upcoming nuptials, clapped his friend on the shoulder. "You'll find a lady to your liking, fear not."

And he continued sipping wine with his companions for some hours, for after all there was no need to hurry himself to Almack's to woo a chit who was already won.

2

THE ROWDON CARRIAGE had, when first constructed, been a grand one, equipped with gold trim and purple paint, and velvet squabs to match. However, the years had not been kind to it.

The springs now sagged mercilessly, the paint was badly chipped, and the trim tarnished. Moreover, the horses did not match, not even in the faint moonlight, and should have been put to pasture years ago.

It was imperative that the contraption tonight resist its tendency to break down, reflected the Countess Anna Rowdon, turning her head to glance at her silent daughter and nursing her pride as the carriage creaked toward Almack's. For if her plans succeeded, Sarah would soon be well wedded, with plenty of carriages. And certain members of the *ton* would come to regret their many slights and snubs.

"Oh! Hawkins, do be careful!" she snapped through the window as the carriage lurched over a pothole. The Rowdons would certainly be replacing some of their servants, she thought with grim satisfaction.

These past three years had been difficult ones for Anna Rowdon, once a much-admired beauty who had made a brilliant match, or so everyone said. She could hardly have foreseen that her Arthur, the dashing Earl of Rowdon, would dissipate both his fortune and his looks in gaming-hells.

His dissolute ways had driven a wall between them, yet Anna still hoped he might reform. He had promised to give up gambling, and although that was not the first time he had made such a promise, she could not help believing he would keep his word at last. If only their daughter would make a brilliant match, all might yet be put right.

Sarah uttered a small noise that might have been a sigh, and Lady Rowdon rapped her daughter sharply on the arm with her fan.

"Do sit up straighter!" she commanded. "Merely because you must wear a gown made over from last year does not mean we have no pride. How you wound me when you slump so! Is our plight not difficult enough, that you must shame me by such posture?"

Sarah obediently squared her shoulders, without raising her eyes to meet her mother's gaze. What did the chit think about when she became lost in contemplation that way? her mother wondered, not for the first time. The girl became quite oblivious to those around her in a manner that was positively embarrassing.

"It's a pity you've no spirit, or we'd have found a splendid match for you years ago," reproved Lady Rowdon, but Sarah made no reply.

It was difficult to believe the chit had turned out to be such a disappointment. As a child, she had conformed beautifully to her parents' expectations. Everyone said she possessed the most exquisite manners, and the promise of great beauty as well, with her dark brown hair setting off eyes an unusual shade of light green.

True, in her earliest years she had sometimes ventured to disagree with her mama, but Anna had squelched most signs of rebellion by clutching her heart and declaring herself near death's door from vexation. And Arthur . . . well, she was forced to concede, his quiet talks had succeeded even where her methods had failed in persuading Sarah that not only her duty but her love of family required her obedience.

Unfortunately, her meekness did not serve so well once she entered society. While there was much to be said for discretion, Sarah was entirely too well behaved to attract any notice at all.

Her only attempt at disobedience had come after she received an offer from that nobody, Kenneth Link. How she had cried and stormed when her parents refused the match!

Well, she had come round soon enough, after her mother swooned and Arthur explained that despite their appearance of wealth, the family finances would not sustain them for more than a few years. Their only hope of escaping poverty was for Sarah to marry well.

Unfortunately, Arthur's gambling had intensified, with the result that their slide into debt eventually became common knowledge. Thanks to that, and to Sarah's pallid demeanour, no acceptable suitor had appeared for four years, until Sir Lindsay Manx, and he was a lukewarm prize.

She felt a momentary twinge of concern at the thought of Sarah married off to the corpulent Sir Lindsay. But the man was pleasant enough, and would not abuse her.

And perhaps the marriage would not be necessary after all, Lady Rowdon reminded herself as the carriage turned into King Street and halted in a line of vehicles jamming the approach to the assembly rooms.

"Mother, I cannot see how I shall do it." Sarah's small voice could scarcely make itself heard above the shouts of frustrated coachmen.

"Oh, do speak up, Sarah! What a little mouse you are!"

The girl tried again, patiently, as if explaining a complicated matter to a querulous invalid. "You know how it hurts me to see you suffer, and to see father worry over bills," she said. "And I am determined to do as father wishes, and accept Sir Lindsay tonight. But how am I to respond if he tries to kiss me? The man is so fat, and wears such outrageous clothing, that I have a disgust of him, Mother."

Only a few words of her discourse penetrated Lady Rowdon's annoyance with the slowness of their progress. . . . *accept Sir Lindsay tonight.*

"Tonight, you say?" she cried. "Tonight? Who says you must accept him tonight?"

"Why, Father does," said Sarah. "Is that not what you want also? You have always welcomed his visits, and Father said he has offered a generous settlement."

"Yes, but you must put him off!" How typical of Arthur, to make plans without consulting his wife! "You must not offend him, mind, but you cannot accept him yet either."

"I don't understand." Confusion writ plain across her lovely face—and it was lovely, Anna conceded silently, although sadly lacking in animation—Sarah awaited her mother's instructions.

"Have you not listened to anything?" said Lady Rowdon. "One speaks of nothing else but that Lord Broadmoor is to be at the ball tonight! He was your admirer once, and you can attach him again. But of course you must not let go of the baronet until all is assured."

Her daughter's eyes widened in dismay. "Attach him again? Indeed, I cannot. I will not! Mother, I would do anything for you, but do not ask this, I beg of you. You cannot imagine how I—how angry he was, and my own feelings—oh—I simply cannot do it!" Tears sparkled in her eyes, catching the gleam of gas lamps from outside.

Anna pressed a handkerchief to her temple. "To think that my own daughter would have so little care for parents. I am not feeling at all well."

"But Mother, I have said I am willing to marry Sir Lindsay. Indeed, I have done nothing but weep and pray for three nights, to bring myself to obey Father. But to display myself before Kenneth . . . before Lord Broadmoor, I cannot do it. And I cannot think why you should wish it."

A complicated business, this! Lady Rowdon moaned as if in pain, to give herself additional time to think. The chit must be brought round, yet she must not discourage Sir Lindsay. Not until her mother had a chance to see which way the land lay.

"Sir Lindsay is a good man," she whispered hoarsely, in a tone that bespoke great agony and never failed to wrench her daughter's tender heart. "The sum he has proposed to settle on you would greatly ease our difficulties for the present. But he is not so wealthy, nor so generous if he were, as to assure us of a secure future. The Marquess of Broadmoor, on the other hand, possesses great fortune."

The carriage lurched forward a few feet and then halted again. This wretched mess of carriages would indeed give her the megrims, thought Lady Rowdon.

"Do you think he would wed me, if he knew it was only for his money?" Sarah pleaded with her mother. "He would not even wed me if he knew—well, that is of no consequence. But I tell you, he will snub me if I speak to him, and then I will be disgraced."

This was an argument Anna had not considered. If the marquess were to cut her daughter in full view of the assemblage, Sarah's reputation would be ruined. The few invitations they still received would cease altogether, and Sir Lindsay might even withdraw his offer of marriage.

"Everyone will be watching to see what passes between us," Sarah pressed on. "I think I should faint dead away from the humiliation, if he slights me."

Her words, far from achieving their desired effect, gave Lady Rowdon an idea.

"That is what you must do!" Her feigned headache forgotten, she all but bounced upon her seat with delight. "You must contrive to be near him somehow, perhaps in the same set upon the dance floor, or you must stand near him. And then on some pretext or other you must faint into his arms."

Sarah tried to speak, but no words issued from her mouth.

"He cannot refuse to aid you, for that would be ungallant," Anna continued happily. "Furthermore, I am convinced he still wears the willow for you, for he has not ventured back to London in all these years until now, when he must come to take his seat in the House of Lords."

"But such deception is foreign to me," Sarah managed to protest, the words seeming to stick in her throat before breaking forth. "It is dishonest, and I cannot abide falseness, nor can he."

"Then he must not know it is false," said Lady Rowdon with what she considered clear logic.

"And even if he is forced to acknowledge me, owing to my indisposition, he will quickly escape from my company," Sarah pointed out. "It's a mad scheme, Mother, and sure to be my undoing."

"Nonsense! Once he has acknowledged you, he can hardly snub you, now, can he?" Seeing her daughter about to protest more forcefully, Lady Rowdon uttered a pathetic cry. "How my head does pain me! This arguing, it grieves me, Sarah. I cannot bear any more."

"Perhaps we should not go in," said her daughter, unable to disguise a note of hope. "We shall return home." She leaned out the window and called, "Hawkins!"

The creaks of the carriage starting forward again drowned her voice, and moments later they arrived at their destination.

Ignoring her daughter's continuing offers to forgo the evening's enjoyment, Lady Rowdon descended grandly with the assistance of the coachman. She had no doubt her persuasions would work upon her daughter, as they always did.

Neil Gow's band was already playing when they entered, the gay music and the bright colours of the gowns compensating for the dullness of the rooms themselves. A furtive glance at the dancers assured Sarah that Lord Broadmoor had not yet arrived.

What a crush there was! It seemed everyone in London had turned out tonight, all laughing and gossiping as they consumed the weak lemonade and stale cake for which Almack's was notorious. The din racketed through her bones, making her long to be home again.

To Sarah's dismay, dozens of pairs of eyes followed her and her mother wherever they moved. Distant acquaintances, moved by curiosity, shoved their way through the crowd to speak to them, when all she wanted was to find some corner to languish in so that she might think.

This was a mad idea of her mother's, and she would not carry it out!

She was willing to sacrifice herself to spare her family suffering; had she not proved that four years ago, by giving up the man she loved?

If it would save my parents from grief, I would gladly humble myself before him now, but it would serve nothing, she thought. How he must despise me! Pray let Sir Lindsay come quickly, and make his offer, and I will accept him as I promised Father. Once it is done, Mama must resign herself to it.

Lady Rowdon's arm in hers, pulling her forward to make way for new arrivals, restored Sarah to the present. The throng parted as the two ladies moved, then closed in around them once again.

Why must they stare at her so, these gentlemen and ladies who came pushing round, resplendent in French silks and Italian crepes, embroidered gauzes and beaded sarsenets? She was only too aware that her own gown of light green striped satin had been purchased a year ago, and despite a few renovations was sadly out of style. Past its first youth—as indeed am I, she thought wryly.

Sarah curtseyed to the Countess Lieven, wife of the Russian ambassador and one of the patronesses of Almack's. It was she who had introduced that daring new dance, the waltz, to these assembly rooms.

"You are the centre of attention tonight, no?" said the countess frankly, for her eminence in society carried with it the right to display a directness that in others might be considered rude. "The new marquess, has he called on you?"

"No," said Sarah, ignoring a scorching look from her mother.

"But then, he has scarcely had time to settle in," Lady Rowdon assured the countess. "Perhaps tonight he will remedy the matter."

"I have no doubt of it," said Lady Lieven.

She nodded and relinquished her spot to Lady Castlereagh, wife of the Foreign Secretary, who proceeded to probe with greater subtlety but no less determination into whether Broadmoor had given sign of renewing his courtship.

Sarah lowered her gaze, allowing her mother to cloud the air with half-truths and innuendos.

Through the clacking of hundreds of tongues, she perceived, or thought she perceived, snippets of conversation that stabbed at her heart.

". . . a bit of new lace, perhaps, but I'm sure it's the same gown . . ."

"What did he ever see in her? Why, she's . . ."

"How she must rue the day . . ."

". . . can't wait to see whether he notices her at all."

How much easier life seemed in the books Sarah loved to read, where the heroines faced only ruined castles and caped villains, ghosts and near-fatal illnesses!

I should deal well enough with that sort of business, Sarah reminded herself. And I'd not languish weakly until I was rescued, either!

His cloak whipping about him in the chill night wind, Lord Evilwit chuckled madly as his cruel gaze raked Lady Sarah from top to toe.

"Soon you will be mine, my sweet," he murmured. "You have no choice but to wed me."

"Never!" cried the heroine, her back to the cliff. "I should cast myself into the depths sooner than submit to you!"

As he leered again, she leaped forward, grasping a corner of his cape and pulling it across his eyes, momentarily blinding him as she . . .

"Sarah, whatever are you doing?"

At the sound of her mother's voice, filled with vexation, Sarah's gaze cleared and she realised that she had involuntarily reached out and was even now fingering the material of a gown worn by Lady Mansfield.

"I . . . I was only admiring this beautiful silk," she stammered. "What a becoming shade of blue, Lady Mansfield."

Ice-grey eyes acknowledged the compliment with lowered lashes. "You are very kind," said the cool blonde woman.

Mercifully, they were interrupted at that point by an elderly gentleman, requesting a cotillion with Sarah. She agreed at once.

When that dance ended, other partners kept her busy with Scottish reels and gavottes. At how many balls these past few years had she attempted to merge herself with some potted plant, from shame at not being sought after; yet tonight, with her dance card filling rapidly, she longed to be left alone to sort through her tangled emotions.

Where was that capricious Sir Lindsay? Often before, the sight of his gross figure had filled her with dread, but now she longed to see him. What a night for contrarieties this was turning out to be!

A hushed murmur soughed through the assemblage as the band played the first strains of a waltz. Sarah turned her head toward the door in time to see it filled by the wide shoulders of Kenneth Link, Marquess of Broadmoor.

Circling the room in the unsteady arms of a rail-thin young man, she caught only frustrating glimpses of the man she still loved with all her heart.

These four years had changed him. He moved with more confidence than before, and held his head more proudly, displaying a small scar across the cheek doubtless earned at Waterloo. No longer unruly, his light brown hair had been close-cropped in the latest fashion, and his dark eyes burned with unfamiliar intensity as they swept the room.

Sarah hoped the movements of the dance hid her trembling as that gaze passed over her. Passed without a blink, and moved on. Had he seen her and deliberately ignored her? Or did she mean nothing to him any more, so little that he even failed to recognise her?

Surely everyone else in the room had noticed the coldness with which he disregarded her presence. Surely even her own mother must realise the cause was hopeless and abandon the field.

As if unaware of the stir he was creating, Lord Broadmoor turned to Lady Jersey and asked her to dance. A diplomatic move, for although the matron already ruled London society, she was surely flattered at being thus distinguished.

The room filled again with chatter, and Sarah was grateful that the music prevented her overhearing any conversations. She felt herself blushing in shame at the thought of what those tongues must be saying now. Where was that dratted Sir Lindsay?

The dance ended at last and her partner returned her to Lady Rowdon.

"Mother, we must leave," Sarah gasped in an undervoice. "You can see he will cut me dead."

"Nonsense," replied her mother, also very quietly, while nodding brightly at Mrs. Drummond Burrell, another of the patronesses. "Remember our plan. It will not fail."

The evening took on a nightmarish quality as Sarah moved dutifully through dance after dance, making polite but monosyllabic conversation with her partners and enduring with difficulty the uncharitable stares and smirks of other ladies.

At every moment, she knew within a hair's-breadth where the marquess was and what he did.

She knew when he partnered Lady Mansfield through a quadrille and smiled at her. She knew when he bent to kiss the hand of an aging duchess, when he favoured the rapier-tongued Miss Kitty Williams with a dance, and when he delighted her cousin, Miss Mary Beth Williams, by asking for her first waltz and securing permission for her from Lady Jersey.

She missed not one expression of those eyes that had probed into hers during their first, accidental meeting at a house party; not one amused twist of the lips she once had kissed, in a moment of overwhelming happiness, in her family's garden; not one gesture of the strong hands that had clenched into furious fists when she told him the agonising news, that she could not marry him.

If only she had dared tell him the real reason, her family's precarious finances; but to do so would be to betray her own father. So she had been forced to remain silent when he accused her of the worst sort of snobbery and insult, of toying with his affections while scorning him as a worthless fortune hunter.

Now, when the movements of the dance brought her near to him, Sarah sensed her mother's silent command, and shuddered. Faint into his arms? He would cast her to the floor if she did!

She gazed about, praying for the sight of Sir Lindsay. It must be nearly eleven o'clock, after which no one, not even the Prince Regent himself, would be admitted to Almack's. Perhaps her suitor had changed his mind, leaving her alone to face the barely concealed ridicule and scorn of the beau monde.

How she longed for a clear-cut enemy, one she could confront and defy . . .

Lady Sarah drew herself up straighter as she faced the foul den filled with cutthroats and thieves. "I will never tell you where the fortune is buried," she declared, "not if I must die a thousand deaths!"

"By the time we are finished with you, my dear, you will beg to die!" cackled an aged crone, brandishing a torch that seared perilously near Lady Sarah's delicate face.

"Torture me then, but it will avail you nothing!" Even as she spoke, Lady Sarah's keen mind sought some means of escape from this horrid chamber. A current of air on her ankle alerted her to a narrow doorway behind her.

With a suddenness that took her captors unawares, she flung herself backwards . . .

The startling and very real sensation of hurtling backwards awoke Sarah from her revery too late. With a shriek that silenced even the band, she flailed her arms, making one last, futile effort to recover her balance before she landed with a thud against Lord Broadmoor who, caught unawares, collapsed beneath her.

=3=

UNTIL THE MOMENT when he found himself unceremoniously hurled to the floor, the evening had fallen considerably short of Lord Broadmoor's expectations.

During his years of self-imposed exile from London, his sentiments toward the faithless Lady Sarah had undergone a transformation, from fury to scorn to indifference. Or so he had assumed, until the unexpected legacy and his return to London.

A casual mention at White's revealed to him that, far from marrying some eligible gentleman years ago as he had assumed, Lady Sarah had remained single. In addition, her family had lost the fortune that once had placed her so far above him.

Along with this information came the news that the young lady was expected to marry at last, her intended being a baronet of attractive means if not looks.

This information displeased the marquess, although he was hard put to determine why. The reason could only be that, despite her family's ills, Lady Sarah had never suffered as he had, never undergone that torment of the heart and blighting of the spirit that had haunted him for years and prevented his forming an attachment to any other woman.

His rise to prominence and the stir created by his return to London gave Broadmoor a cherished opportunity to even the score.

Thus he cast aside his instinct to avoid society and determined instead to lionize it. He would be seen with the most beautiful and fashionable women of the *ton*; his name would perch on every tongue; and Lady Sarah, mercenary creature that she was, would soon regret her heartless conduct toward him.

What a crashing bore it had been, enduring those fittings with his tailor, opening up that big house instead of taking comfortable rooms as he originally planned, and parading himself about in a phaeton that verged on the gaudy. But he intended to play this role to the fullest.

Tonight at Almack's was to be the climax. At first, all had gone according to plan. London buzzed for days in advance; Broadmoor's entrance to the assembly rooms created a sensation; even Lady Mansfield, as ravishing as ever in her widowhood, gave indication that she was available to be courted.

What spoiled it in the end was Lady Sarah herself, the heartless wench! Not one whit changed from four years ago, she whirled blithely in the arms of one man after another, taking no notice of the marquess at all.

Despite his seeming lack of interest, Broadmoor could not help remarking to himself on the grace with which she danced and the soft, dreamy expression that had always mystified and intrigued him. It was as though Lady Sarah were merely a visitor to this world, a faery descended for a few hours to brighten the drabness around her.

Doubts began to plague him, along with memories he had ruthlessly suppressed. He could still see her, that last evening, sitting in silence on her drawing-room sofa as he railed at her, with nary a word in her own defense.

Had he misjudged her? When he demanded an explanation, why did she reply only that her parents would not countenance the marriage, and say nothing of her own feelings? Why did she refuse to elope with him, if not because she disdained his low station and the prospect of having to live on his meagre salary? The only possible conclusion was that she never considered him a serious suitor in the first place, that her professed affection for him was mere pretense.

Yet now, how tedious the other women seemed by comparison. Miss Kitty Williams conversed only about gowns and carriages and who was to sing at the opera. Miss Mary Beth Williams passed their entire waltz together expounding at length on what a wonderful time she was having in what, she continually reminded him, was her first season.

Lady Mansfield offered more tolerable companionship, yet the woman's studied elegance rubbed unpleasantly compared to Lady Sarah's freshness. But surely, he reminded himself, that seeming innocence was only a gambit.

Thoroughly annoyed at his own contrary emotions, Lord Broadmoor determined to end the evening and give up his planned revenge as a bad job. Henceforth he would follow his natural desire to avoid the social scene, and Lady Sarah with it.

Duty required that he submit to one more reel, with a Friday-faced friend of his late mother's. His irritation was compounded by the nearness of Lady Sarah, who seemed blissfully oblivious as she danced with her back toward him.

Then, without warning, what had been an unpleasant evening was transformed into a thumping disaster when the young lady inexplicably flung herself into him, knocking Broadmoor to the floor.

"What the devil!" he cried, simultaneously becoming aware of a throb in his ankle, a hubbub from the crowd, and the surprisingly agreeable warmth of Lady Sarah pressing on top of him.

"Oh, my Lord!" Her cheeks framed by a tangle of dark brown curls, the chit, still seated on his chest, looked down and met his stare. Had he truly forgotten that her eyes were that fascinating shade of light green?

"What, may I ask, is the meaning of this?" he demanded in as dignified a manner as possible, given his position.

"I . . . I can explain . . . Oh, dear, what a great gawk you must think me." She bit her lip and regarded him in confusion, as if just awakened from a dream.

"I will think far better of you if you will cease using my person as a settee."

"Oh!" Blushing crimson, she accepted the assistance of her erstwhile partner in rising.

Dusting himself off, the marquess rose also, trying not to wince as he put weight on his injured ankle. Half the assemblage, it seemed, had gathered round, with Lady Jersey fussing and squawking in the foreground.

"There has been no serious harm done," Broadmoor informed the lot of them. "Pray resume your dancing." Before Lady Sarah could take herself off, he reached out and clamped one hand about her wrist. "I believe I was promised an explanation."

Pulling her behind him, he shouldered his way across the room, doing his best to ignore the fascinated stares of onlookers.

At last they reached a relatively quiet corner of one of the gaming rooms. The gentlemen in the center of the chamber were far too absorbed in the cards laid out upon the green tables to pay heed to new arrivals.

"Well?" said Lord Broadmoor. "I await your accounting, Lady Sarah."

"Have I apologised yet?" she asked uncertainly.

"At length."

"And you want me to tell you why I cast myself into you on the dance floor and knocked you down?"

"That was the idea, yes." He folded his arms and glared at her with as much fierceness as he could muster when confronted with such a wide-eyed, taking little thing.

Lady Sarah looked down at her feet, as if considering placing the blame on them, but appeared to think the better of it.

"I was trying to escape from the cutthroats and thieves," she said at last, without looking up.

Lord Broadmoor did not immediately reply. Indeed, so taken aback was he that he did not quite know *how* to reply. "What cutthroats and thieves?" he said at last.

"The ones I was dreaming about."

"Oh, *those* cutthroats and thieves." He could not resist cupping one hand under her elfin chin and forcing her to meet his gaze. "Do you mean to tell me, Lady Sarah, that all those times when your mind appears to have wandered, you are imagining yourself the heroine of some harebrained romance?"

"Not harebrained!" she declared. "I am wonderfully brave, you see, but in real life, I never have a chance to show it."

This conversation was not going at all the way he had expected. "Do you wish me to secure for you a commission in

His Majesty's service?" inquired his lordship. "Perhaps a post might be obtained for you aboard some ship."

"Nonsense," said Lady Sarah. "They have no ruined castles on ships, though I've no doubt there are villains a-plenty."

Lord Broadmoor had crawled under fire across a battlefield in Spain to rescue a wounded comrade and fought hand-to-hand with a sabre-wielding Frenchman at Waterloo, but the most difficult thing he ever did was to refrain from kissing Lady Sarah at that moment.

Instead he said, "And when you are having these madcap dreams of yours, do you always act them out upon whatever hapless soul finds himself nearby?"

"I'm afraid I do," she admitted. "Why, I nearly tore Lady Mansfield's dress earlier this evening, thinking it was a villain's cape. She'd not have liked that by half, would she?"

"She might have considered it rude," agreed the marquess, unhappily remembering more and more each moment exactly what it was about Lady Sarah that had made him fall in love with her in the first place. "Tell me, have you always had these fancies, or is this something recent?"

She considered thoughtfully. "Now that you tax me on it, I recall that for many years my dreams centered on matters nearer at hand. When I was in the schoolroom, I thought mostly about my come-out, and what a pleasant time I should have."

"But life proved a disappointment?"

"I'd never thought before about precisely when I began imagining these scenes," said Lady Sarah. "Now that I consider, it must have been when . . ." She stopped abruptly.

"Pray continue."

"A few years ago."

"When your family lost its fortune?" He regretted the question when he saw how pale she became.

"More or less," said Lady Sarah. "But I'm sure it's a matter of indifference to your lordship. I—I haven't congratulated you on your good luck, if it's good luck to have three of your relatives stick their spoons in the wall within a year. Oh, dear, that didn't come out the way I meant it. At any rate, I am pleased for you."

Broadmoor shrugged. "Wealth and position are not something I had ever aspired to, but I cannot say I would now willingly give them up."

"Do you know," she said as if making a great discovery, "talking to you is even more agreeable than having one of my dreams?"

"Then I trust I needn't fear that you will rend my garments or knock me to the floor again?" he enquired.

"Certainly not . . . Oh!" Her mouth hung open as if she had seen an apparition, and Lord Broadmoor turned to look at the doorway. Standing in it, taking a pinch of snuff, was a fat, middle-aged gentleman with the atrocious taste to wear a yellow jacket with a green and gold striped waistcoat.

"That's Sir Lindsay," confided Lady Sarah. "He's . . ." She stopped in midsentence, as if recalling something alarming. "He's . . . a friend of Papa's. Pray excuse me." She all but dashed past the marquess, catching the rotund baronet by the arm and pulling him through the door so unexpectedly that he snorted out a spray of snuff.

Could this fat fop truly be the man she intended to marry? It took all of Lord Broadmoor's self-restraint to keep from striding across and commanding the impudent fellow to be gone from these rooms and from Lady Sarah's company forever. The thought of her wedded to that travesty of a man turned his stomach.

Yet there was some mystery here. He lowered himself onto a straight-backed chair, trying to ignore the pain coursing through his injured ankle.

Blast Lady Sarah! She'd thrust herself back into his life in front of Lady Jersey and everybody, and made him fall half in love with her again. How the blazes had she managed to do it?

And why was she contemplating marriage to Sir Lindsay? True, the man had money, but surely Lord Rowdon would never force Sarah to take a husband against her will. Yet if she loved the man, why had she flirted so openly with Broadmoor?

The game in the center of the room was breaking up. The noise roused the marquess. One unfortunate aspect of his much-cherished popularity was that his absence on the dance floor had surely been remarked upon, he realised.

The strains of a waltz filled the air as Broadmoor made his return. The Countess Lieven presented herself at hand, and he promptly requested a dance, gritting his teeth against the injured ankle. What warrior ever let such a small injury keep him from his duties, after all?

As they took their places on the thronged floor, he caught sight of Lady Sarah, speaking earnestly as she danced with that lump of a baronet.

"Do you not wish at times you could read minds?" inquired the countess.

The marquess nodded, wondering if she had noticed the object of his curiosity but deciding to direct the conversation into safer channels. "Especially those of enemy soldiers. Now that would have been a useful talent."

His partner smiled enigmatically. "Society is also a kind of battlefield, my lord, and there are many strategies. You are new to this sort of conflict, I think."

"Indeed I am," said Broadmoor. "For example, I have the strong sensation that you're trying to tell me something and I haven't the least notion what it is."

"Precisely." The countess followed smoothly as he spun her across the room. "You must learn to perceive what is truly meant, rather than what is said—or what you can hear."

"If only I had such a skilled instructress as yourself," he said politely.

"I shall do you a favour." The countess nodded with her chin toward Lady Sarah. "That young lady is very surprised that you noticed her, and very flattered."

"Oh?" The countess had his full attention now.

"That man, perhaps you know, is Sir Lindsay Manx," she continued. "I have it on the authority of a good friend of his, one who dined with him earlier, that he is to propose marriage to her tonight."

"And has he done so?"

"Yes, I believe he has." The countess studied the other pair of dancers for one moment further. "Yes, and she is replying to him."

"What is she saying?" Broadmoor hoped she couldn't detect the dryness in his throat.

"She is saying neither yes nor no," said the countess. "An hour ago, she would have accepted him. But now you have renewed her hopes for you, and you are a much bigger prize, if I may be frank, my lord. Yet she does not wish to let her fish from the hook so quickly, for perhaps she will not catch another. And so she makes excuses, to put him off until another day."

"How can you be so sure?" Broadmoor demanded.

His partner gave him another of her mysterious smiles. "I have been many years in society, my lord, and I can read more in the flicker of any eye than most people can gain from an hour of conversation. Believe me, what I have told you, it is so. The question is, what will you do about it?"

"And what an interesting question that is," said the marquess as the music ended, giving him an excuse to escort the lady back to her friends. As he walked away, he heard her snap her fan in frustration.

The marquess's head was beginning to spin from the heat, the chatter, and his own confusion about Lady Sarah, and his ankle demanded relief. Deciding that the time for his departure had come, he made his way toward the door.

A familiar face caught his eye. Sarah's mother, Lady Rowdon, preening herself beneath the flattering attention of Lady Jersey.

He noted with distaste Lady Rowdon's smug expression, as if she had pulled off some great trick. Was he the target of it? He glanced back at Lady Sarah, and saw that she was still speaking earnestly with Sir Lindsay.

What was it Lady Lieven had said? Something about a fish on a hook, and wanting to trade one for another. So Sarah intended to keep the baronet dangling, toying with him as she had once done with a naive young officer.

Striding out into the warm night, Broadmoor felt the truth of the matter smite him full-face. However it had come about that Lady Sarah knocked him down—and he could not quite believe she would have dared do it intentionally—she had unquestionably taken advantage of the situation to use her wiles upon him.

She knew all too well how to blend shyness with candour, a combination of traits that made for the appearance of charming spontaneity. That was just as she had behaved years ago, when she managed to wrap him round her finger and bring him to propose. Then her coldness, her refusal to elope or explain why she would not, had made it clear the matter was merely a game to her. Once she won, she lost interest.

Tonight she had very nearly deceived him again.

What a fool she must think him! It was a shame that, no matter how cruelly and shamefully she behaved, one could not challenge a lady to a duel.

More of the countess's words came back to the marquess as he sent his groom scurrying to fetch the phaeton. "Society is also a kind of battlefield, my lord, and there are many strategies."

It would be easy enough to avoid Lady Sarah, but why let the scheming chit escape so easily? No, the marquess reflected, he would join the game of hearts and lead her along as she had once done with him, then crush her hopes with the same silent unconcern.

But the matter must be handled skillfully. He must not seem too easily won . . .

Musing deep on his battle plans, the marquess bolted up into his seat on the phaeton and cracked his whip in the air to set the matched black horses on their way.

=4=

SIR LINDSAY, So long awaited, had arrived at the worst possible moment: just in time to see Sarah crash into Lord Broadmoor and make a spectacle of herself in front of the entire gathering, as he was quick to point out to her.

"Thought of you as a quiet sort of chit," he grumbled as they joined the crowd on the dance floor and began to move about more or less in time with the music. The baronet's awkward swaying could scarcely be classified as dancing, Lady Sarah could not help reflecting, despite her resolve to appease him.

"Then going off that way with Broadmoor—damn smokey, if you ask me," Sir Lindsay continued in his nasal voice. "What were you two talking about, then?"

"I was apologising," said Sarah, wishing the agitation in her mind would settle down.

The encounter with Kenneth—no, she must not think of him as if they were still on intimate terms—with Lord Broadmoor had shaken her badly, and it took all her strength not to stare at him now as he partnered the Countess Lieven.

Why did he have such a devastating effect on her? She hadn't meant to tell him of her fantasies; indeed, she had never told anyone else, and was startled to find herself pouring out the tale within minutes after renewing an acquaintance so long and so bitterly severed.

Yet he did not seem to hate her—gave the impression, even, of welcoming her company. Dared she imagine there might be some hope of reconciliation? Only if she were a dimwit! she chided herself.

Her duty was clear: She must not linger with Broadmoor when her family's well-being depended on her acquiescing to Sir Lindsay.

But I can't! she realised, miserably aware of his pudgy hand on her waist as they danced.

How could she agree to share his life, while Kenneth was dancing right in front of her eyes? Perhaps, after all, the best thing was to follow her mother's advice.

"I suppose there's no harm done," the baronet said, evidently mistaking her silence for contrition. "Look here, Lady Sarah, I've had a talk with your father. I suppose he told you about it, eh?"

She could only nod stiffly.

"So. Can we consider the matter settled?"

"The matter? Are you proposing to me, Sir Lindsay?" Don't make a fuss, you ninny, she scolded herself. Did you really think he would do it properly?

He knelt before her in his white cape and took her delicate white hand lovingly in his. "Lady Sarah, dare I hope that you might consent . . ."

That might be the way heroes did it in books, but she must admit Sir Lindsay in that position would be anything but romantic.

"Proposing? What else would I be talking about?" said the baronet. "Shall we set the date?"

"But I haven't agreed yet!" she said.

"Turning missish on me, are you? I've a good mind to abandon the entire matter!" he said. "Your papa assured me you was an obedient girl, but I'm not so sure he wasn't gammoning me."

"But I am obedient!" said Sarah. "It's only . . ." Only what? *"Come away with me, Lady Sarah," said the man in the white cape, his eyes burning into hers* . . . This was no time for daydreams! "It's my mother!" she blurted.

"Eh? What about your mother?" The baronet glanced across the room at Lady Rowdon, who stood arm in arm with Lady Jersey. "You mean she don't approve the match?"

"Oh, she's delighted with it!" said Sarah. "It's her health, I mean. She needs me home for the time being, to care for her."

"Looks well enough to me," remarked the baronet, beginning to perspire as the waltz neared its end.

"She's a great gun; insists on forcing herself from her sickbed to chaperone me." Sarah began to feel desperate. If he refused to believe her excuse, she would have to accept him, and her heart pinched at the thought.

"Your father said nothing of this." Sir Lindsay eyed her suspiciously.

"She attempts to hide the gravity of her condition even from him." Thank heaven the dance had ended! Lady Sarah felt herself out of breath from the effort of contriving to put off her suitor without alienating him.

Fortunately, Lord Quires appeared just then to spirit Sarah away for a quadrille, leaving the baronet staring ominously after them. However, her relief was short-lived, for it soon became clear that the viscount's gallantry stemmed from his wish to learn what had transpired.

The dance did not allow for protracted conversation, but his lordship conducted his probing smoothly, his tongue like a fine needle that passes through delicate cloth without leaving a mark.

"Sir Lindsay's looking a bit down at the mouth," observed Quires. "Having one's offer rejected will do that to a man. But he'll get over it."

For all her wool-gathering, Sarah was not insensible of the currents that eddied through London society. Having once, some years ago, been courted briefly by Lord Quires, she had noticed how quickly anything said to him reached the ears of Lady Jersey and Lady Lieven.

"Why are you so certain he offered for me?" she asked when next the pattern of the dance brought them together.

"Told me he would, at dinner tonight," replied her partner.

"Ah," said Sarah.

In desperation, she pulled the sword from the hand of her injured hero and turned to face the villain. "It is not in my nature to fence with you," cried Lady Sarah, "but I will do it to save the man I love!"

"As a matter of fact, I did not refuse him," she told the viscount. "The waltz finished before I had a chance to reply. Which, you must confess, is one of the disadvantages of proposing marriage on the dance floor."

Once again the quadrille separated them. She could not help noting the marquess's departure from the assembly rooms, but quickly transferred her gaze to Sir Lindsay, for she knew how closely she was watched.

When they were rejoined, the viscount said, "Then you mean to accept him? One might suppose otherwise, seeing the attention shown you by Lord Broadmoor."

"He and I are old friends," said Sarah, rather proud of how neatly she sidestepped his questions.

Quires accepted defeat gracefully and bowed low over her hand when the dance ended before returning her to her mother.

"Such a wonderful evening!" exclaimed Lady Rowdon when he had taken himself off. "However, now Lord Broadmoor has left, I think we might go also."

"But I must speak again with Sir Lindsay," Sarah protested weakly. "Mother, he offered for me, and I had not time to give him my reply."

"All the better," said Lady Rowdon. "And as I see him coming our way, we must be off at once."

The haste with which her mother pulled her outsie filled Sarah with humiliation. What a havey-cavey business this was! True, she had no great desire to confront Sir Lindsay, and no brilliant plan for keeping him a-dangle without rousing his fury. Nevertheless, she disliked scheming and dishonesty.

"Perhaps it would be better if we left London entirely," she told her mother as the groom assisted them into their carriage. "We could live far more cheaply in the country, and perhaps I need not marry anyone at all."

"What nonsense is this?" Her mother's tone dismissed the suggestion beyond all redemption. "Go to the country? Indeed, we shall not. Sarah, your season is made! Lord Broadmoor has noticed you, far above anyone else at the ball."

"Only because I fell on him," Sarah pointed out.

"And how cleverly you contrived that," said Anna Rowdon in a tone far more cheerful than Sarah had heard in some time. "I meant to compliment you upon it. Had I not known better, I should have thought it purely accidental."

"It *was* purely accidental," Sarah assured her. "I could have been ruined, if he'd taken offense."

"But he didn't," said Lady Rowdon. "Indeed, Lady Jersey was speculating that he may renew his suit. Wouldn't you prefer that to marrying Sir Lindsay?"

"Of course I would." Sarah stared down at her hands miserably. "But he won't."

"Why not? He offered for you once," said her mother.

"But I refused him!"

"Many ladies refuse many gentlemen, but that does not mean they give up all hope of winning in the end," Anna pointed out. "You refine on this too much, Sarah. No doubt he has remembered why he once doted upon you, and sees that now he may hope for success."

"But he isn't like that! He's proud and—and he felt that somehow I betrayed his trust," said Sarah. "Can you not understand, Mother?"

"I understand what I perceive with my own eyes," was the answer. "Now, we must decide about clothes. It is becoming obvious that we shall have a busy month or two ahead of us, and we must have new clothes."

Her other thoughts flew out the carriage window and disappeared into the shadows of the street. "New clothes?" cried Sarah. "Mother, we can't afford them! And we haven't time to make any ourselves. You know how wretched I am with the needle."

"Indeed we shall not make them ourselves," said Lady Rowdon. "We must have the very best! Madame Therese in Curzon Street, perhaps, or something by Fanchon. Your pelisse is in a frightful state, and we must have new shoes, and shawls, and . . ."

"But we haven't the money," Sarah said. "We should require hundreds of pounds to put things right in our wardrobes, and we've been on short rations for ages. Father says . . ."

"If your father is so concerned about our finances, he had better stop . . . well, never mind that." Anna spoke with even more than her usual sharpness. "We shall borrow the money, if need be. You see, Sarah, even if Lord Broadmoor doesn't come up to scratch, we can put ourselves in a position to attract some other suitor even more eligible than Sir Lindsay."

"Then I shall refuse the baronet straightaway," said Sarah, relieved.

"Goose! You don't toss away an egg because you've seen a chicken on the horizon," said Lady Rowdon. "You must play him along for a bit."

Sarah held her tongue until they arrived at the modest town-house off Clarence Square. She had no doubt Father could make his own arguments well enough.

To her surprise, he was already home, ensconced before a roaring fire in the library. Generally her father remained late at his club.

Her mother, breezing into the room full of news, failed to note what the earl was reading, but Sarah observed it. Open in his lap was an account book, and he held in one hand a letter bearing the imprint of a firm of solicitors.

Lord Rowdon's face, which normally wore either the placid smile of a man happily soused or the grimace of one who has been frustrated at yet another venture but means to fight again, was set now along grim and solemn lines. How old and worn her father looked, Sarah thought worriedly.

"Your daughter has met with the most amazing success!" crowed Lady Rowdon. "You should have been there, Arthur! All London is talking about it."

"Damn success and damn London!" retorted his lordship. So he had been drinking, his daughter observed unhappily. "What I want to know is, did Sir Lindsay offer for you, Sarah?"

"Yes, Father," she said.

"Good." The earl, who had not bothered to rise, leaned back in his wing chair and raised a glass of port. "We are saved, then."

"Saved?" said Lady Rowdon. "Whatever are you going on about, Arthur? Naturally, she did not accept him."

"What!?" The earl roared to his feet, stamping across the room to catch Sarah by the shoulders. "You refused him? You ungrateful child, what of your promise to me? Do you realise what you have done?"

Her father's unfamiliar harshness set Sarah quivering inside. "But Father!" she cried. "How can you think so ill of me? I did not refuse him!"

"Eh?" Lord Rowdon let go of her. "What is the meaning of this? Didn't accept him and didn't refuse him either?"

"I hadn't time," said Sarah. "He asked me while we were dancing, and the dance ended before I could answer him."

"Well, that's all right then." The earl made a show of clapping her on the back, rather as if she were one of his hunting cronies. "He'll be round tomorrow, I expect, and we'll set the betrothal then."

"We most certainly shall not!" Lady Rowdon drew herself up to her full height, which was near that of her husband, and considerably more than Sarah's. "Attend me, husband! Your daughter has been noticed by Lord Broadmoor."

"Broadmoor?" Lord Rowdon said. "Fellow died, didn't he? Who holds the title, then?"

"That's the beauty of it," declared his wife. "It's Captain Link. Remember him? He offered for Sarah once."

The earl resumed his chair, and Lady Rowdon took the only other one at hand. Sarah's feet were beginning to ache from all the dancing, but she was glad to see her parents rest as they ought.

"Link," mused Rowdon. "Now I think on it, yes, I do. Didn't know he had any prospects, though."

"If you listened to gossip instead of . . . instead of spending all your time on business matters, you'd know it was only by a fluke that he succeeded to the title," said Lady Rowdon. "But that's neither here nor there. The point is, my dear, he's fearfully rich, everyone who matters is trying to snare him, and he spent at least ten minutes speaking privately with Sarah! I heard Lord Quires tell Lady Jersey his lordship looked quite entranced during the entire conversation."

The earl drummed his fingers on the arm of his chair. "He's not spoken of marriage though, I presume?"

"Well, he could hardly . . ."

Lord Rowdon lifted the letter and waved it at his wife. "Do you know what this is, my dear? A missive from our creditors' solicitor."

"Our creditors?" said Sarah. "Have we borrowed money then, Father?" She had known their own resources were almost exhausted, but to be in debt was an ignominy she had hoped they could avoid.

"Unhappily, yes, I have been forced to seek the assistance of these scoundrels," he answered. "They state herein that unless they are paid the sum of . . . well, never mind the exact amount, but it's more than I can raise. At any rate, unless they are paid within the next thirty days, they shall seize this house and all its contents."

"Put them off," said Lady Rowdon airily. "We've done so before."

"We have?" The conversation filled Sarah with dread. She had never dreamed their situation was so dire as this. That they were reaching the end of their means, yes, but this could mean debtor's prison for Father and destitution for herself and her mother.

"They'll not be put off again," growled the earl. "Says so quite clearly. So you see, Broadmoor's prospects mean nothing unless they pay off in less than thirty days, and that hardly seems likely. Else we shall be completely ruined, and no one will have her."

"This is dreadful!" cried Sarah. "Father, Mother, I know what we must do. We must sell this house at once—or surrender it for the debts—and return to the country. We can live quite comfortably there, with the rents from the tenants."

Her parents exchanged meaningful looks.

"What is it?" A black cloud of panic welled up in Sarah's throat and threatened to choke her. "There's something you've not told me!"

"Yes, my dear, I'm afraid there is," said her father gravely. "The house in the country was gone for debts long ago."

Sarah leaned against a bookcase, trying to absorb what he'd said. Gone for debts, the house where she'd grown up, where she'd played with the kittens born each spring in the stables, where she'd learned to ride and where she'd passed joyous hours on rainy days, listening to the cook recount tales of her many outlandish relatives.

"Why didn't you tell me?" she asked.

"We had no desire to sadden you," said her father gently.

"Nevertheless, I think you will be gravely in error to insist that Sarah marry Sir Lindsay without giving Lord Broadmoor an opportunity," said Lady Rowdon. "The settlement is barely adequate to our needs, and what of the future? We have no other daughters, you know."

"If only there were a son!" The earl glared at his wife.

"And what could he have done?" she demanded. "It's your . . ." She caught herself and drew back. "This argument is pointless. Now, as I was saying. Sarah can keep the baronet at bay for a few weeks, until we know which way the wind blows."

"But Kenneth will never offer for me again!" Sarah blurted. "No matter how politely he behaves toward me, he will never forgive me! I know him well enough for that."

"Hush, girl." Her father examined the letter one more time and cast a despairing glance at the account books. "It's true that Sir Lindsay can keep us from prison, but as your mother says, how shall we live then? No, we must take the gamble."

"I thought you would see it that way." Lady Rowdon smiled, but her eyes were cold. "Now go to bed, Sarah. You are looking tired, and we must not have wrinkles."

"But you have forgotten about the clothes," said her daughter. "There can be no question now of our borrowing money to put feathers on our backs."

"Do you expect the marquess to bend his knee to a lady dressed in rags?" was Lady Rowdon's reponse.

"Father . . ."

"Your mother is right—twice in one evening," he observed. "The heavens may fall in, eh? Yes, you must have clothes, Sarah. What are a few more hundred pounds, with all this? One must take risks to get ahead in this life."

"Or behind," said Lady Rowdon, then turned to her daughter. "Go on up to bed, Sarah. Your father and I wish to speak privately."

"Good night, then." Sarah kissed them both on the cheek and fled up the stairs, to pass a restless night dreaming of the marquess taking her in his arms and making everything right again.

=5=

"I've a Mind to call it off, here and now," muttered Sir Lindsay as his curricle wedged itself into Hyde Park, this being the five o'clock hour when the *ton* crowded into the park to see who might be riding with whom.

"Shocking behavior," agreed Mr. Lenham, who was in fact scarcely listening, so busy was he attempting to determine whether any of the carriages contained the exquisite form of the very young and very wealthy Miss Mary Beth Williams, who had captured his heart the previous night during a single cotillion.

"Hard to countenance, her running from Almack's that way," the baronet continued, guiding his team between two young men on horseback and a lumbering landau filled with old ladies. "Practically fled out the door. I'd have had my answer, though, had it not been for Quires. What the deuce was the fellow thinking of, snatching her off like that for a dance? He could see what we was discussing."

"Do you observe that chaise over there?" inquired his companion. "Can you see who is in it?"

"Couple of cits," said Sir Lindsay. "Jumped up merchants' daughters who live in the City, looking for a husband. Got plenty of blunt, lad, but they'll only spend it for a title."

"It's rotten, ain't it?" sighed Franklin Lenham, leaning back and letting the April sunshine bathe his face. "It ought to be a law: A person should be born either wealthy or titled, or possibly both, but certainly not neither!"

He was jolted nearly out of his seat a moment later as the baronet cracked the whip and sent his horses dashing through an opening in the welter of carriages. "What the blazes?"

"Quires," said Sir Lindsay grimly. "Got a bit of explaining to do."

"Or news," said Mr. Lenham hopefully, hanging onto his seat for dear life. "He's always got the latest bit of tittle-tattle."

The viscount, as it happened, was strolling on foot, or at least standing on foot, beneath a tree. The fact is that his beefy form scarcely ever moved under its own power. He had chosen this means of transportation purely because of the ease with which he might be taken up into carriages, to learn the latest *on-dits* from one acquaintance or another.

"Quires!" shouted the baronet, pulling up alongside his friend. "What were you about, last night? Practically tore Lady Sarah from my arms, just as she was about to accept me! Dash it, man, what was the meaning of that?"

"My mistake," said Quires pleasantly. "Thought she'd already accepted you. You didn't call on her this morning? I thought surely you would have done so."

"Do you mean to say people go calling the morning after a ball?" Sir Lindsay gaped down at him from the seat of the curricle. "One can hardly pry oneself from bed before noon, now can one? Thought I'd go round tomorrow, unless you know something I don't."

"The lady gave no indication of interest in any gentleman save yourself," responded the viscount. The baronet appearing lost in thought and giving no sign of wishing to continue the discussion, Quires turned to the younger man. "Well, Franklin, did you find your heiress at Almack's?"

"Yes, and I must talk with you." Lenham moved round to the back of the curricle to make room for Quires, who climbed up with a fair amount of wheezing. Lenham feared at first that the combined weight of the two older gentlemen in front would throw the light vehicle off balance, but the fearful creaking of springs settled down as the horses started up.

"Now," continued Lenham. "Lord Quires, you must help me win the hand of Miss Mary Beth Williams. Do you know her?"

"I've seen her," replied his lordship. "Pretty thing, and flush enough for you, too. Have you called on her?"

"I left my card this morning," said Lenham. "She was not yet awake, or so the butler said, but it was after one o'clock. Do you suppose she would refuse to see me?"

Quires considered. "Most unlikely. A girl in her first season rarely refuses to see anyone, unless he has given direct offense. Could be her aunt and uncle, however. They're on their guard for fortune hunters."

"I certainly hope I shouldn't be classed as such! I've a genuine fondness for the lady," protested Lenham.

"Of course you do," soothed the viscount. "But it might be best if you were to encounter her by chance a few times first. If a friendship were already established between the two of you, her family would find it more difficult to put you off." He lifted his hat to a passing acquaintance, making note mentally that the lady appeared wan. An unhappy love affair, perhaps, or a lingering illness? He must make inquiries.

"But that could take months, and the season will be over by then!" said Lenham.

Quires issued an exaggerated sigh. "The younger generation," he said. "Don't you know that accidents can be arranged, my dear fellow?"

"Arranged?"

"One sets one's manservant to learning the lady's plans," said the viscount. "Wherever she goes to call, one happens to call also. Do you understand?"

"You're amazing." Lenham watched appreciatively as Quires bowed toward Lady Lieven's equipage. "You have an answer for everything."

"Does he now?" said Sir Lindsay, roused from his contemplations. "Then tell me, Quires, what is Lady Sarah about? Does she mean to put me off and try to snare herself bigger game? I'll not have it!"

The possibilities offered by Lady Sarah's romantic entanglements were the most intriguing the viscount had come upon during an otherwise dull season. He had no wish to spoil the fun so early by seeing one of her prime suitors chased off.

"I think it more likely it's Rowdon and his wife, not his daughter, who wish to ensnare Lord Broadmoor," said Quires. "Lady Sarah seems to me a dutiful miss."

"Hmmph," said the baronet. "Then Rowdon has played me false. Devil take him! I'll not have that either! Does he think I'll hang about for months until Broadmoor makes up his mind whether he wants her?"

"You'll have your answer in less than thirty days, that much I can say for certain," replied Quires, as Lenham in the rear seat listened with fascination.

"Thirty days?" said Sir Lindsay "Why thirty days?"

"Because, my good sir, I have learned—never mind how; I have my informants—that his creditors are about to foreclose on Lord Rowdon's townhouse, and that is the only asset remaining to him," answered the viscount. "His daughter must have a marriage settlement, or the guarantee of one, by that time or it's debtor's prison for him."

For the first time all day, Sir Lindsay smiled. "Then I have him over a barrel, do I not? I shall make good sport of them for the next few weeks. You don't think Lord Broadmoor will actually offer for her, do you?"

"I most sincerely doubt it," said Quires. "Did you notice that he danced twice last night with Lady Mansfield? He was enamoured of her once, you know, before she was married. I must call on her tomorrow to learn how it is going. That is where I would place my bet, gentlemen."

"You amaze me, my lord," Lenham commented from behind them. "There is not a word exchanged, or a penny either, I warrant, in all London that you do not know about. But have you never thought to marry yourself?"

"Marry? I?" said Quires. "What, and break the heart of my greedy young nephew, who is my heir? No, thank you, I prefer to take my companions at Covent Garden, where one pays for the night and not for the rest of one's life."

The viscount was set down again beneath the same tree. Lenham, glancing back a short time later, saw him taken up by Lady Jersey's carriage and borne away.

"Perhaps he will call again today." Mary Beth looked up from her kippers and curried eggs to examine the card left her on Thursday by Mr. Franklin Lenham. "A nice-looking fellow, rather charming and most interested in my conversation."

"Child, the man is a fortune hunter!" Kitty sipped at her morning coffee, for although it was past two o'clock in the afternoon, the pair had slept late. She was enjoying the role of wise elder, as her parents had both left the house earlier on errands. "We must not be at home to him when he calls. He's not the first to come sniffing round you for your money, you know."

To her surprise, Mary Beth glared at her. "Does it not seem to you, cousin, that a fellow might like me for myself? Can you not imagine that some factor other than money might attract the man?"

"Oh, Mary Beth, do not mistake me." Kitty, seeing she had gone too far, leaned forward with a conciliating smile. "I only wish to protect you. Of course, many men will fall in love with you, but your husband should be at least your equal in wealth and station, for your own protection."

"I suppose that may be true." The younger girl took a second helping of toast. If she kept eating that way, she would soon outgrow all her gowns, Kitty thought, but minded her tongue. "Naturally, I should prefer Lord Broadmoor. Did you see how he sought me out for a dance?"

"He danced with me also," sniffed Kitty.

"Oh, yes, naturally," said Mary Beth. "You looked very distinguished dancing together. But did you notice how indulgently he smiled at me? He assured me I should readily come to feel at home in society, and said it was charming to meet someone as young and naïve as I. Was that not kind of him? Perhaps he will come to call."

Had he really paid her such heed? Kitty could not credit it. She recalled quite distinctly how taken with *her* the marquess had been during their dance. He listened intently to her knowledgeable talk of society and complimented her on her worldliness.

"What do you think he said to Lady Sarah when they were alone?" asked Kitty, who would have given the rings off her fingers to know the answer.

Mary Beth shrugged. "At her age, perhaps he inquired after her rheumatism."

The cousins giggled.

"I have it!" said Kitty, who wished to take her cousin out of the house. Her parents had left strict instructions for her to make sure that Mary Beth did not see Mr. Lenham should he call again, and that was the simplest means of carrying out their command. "We shall call upon Lady Sarah! Perhaps we may learn something of interest."

"Do you think Broadmoor will be there?" asked Mary Beth.

Kitty slammed her empty coffee cup down in the saucer with such force that it rang out sharply. She shook her head at the footman who offered to fill it, and he resumed his impassive position behind her chair.

"I heartily doubt that Broadmoor will call upon *her*," said Kitty, annoyed that he had not yet shown his face at her own door. "She made a spectacle of herself Wednesday night, and think how cruelly she treated him four years ago! I merely wish to know how matters stand with her."

"They say she will have to marry Sir Lindsay Manx." Mary Beth wrinkled her nose. "Did you see how he was dressed? All those stripes, and such a stomach!"

"Mary Beth!" rebuked Kitty. "He is a man of fashion, and wears what fashion dictates. And a man of means as well. We are not all so wealthy as you. Even I, although I have a respectable portion, cannot call myself an heiress, for most of father's wealth must go to Joseph."

Her older half-brother was a sore point, and Kitty felt relieved when Mary Beth rose from the table and said, "Let's go upstairs and decide what we should wear to visit Lady Sarah!"

Kitty joined her, but knew already she would choose her best sprigged muslin morning gown. After all, there was just the slightest chance Lord Broadmoor would appear after all. Moreover, Sir Lindsay would almost certainly be there, and she did not wish him to think her lacking in style.

"He will not come." Sarah stared bleakly out the window, uncheered by the bright midafternoon sunshine. "It is already past four and we shall be having tea soon."

"Nonsense." Behind her, Lady Rowdon sorted with satisfaction through the cards their callers had left already that afternoon and the one previous. "A gentleman of fashion may spend hours getting himself properly dressed before making his calls. And look who has been here already—the ladies Jersey and Lieven . . ."

"Gossips," said Sarah.

"Four unmarried young men . . ."

"All penniless."

"Three respectable young ladies and their mothers . . ."

"Hoping to meet eligible gentlemen."

"Sarah, you are impossible!" declared her mother stoutly, although to Sarah's ears her voice rang hollow. "You scarcely smiled all day yesterday. If you could not enjoy the company, did you take no pleasure in the pattern for your new ball gown? The material was splendid, and only just arrived from Paris. Did you not like it?"

"Oh, Mother!" Sarah turned away from staring at the quiet street. "You know as well as I that it is who did *not* call that matters. Neither Lord Broadmoor nor Sir Lindsay has come anywhere near this house in the past two days! And how can I take pleasure in gowns bought with money that is not ours?"

"Half the *ton* buys on credit," replied Lady Rowdon. "This at least is in the nature of an investment."

"This is in the nature of folly!" said Sarah, with an unusual display of spirit. "Now I fear we have lost the baronet. Mother, what will happen to us? I cannot bear to think of Father in prison."

Setting aside the cards, the countess walked over to face her daughter. "That has always been the trouble with you, Sarah. You are inclined to worry and fret over the smallest problem. While I do not hold with your father's views of life as a gamble, it is my belief that wealth, beauty, and position are attracted to their own kind. We must maintain our station, whatever the cost, to the very last possible moment."

"But surely you must worry!" Sarah had not missed the lines of fatigue in her mother's face that morning, nor the frown she wore at supper last night. "It affects your health, Mama, and you have never been strong. Your sister lives in Torquay, does she not? Surely she would welcome a visit from us. It might be restful for you, by the sea in Devon, and we haven't seen her in years."

"Oh, indeed." Bitterness tinged Lady Rowdon's voice as she turned back to the sofa. "No, Sarah, my family wants nothing to do with us; surely you have perceived that by now. They fault your father for running through my dowry and his own inheritance."

"But he cannot be blamed for what is God's doing rather than man's!" Sarah protested. "Did he cause a ship to sink at sea, or a harvest to go bad? Many others have lost their fortunes through such calamities as ours, and they are not held responsible."

Lady Rowdon kept her face averted and made no response. Sarah would have questioned her further, for this estrangement from her mother's relations had long concerned her, but for the appearance of Henderson, the butler, to announce the arrival of two young ladies.

"Miss Mary Elizabeth Williams and Miss Catherine Williams," he said, then stepped aside just in time to avoid being trampled by the two enthusiastic guests.

"Lady Sarah! Oh, do forgive us for not coming earlier, but we have been fearfully lazy!" cried the girl she recognised as Kitty.

"How very fine you are looking," added Mary Beth. "Are we really late? I am not conversant with these things yet, this being my first season."

"You are both very welcome," said Sarah, wondering at the warmth of the greetings, for she could not recall having exchanged more than a word or two with either of these young persons before.

The two began prattling, and went on so long that Sarah had difficulty restraining herself from daydreaming. So distracted did she become that before realising it she had consented to accompanying the two cousins to Vauxhall Gardens the next night to see the fireworks.

Both of her visitors exerted great effort to keep the conversation from lagging, as if they wished to prolong the visit, she noted as she went to confer with Henderson about serving some sandwiches in the drawing room.

Lady Rowdon joined her, and Sarah inquired in a whisper, "Are they hoping Lord Broadmoor will call? Perhaps I should make it clear . . ."

"Nonsense!" Her mother glared at her, and Sarah felt her courage retreat. "Do you want everyone in London to say you are abandoned? Further, Mary Beth is known to be an heiress, and will herself serve as an attraction. It would be best for you to become her bosom bow."

So the visit continued until, mercifully, there came the sound of a carriage in the street.

"Someone is calling upon you!" Mary Beth flew to the window. "Do you recognise the vehicle, Sarah, or Kitty? I am not yet well enough acquainted with London to know whose it is."

The other two joined her at the window. "Dimwit," said her cousin. "You can plainly see Sir Lindsay and Mr. Lenham in the curricle."

Sarah uttered a small, relieved sigh. Her suitor had returned, and she would lose no time in accepting him.

"But there is a phaeton come round the corner," proclaimed Mary Beth. "Even I can recognise that one."

The sight of the black and gold vehicle filled Sarah with dread. Lord Broadmoor had come to call, and she could not imagine a worse time for it.

=== 6 ===

LORD BROADMOOR, RESTLESS from dreaming of a lithe feminine shape that repeatedly kicked him in the ankle, spent the day after the ball closeted with his man of affairs, reviewing business matters he had been forced to neglect while preparing for his return to society.

On Friday morning, his ankle and his temper somewhat restored, he turned to the most important business at hand: how to deal with Lady Sarah.

Showing the same flair for organisation that had made him so valuable to Wellington, he encamped in his study with a pad of paper, three goose quill nibs, and a penholder to plot out his campaign, instructing the butler that he was not to be disturbed.

Fully aware that any revealing scribblings could fall into the hands of servants, who might give the game away to the enemy—Broadmoor could not help thinking in military terms—he made sure to note down only key words that would be meaningless to anyone but him.

The object was to make Lady Sarah fall in love with him or, if the cold-hearted wench were incapable of such deep feeling, to make her pin her hopes on him, so that they might be dashed.

Did he also wish to chase off Sir Lindsay as a suitor? That would be fit punishment indeed, and further, the marquess found himself inexplicably disturbed at the thought of Lady Sarah warming that fop's bed.

However, he reasoned, his goal was not devastation but fairness, and he had to concede that Lady Sarah had not in any way harmed his finances or his military career. Therefore, he decided, he would not make any special effort to discourage his rival.

Now, he thought, what other caveats must he observe?

For one thing, Broadmoor saw, he must court the chit without giving society in general so strong an indication of marital intent that he would be judged a cad when he deserted the field. He did not, after all, wish to sully his reputation.

He also noted that forays would not be without danger: He might be captured by the enemy. Lady Sarah had come perilously close to ambushing his heart the night before; only Sir Lindsay's timely appearance and the smug look on Lady Rowdon's face had reawakened his own natural caution.

At this point Lord Broadmoor digressed, laying down the pen and recalling the sweet confusion on Lady Sarah's countenance as she confessed her dream of defying cutthroats and thieves. What a quiz she was, walking about in the midst of such absurd fantasies! But how very endearing, as well.

And to think she had nearly torn Lady Mansfield's dress . . . Lady Mansfield!

Ah, here was a solution to three problems at once. On his pad, Lord Broadmoor wrote: "1. Jealousy. 2. Reputation. 3. Safety."

Jealousy. Yes, Lady Sarah would be jealous if he courted Lady Mansfield at the same time. It would certainly not do for Sarah to assume that he was already in her pocket; she must strive to win him, and thus truly commit herself to the battle. In the end, then, her disappointment would be all the keener.

Reputation. There could be no scandal attached to his throwing over Lady Sarah, if it had been unclear from the start where his affections lay.

Safety. He must, after all, marry someone and produce an heir, and who better than Lady Mansfield? She was beautiful, wealthy, unmarried, and willing. Best of all, keeping a fixed image of her in his mind would provide a shield against Lady Sarah's bombardments.

Done! thought the marquess, folding up the sheet of paper and placing it inside his breast pocket. He would begin by calling on his two ladies. That should set tongues wagging quick enough!

It was almost four o'clock when his lordship alighted at Lady Mansfield's, and he was not surprised to see another carriage already there before him. He did not recognise it, but then he had not been in London long enough to know everyone's equipages.

The butler admitted him with flattering alacrity, and Kenneth found himself ushered into a charming parlour filled with sunlight and furnished in Oriental splendour, with japanned lacquerwork on the tables and chairs, a sofa the colour of jade, and a large vase on the hearth painted with scenes from China.

Sound asleep in a chair tucked away in the far corner was an elderly lady, who gave no sign of having heard him come in. She was apparently chaperoning her mistress during a visit by Lord Quires, the owner of the carriage.

Lady Mansfield rose from the sofa to greet the new arrival, extending two white hands whose delicacy was accentuated by the rich cherry hue of her cambric morning dress. "Lord Broadmoor!" she said. "I am so pleased to see you. You are acquainted with the Viscount Quires, are you not?"

The marquess nodded, shaking hands with the bluff fellow. Here was a lucky chance. The viscount had a reputation for dealing in gossip, of the most accurate and refined sort. His word would be accepted everywhere, and could be invaluable to the battle. He could also be a useful source of information from the enemy camp—or to it.

"Everyone knows Lord Quires, I believe," said Broadmoor, accepting a seat and a glass of sherry.

"Everyone may know me, but everyone wants to know you," returned the other gentleman gallantly.

So his interest is piqued, thought Broadmoor. Very good. Whether he be friend or foe remains to be determined, however. "And what does everyone say of me?" he asked. "For if anyone would know, I think it must be you."

The viscount smiled. "I like to think I am in many people's confidence," he said. "But I would not be, were I to prove myself untrustworthy by revealing their comments."

We understand each other, thought the marquess.

Lady Mansfield did not appear at all pleased to find the two callers in her drawing room more interested in each other than in her. "Naturally, everyone says that you are the most eligible man in London," she told Broadmoor. "And they compliment your bearing and manner, as well."

"Thank you, madame," he said, lifting his glass of sherry in salute of her. "I take the compliments as your own. And everyone says that you, newly emerged from widowhood, are lovelier than ever, and they are right."

"Indeed," said Lord Quires. "It was noticed by many that Lord Broadmoor favoured you with two dances. Some called this sentimentality, as you are old acquaintances, but others consider it a sign of renewed friendship."

"I am sure they attach too much importance to a courtesy." Lady Mansfield's grey eyes narrowed in annoyance.

It was understandable, reflected Broadmoor, that she should resent the viscount's implication of a budding romance, for fear of destroying it before it could bloom. But he himself understood that Quires was in reality seeking information.

"Others, no doubt, remarked upon the length of time I spent conversing privately with Lady Sarah, as well as on her unusual behavior in bringing me low," suggested the marquess.

Quires nodded. "I have no doubt they are laying bets at White's between the two ladies. Barbaric custom, ain't it?"

Their hostess clearly did not like this turn of the conversation. "Tell me, Lord Broadmoor, are you well settled in at Grosvenor Square?" she inquired. "Have you found the servants suitable? Domestic staff can present such difficulties."

"Fortunately, I have brought my own valet, and for the rest, the house seems well enough run," said Lord Broadmoor, who preferred to leave domestic arrangements to the butler, a long-time family employee.

"On one point I must caution you," said the viscount. "One has a tendency to forget that servants have ears, but they can be most indiscreet."

"I have no doubt of that," agreed Lady Mansfield.

"For example, there is an item I have heard that could only have come from a servant, or perhaps some enterprising clerk," Quires continued.

"Perhaps we should not listen to it then," said their hostess, but a hesitancy in her tone indicated she was loath to miss such a titbit.

"Then you may close your ears, my dear, but I think Lord Broadmoor would be interested," said the viscount. "And no harm done, so long as the information does not leave this room."

Lady Mansfield glanced at the snoozing woman in the corner, but her companion gave no sign of waking. "I suppose that's so," she conceded.

"Pray proceed," said Lord Broadmoor.

"This servant, or clerk, or whoever, would have it that Lady Sarah must choose her husband within thirty days, for the creditors are about to foreclose upon the Rowdons' townhouse, and they have nowhere else to go," said Quires. "That would lend some liveliness to the betting at White's, but they shall certainly not learn of it through me."

For that would spoil your fun, in breaking the news to the participants personally, thought the marquess, surmising that Sir Lindsay had already been or shortly would be apprised of the matter.

It did indeed add zest to the battle, to know that the climax would take place in so short a time. He must work more quickly than he had anticipated.

"More sherry?" Lady Mansfield crossed to him and refilled his glass. When she sat down again, she chose a seat nearer to the marquess. So she too wished to proceed more rapidly.

"I must be going." Quires stood and took his leave, adding to Broadmoor, "We must dine together soon. Are you agreeable?" To which the marquess readily assented.

"Interesting man," said Lady Mansfield when he had gone, returning to her seat near Broadmoor. "One learns all manner of things from him, sometimes more than one wants to know."

"Is he a good friend of yours?" asked the marquess.

"Not really. He has called on me only once or twice before, and then in the company of others. No, I think he was seeking information about you, and I am not sure whether he got it."

"He knows that I'm here," said Broadmoor. "That will entertain Lady Jersey and perhaps change the odds at White's, if they are giving odds."

Lady Mansfield yielded up a refined shudder. "The very idea chills me. To lay wagers upon a man's affections, and two women's future! One would think marriage were a sort of horse race."

Here the conversation lapsed for a moment, and the marquess was considering going on his way. However, his hostess clearly had no intention of losing this rare opportunity to rub shoulders with him alone.

"I can't tell you how pleased I am that you are come up in the world," she said. Her eyes met his in a most intimate manner, except that little warmth shone through her natural reserve, and so the effect was rather like weak sunlight on a cool day. "I had always thought you deserved more success in the world."

"Unfortunately, I did not rise so high because I deserved it," said the marquess.

Lady Mansfield leaned toward him. Good heavens, she was flirting with him! "This is that rare occasion, I believe, in which chance has rewarded the right man."

"I am honoured that you think so well of me." Oddly enough, Broadmoor found that he felt slightly uncomfortable and unsure of what to say next. Had he forgotten how to go about courting a woman? The idea was disconcerting, as was the prospect of going through an entire married life searching for topics of conversation over the breakfast table.

"For a man long absent from London, you acquitted yourself well on the dance floor at Almack's," said Lady Mansfield. "And your tailor is impeccable. Weston, may I assume?"

"Naturally." The marquess flicked a speck of dust from his snowy cravat, tied by his valet with much skill in the Mathematical, one of the many elaborate styles popular for neckcloths.

Ah, yes, now it was his turn to say something. "And may I compliment you again on your gown, Lady Mansfield? That shade of pink is particularly becoming. I am glad to see you are out of mourning."

"Yes." She smiled, apparently relieved at finding this new topic for discussion. "I feared perhaps it was too soon, but my companion, Mrs. Buxton, assured me it was not."

At the mention of her name, the sleeping woman issued a loud snort and sat upright. Lady Mansfield frowned, evidently not welcoming a third party to their tête-à-tête.

"Eh? Is Lord Quires gone?" The elderly woman began to rise with some difficulty, and the marquess hurried across the room to assist her. As he took her arm and she straightened, he distinctly heard her knees cracking.

"Gone some ten minutes ago," he assured her. "Allow me to introduce myself, madame."

"Not necessary," she said as he lowered her to the sofa. "You are that handsome Lieutenant Link. You young folks don't think I notice, but I do. You've been dangling after Stella for months, ain't you?"

"Please, Patience!" Lady Mansfield glared at her cousin, then added to the marquess, "She is always confusing past and present."

"Nonsense," said Mrs. Buxton. "I'm not mistaken, am I, lieutenant?"

"Far be it from me to correct a lady." Broadmoor beat his verbal retreat from the field, leaving the skirmish between his hostess and her companion.

"Too bad that your pockets are to let," Mrs. Buxton continued. "Else you might have a chance, eh? But I'll tell you one thing about Stella. Her portion ain't all it's cracked up to be."

"Cousin!" cried Lady Mansfield in horror. "You are giving the most erroneous impression . . ."

"Two of you'd have nothing but love to live on, and that ain't all it's cracked up to be either," Mrs. Buxton said blithely. "So take my advice and bestow your attentions elsewhere. Her family's got a fine gentleman picked out for her . . ."

Lady Mansfield had turned pale with shame, and Lord Broadmoor decided the game had gone far enough. "Mrs. Buxton," he said. "I do believe you have got things a bit mixed up. I often find myself somewhat confused when suddenly awakened also."

"Suddenly awakened?" asked the woman. "Was I asleep? Oh, dear me, must have been, for Lord Quires has taken himself off and I failed to bid him good-bye. How very awkward of me!"

The marquess gave his hostess a reassuring smile. "Try not to be too hard on your cousin, my dear. She is a charming soul, and could never give offense."

Lady Mansfield smiled back shakily. "I suppose I should be grateful she did not speak her piece before Lord Quires, or I would not have been able to hold my head up in society."

"What have I said?" demanded Mrs. Buxton. "I was merely being frank with the lad."

"I shall explain it all to you later," said Lady Mansfield.

"And I shall depart, before I overstay my welcome," said the marquess. With a bow and a thank-you for the sherry, he was on his way, stepping out into the fresh air with a deep breath of relief.

Now, he thought, on to Lady Sarah's.

As he guided his phaeton through the streets, which were filled with vendors of milk and oranges, apple tarts and strawberries, the marquess reflected on the success of his first sortie.

Already Quires would be spreading word of his call to the ladies Lieven and Jersey, and the news would soon reach Lady Sarah.

Matters also seemed to be progressing well with Lady Mansfield herself. Clearly, she would not be averse to receiving his attentions, and her companion might provide enough solecisms to keep him amused.

It was difficult to imagine a lifetime in the smoothly controlled company of Lady Mansfield, but he supposed that matters changed after one was married. Then one had all manner of things in common, from children to estates, to talk about.

Approaching the Rowdon house off Clarence Square, the marquess noted the presence of two other carriages. A coachman and groom waited alongside one; it must belong to a lady or ladies, for a gentleman would have driven himself.

From the other vehicle, a curricle, two men were descending, and Lord Broadmoor identified one of them immediately as Sir Lindsay.

What a stroke of luck! he thought as he drew up alongside and tossed his reins to his groom. Sir Lindsay and Lady Sarah both on hand for the battle. What a splendid conflict this promised to be.

7

SARAH WISHED AT that moment that she might be three people, so that she could placate the baronet, flirt with the marquess, and send her real self scurrying into the deepest hole she could find.

But there was no escape, not with her mother rooted firmly at her side and her mind filled with the image of them all being cast into the street by creditors.

"How kind of you to call," Lady Rowdon was saying as Sir Lindsay and Mr. Lenham entered, the latter gentleman making immediately for Mary Beth's side. "We are delighted to see you both."

"Sir Lindsay, how very fine you are looking!" exclaimed Kitty, although Sarah could not see what was so fine about a maroon coat over a pink and grey satin-striped waistcoat with grey trousers. The ensemble gave the hefty Sir Lindsay the appearance of a walrus, all shoulders and stomach.

The marquess would enter at any moment, Sarah thought, glancing toward the door apprehensively. That would certainly not help assuage the displeasure Sir Lindsay must already feel toward her. However, the baronet's cheerful countenance dispelled Sarah's worries momentarily.

He turned to speak to her mother. "I have come to show there are no hard feelings. Some men might perhaps take offense at the manner in which my proposal was treated, but I am not one of them. I hope that Lady Sarah and I may always be friends."

"Friends?" Lady Rowdon looked as if she might perish of the apoplexy. "But my dear sir, she did not refuse to be your wife! Come here, Sarah!"

As she dragged her unwilling feet across the room, Sarah noted its other occupants listening intently. What a dreadful tangle this was!

"Good afternoon." Sir Lindsay bowed to her, looking more jovial than she had ever seen him. "Indeed she did not, Lady Rowdon, but I am not a fool. When a lady all but runs from the ballroom, I do not take it as indication that my suit has been successful."

"Run from the ballroom?" Lady Rowdon gasped. "Oh, good heavens, I fear the blame was mine, sir. I felt ill, and my daughter places my health above all other considerations, even her own happiness."

"So she was explaining to me as we danced," said the baronet. "Well, then, Sarah, does this mean my suit is well received?"

"I am honoured by your visit, and deeply regret if I have given the wrong impression," Sarah managed to say, under her mother's stern eye. "I hoped I might have some time to consider."

"Oh, indeed yes," boomed the baronet, clearly not troubled that his audience also included his friend and the other two ladies. "There is no hurry at all. Perhaps it would be agreeable if I withdrew my offer, and we resumed our acquaintance as it was? Then if you should at some point decide that we could make a match of it, you might so indicate, and if my heart has not become otherwise involved, all will be settled."

"I do not think anything so drastic is necessary." Lady Rowdon glared at her daughter, although it seemed to Sarah that Sir Lindsay was being intentionally difficult. "Surely my daughter can give you her answer within, say, a few weeks?"

"Does that not seem a rather long time to you, my love?" asked Sir Lindsay of Sarah. "A few days is generally enough for young ladies, I believe."

"Yes, but . . ." Lady Rowdon was not permitted to finish whatever she intended to say.

"The Marquess of Broadmoor," announced Henderson.

Sarah's heart performed an alarming series of leaps and plunges at the sight of the marquess, of his intent dark eyes and of the symmetry with which he moved. He was instantly engulfed by Kitty and Mary Beth, who had been eagerly awaiting this moment.

"How very good to see you again," said Kitty, as if this were her own home and he had come expressly to see her. "Everyone has been wondering where you were yesterday, for you were not seen in Hyde Park, nor even at your club, so I'm told."

"What chance that we should meet this way," added Mary Beth. "My acquaintance in London is not yet great, your lordship, as this is my first season, and I had not expected to encounter you again so soon."

The marquess merely smiled politely, as if he had been introduced to a pair of gnats and was restraining himself with difficulty from swatting them. "Sir Lindsay," he acknowledged. "And, ah, Lenham, I believe? Lady Rowdon, a pleasure to see you again."

He bowed to her and to Sarah. What was he doing here? It did not seem possible that he wished to renew his suit, despite his inexplicably friendly behaviour at Almack's.

Sarah peeked at Sir Lindsay, expecting to see an angry glower, but his face displayed only good fellowship.

"Broadmoor! Glad to see you here. What a splendid job your valet has done with that cravat. What do they call it?"

"The Mathematical," said Broadmoor. "And yours is . . .?"

"My own design," replied the baronet. "Come aside, and I will tell you how it is done. You are the first in whom I have confided. I ask only that you identify it in future as the Manx. Are we agreed?"

Broadmoor, who Sarah would have sworn cared not a fig for his cravat, accepted this invitation at once and went off to a corner with the baronet as if this were the sole purpose of his visit.

Kitty assumed a vexed expression, but Mary Beth turned gladly enough to Mr. Lenham, who was full of compliments.

Meanwhile, Lady Rowdon had recovered herself enough to order refreshments all round. "Be on your guard," she advised her daughter sotto voce. "We must not lose Sir Lindsay. Lord Broadmoor is by no means caught."

"Nor will he ever be!" said Sarah, then backed up a step as her mother opened her mouth to scold. "But I will do my best, I assure you."

She retreated to a chair. Kitty for once had nothing to say, being occupied with staring across the room at the marquess, and her cousin was fully occupied with her young suitor, leaving Sarah a moment's peace.

She gazed nostalgically about the room, with its large Regency bow window and delicate French furnishings. She must win Sir Lindsay back—for she had no real hope of attaching Lord Broadmoor—or all this would be taken from them. No doubt their creditors would descend upon them in black capes, ready to cast her parents into prison . . .

Lady Sarah took a firm stance in the doorway, trying to hide the palpitations of her heart. "Stay, gentlemen!" she cried to the black-clad hordes. "Take not my innocent father and mother to the Fleet. I will go in their stead, since it is I who failed to find a wealthy husband."

The foremost of the creditors leered at her. "Prison, my dear?" he hissed. "It is your virtue we will have instead. Now come away from the door." He reached up to take her arm.

"Fiend!" Lady Sarah flung off his hand . . .

A hard grip on her wrist stopped the motion. A footman stood gaping at her scarcely two feet away, holding a heavy tray of china and sandwiches that had narrowly escaped being dashed to the floor by her impulsive gesture.

Sarah looked up to see Lord Broadmoor grinning at her from above as he released her wrist. "Barely caught you in time, I see," he murmured. "Dreaming again?"

She nodded, feeling a blush infuse her cheeks. A quick survey of the room assured her that, thankfully, no one else had been watching.

The marquess pulled up a chair beside hers as the footman proceeded to arrange the luncheon on several small gilt tables in the center of the room. "What was it this time?" asked Broadmoor. "More cutthroats? Or pirates, perhaps?"

"Creditors," said Lady Sarah, and then flushed even more deeply.

The marquess regarded her thoughtfully. "They trouble even your daydreams?"

Sarah glanced at her mother, but fortunately Lady Rowdon was involved in animated conversation with Sir Lindsay. "It is chiefly my mother's health that worries me. I know she appears well enough, but sometimes she suffers alarming attacks. I would do anything to relieve her mind."

"Anything?" asked the marquess in a strange tone she could not interpret.

As Sarah nodded and gazed up into his mesmerising brown eyes, she recalled the words of the imaginary creditors: "It is your virtue we will take instead."

A brilliant idea flashed into her mind. Of course! It was the perfect solution to all their problems.

Lady Rowdon began serving the guests their sandwiches and tea, along with cunning little peach and apple tortes that Cook had devised. Broadmoor was, like the others, momentarily occupied with being served and eating these delicacies, and Sarah was spared a few moments to meditate on her wonderful new plan.

Harriette Wilson, the most famous and beautiful of the Fashionable Impures, turned to her companion at the Opera. "Who is that exquisite woman over there?" she asked.

"Why, that is Lady Sarah Rowdon," he said.

"A lady?" Harriette studied the slender figure. "But she wears rouge, and she is unaccompanied."

"Ah, she is awaiting her paramour, the Marquess of Broadmoor," said the companion. "She has consented to be his mistress, to save her family from poverty and herself from an unwanted marriage with Sir Lindsay Manx."

"How very clever of her," said Harriette. "And noble, as well . . ."

"I must ask that you not make any sudden movements, for I've no wish to find your cup of tea in my lap," said the marquess.

"I beg your pardon?" She blinked at him, then at the plate and teacup that had mysteriously come to roost in her hands.

"The distracted expression gave you away." Broadmoor kept his voice low so the conversation would not be overheard. Lady Rowdon had once again cornered Sir Lindsay, no doubt with the intent of giving Sarah a clear field with the marquess. "I knew that you were dreaming, and would inevitably begin making wild gestures."

"Not at the opera!" said Lady Sarah.

"Ah. The opera?" The marquess cocked his head musingly. "Were you being attacked there? I would offer to rescue you, but I gather that in these fantasies you are quite capable of rescuing yourself."

She could hardly confess to him what she had been doing there. In fact, Lady Sarah was at a loss to know how to secure for herself the position of his mistress. She was not even certain what a mistress did.

"Do you know Harriette Wilson?" she asked.

The marquis looked startled. "I know who she is—but you should not. That is hardly a matter for delicate young ladies."

"But she must lead a fascinating life, don't you think?" Sarah persisted. "She has so many admirers. I've seen her in Hyde Park; all the gentleman ride alongside her carriage, hoping to be noticed."

"You are the most unpredictable woman I have ever met," said the marquess. "I never know what the topic of conversation will be. Could we not discuss the weather, or the latest fashions?"

"Are you interested in the weather or the latest fashions?"

"No."

"Well, neither am I." Sarah considered that matter settled and returned to her former topic. "How do you suppose Harriette Wilson got to be that way? Did she have to have special instruction, do you think?"

Broadmoor looked as if he might choke, and took a quick sip of his tea. "No, I don't suppose she did."

Sarah had hit a stumbling block. She could hardly come right out and ask the marquess if he were interested in taking a mistress. It seemed unlikely that he had one already, newly returned to London as he was, so at least she needn't worry about that.

However, this might take more planning than she had imagined. Were she to enquire directly, the marquess would likely be shocked, or amused, but certainly he would not take her seriously.

She must devise other means of drawing his attention, and in haste, for only a few weeks remained before she must otherwise consent to Sir Lindsay, if his offer still held good.

How much simpler it would be if she and Kenneth could marry. Tears clouded Sarah's vision as she allowed herself one wistful recollection of the time when such happiness had seemed within grasp. But now he was Lord Broadmoor, and she was the one girl in London he surely would never court.

True, he had come here today, and from this fact her mother would draw the conclusions she and Father wished. Sarah knew better. The marquess might have been passing in the street and seen the other carriages, and called from curiosity or a perverse desire to set tongues wagging. But he would never forgive her for what he had made quite clear he saw as a violation of his trust and affection.

"Such a variety of expressions have marched across your face these past few minutes that I am at a loss to interpret them," said the man in question. "Just now you appeared terribly sad, Lady Sarah. Is something wrong?"

This would never do. What gentleman would want a mistress who depressed his spirits? "Not at all." She lifted her chin and tossed back her dark curls. "Tell me, now that you are back in London, my lord, do you plan to mix much in society? May we hope to see you at balls and Vauxhall Gardens and the theatre?"

For she must know where to find him, so that she could formulate her plans, thought Sarah.

"You are seeing me here, right now," said the marquess. "Is that not sufficient?"

Sarah frowned at him. "You are making this most difficult, my lord."

"Making what difficult?"

"I am trying to learn your habits, what places you plan to frequent."

Broadmoor, having finished his refreshments, handed the plate to the footman and settled back in his chair. "Why should you want to know that?"

"If I don't know where you are going to be," said Sarah, "how can I arrange to happen upon you from time to time?"

"I will give you the information you seek, if you will tell me why you should want to follow me about," the marquess continued with a glint in his eye, as if this were an intriguing sport.

"You would never believe me," said Lady Sarah. "What about Vauxhall? Surely you will be there tomorrow night. They are to have a splendid fireworks display, and everyone is going."

"Will you be among them?"

She nodded. "I will be accompanying the two Misses Williams."

"Are they very great friends of yours?"

"Actually, no, I think they have only come today to see if you would be here," Sarah admitted.

"Then why did you agree to go with them?"

"I was on the point of being engulfed by a daydream, and did not know what I was saying," she said, and was embarrassed at the hearty laugh that greeted this confession.

"Well, well, you two are getting on splendidly, I see," said the faintly nasal voice of Sir Lindsay, who had come to stand before them. "I regret that I must take my leave, for I have been having the most enchanting conversation with your mother, Lady Sarah."

She stood up immediately, guiltily aware that she had neglected him. "Sir Lindsay, you are not departing already? But we have scarcely spoken."

"Oh, no offense taken." He waved away her objections. "Lenham, if you can tear yourself from the lovely young lady"—for his friend was gazing rapturously into Mary Beth's eyes—"we shall be on our way."

"And we must be gone also," said Kitty.

A flurry of farewells, and the room began to empty. Just before withdrawing, Lord Broadmoor said quietly to Sarah, "It is to be a masquerade tomorrow night, you know. How will I recognise you?"

"No doubt I will stumble into someone, or rip some lady's dress, or smash the dishes." Sarah had not meant to be witty, but he was still laughing as he went out the door.

"Well!" Lady Rowdon stood in the bow window, watching the carriages move off down the street. "What a strange afternoon that was."

"Why strange, Mama?" Sarah watched longingly as the black and gold phaeton disappeared from view. Someday she would ride there at his side, but of course her parents would not speak to her then, for she would be fallen from grace. She would have to pass by this house, knowing that she had saved it for them, and yet never be able to enter again . . .

"I do not mind," Lady Sarah told her dresser-maid, who was fastening the clasp of a diamond and gold necklace. "It is enough for me to be certain they are well and lack for nothing. But if only, one more time before I die, I could hear my mother's voice . . ."

"Sir Lindsay was in the most peculiar mood," said Lady Rowdon. "Very merry indeed, and not seeming at all eager to be wed. Odd, how he kept saying that your decision might be put off after all, that there was no rush. Almost as if he knew we could not wait long. But no matter. What a splendid success you were with Lord Broadmoor!"

"Was I?"

"Kitty Williams stared daggers at you the whole time," said the countess cheerily. "She loves to gossip, although she is a very common sort of girl and has no one's ear, no one of significance. Still, no doubt word will somehow or other reach those who matter, and you shall be given all the more importance, just as you deserve."

"I do not care for importance." Sarah looked down at her hands. She wished she dared confide in her mother about her plans, but then no doubt she would be hustled off to marry Sir Lindsay at once. And the more she saw of him in the presence of the marquess, the more she thought she could not bear to be his wife.

"Did Lord Broadmoor say he would call again?" Lady Rowdon turned away from the window, and Sarah was obliged to follow her through the room and up the stairs. "Will he come tomorrow?"

"He will be at Vauxhall, and I am going with Mary Beth and Kitty," said Sarah. "Shall you come too, Mama?"

"No, your father and I have invitations for a dinner at Lady Cowper's—very tedious, but of course we could not refuse, as it is all the crack," said Lady Rowdon. "I am sure the Williamses do not let their girls run about unchaperoned, so you will be well enough with them."

"Oh, I am glad you and Father were invited to Lady Cowper's," said Sarah. "It means you may take your place in society again, does it not? How very gay you look, Mother. I was becoming worried."

"Gay? Of course I am gay." Lady Rowdon led the way to Sarah's room. "My daughter is to marry a marquess—and hush, I'll not hear otherwise. Now, we must decide what you are to wear tomorrow night."

8

LORD QUIRES WAS not in the best of moods when he emerged from Betty's, the St. James's fruiterers, on Saturday afternoon.

He had gone to the shop, noted for its social atmosphere, to dispense sought-after titbits about Lord Broadmoor's visit to Lady Mansfield on the previous day, only to be cast into the shade by that jumped-up chatterbox, Miss Kitty Williams.

She was describing at length how the marquess called upon Lady Sarah, and spent above a quarter of an hour speaking with her in a low voice and laughing merrily at her sallies. Furthermore, Miss Williams declared, Lady Sarah was to accompany her and her cousin that very night to Vauxhall, and who knew what might transpire there?

Quires took a seat in his carriage and ordered the coachman to take him to Gunter's, where he would soothe his vexation with an ice, the day being quite warm for April.

Naturally, he would attend Vauxhall himself that night, although it was a rather common place where even ruffians might enter for a shilling. But how was he to learn anything of interest, off by himself while Miss Williams strolled arm in arm with Lady Sarah?

He contemplated the merits of dropping round Sir Lindsay's rooms and suggesting they attend Vauxhall together. But the baronet's story could take only a poor second place to the main interest, the progress of the relationship between Lord Broadmoor and his former inamorata, and how was Quires to manage to sit center stage?

It was one of those times when a weaker man might have given up entirely. But the viscount was merely winded, not out of the race.

By force of habit, Quires scrutinised the other carriages while he sent his coachman into Gunter's, it being his preference to eat in the privacy of his carriage when he could not be seen with someone of note.

Thus it was that he recognised the blue and white equipage of Lady Estelle Mansfield as she and her companion sat waiting for their ices.

Here was a rare opportunity indeed. Of all the players in this most exquisite drama, Quires preferred the estimable Lady M., as having a refined air that blended perfectly with her elegant beauty, although he deplored her customary reluctance to indulge in *on-dits*. This time, however, she might perhaps be persuaded to take him into her confidence, if he could demonstrate that it would work to her benefit.

Without hesitation, the viscount lowered himself to the street and strolled toward them. His coachman, who was experienced in such matters, would not be long finding him.

"Good morning." Quires doffed his fashionable beaver hat. "How very lovely you are looking, Lady Mansfield. Mrs. Buxton, always a pleasure to see you."

He was politely invited to join them, and did so without demur. The carriage was a commodious one, lined in blue velvet; he had not ridden in it before, since Lady Mansfield did not seek him out in Hyde Park.

"I trust you have had an enjoyable four-and-twenty hours, my lord," said Lady Mansfield. "I have no doubt Lady Jersey and Lady Lieven were most curious to hear about Lord Broadmoor's visit to me."

"Do I detect a note of disapproval in your voice?" The viscount adjusted his kid gloves, which were cut a bit low for his taste and gave the sensation of continually creeping down. "But you know, my lady, I not only give information, I also collect it, and it happens that I have something of interest to you."

"Strange business." Mrs. Buxton, who had been staring out the window, looked round at her companions. "You go about buying and selling information, do you, sir? An unusual occupation, if I am not mistaken. But you do bear a powerful resemblance to the Viscount Quires, now I get a better look at you. Perhaps that aids you in securing clients."

"My dear Patience, this *is* the Viscount Quires," said Lady Mansfield. "He is about to tell us something for which I am expected to pant eagerly, as if I were some young miss fresh from the schoolroom. But in fairness, I must concede that he does not buy and sell information, he trades it."

"Quite." The viscount considered departing in a huff, but decided this opportunity was too good to pass up. "For example, I learned this morning that directly he left your house yesterday, madame, Lord Broadmoor paid a call on Lady Sarah."

Lady Mansfield did not look at all pleased at this news. However, her response was interrupted by the return of her footman, the approach of the viscount's coachman, and the fuss attendant on taking the ices into the carriage.

When they were settled once more, her ladyship fixed a stare on Quires and said, "If you plan to run to your friends with an account of my shocked reaction, or my distress, I fear you will be disappointed."

"You mistake me, Lady Mansfield," said Quires. "The currying of news is to me as fine an art as was the collecting of ancient marbles to Lord Elgin. I wish my treasures to be as genuine as his. Shopgirls' chatter will not do, and I would not lower myself to betray a friend. You may react to my news however you will, and no one shall hear of it."

"Then what is it that you wish, for I do not flatter myself that you seek out my company from admiration for my person?"

The viscount regarded her musingly. She was not a cooperative spirit, but if he could bring her round the result could be to thrust him well ahead of that encroaching Kitty Williams.

"It has occurred to me that we could be of mutual benefit in this affair," said Quires. To her sceptical look, he continued, "You wish, if I am not mistaken, to bring the marquess up to scratch."

"Yes, she does." Mrs. Buxton appeared oblivious to her mistress's fiery glare. "Told me herself they was to be wed. Won't let me send in the notices until he's asked her, though, and I hope it's soon. I've got them all written up and if it takes long, I shall forget where I've put them."

"Cousin, you are most vexing." Lady Mansfield spoke between gritted teeth.

"Not a word of this shall ever pass my lips," Lord Quires assured her. "It is the most natural thing in the world for you to seek such an advantageous marriage. There I can help you."

"Oh?"

"Do not forget, I have Lord Broadmoor's agreement to dine with me shortly, and so I have his ear. Furthermore, I have already learned something of his plans for tonight. It cannot hurt to be seen by him, especially as Lady Sarah is also to be at Vauxhall tonight."

"Vauxhall?"

"You had planned on going, perhaps," suggested the viscount.

"To a common masquerade? Indeed not. But I may change my mind." Lady Mansfield finished her ice thoughtfully. "There is some truth in what you say, that you could assist me, if you promise to be discreet. But how am I to repay you?"

"Allow me to accompany you tonight," said Quires. "And to join you at times for other entertainments. That way I may observe from a front-row seat how the play comes out. And may I add that my sympathies lie with you."

"I make no promises for the future." Lady Mansfield held her head high—charming minx she was, too, thought the viscount. "This alliance goes against my instincts, but I can see some merit in it. You will come round for me, then?"

Quires assented readily and bowed himself out of the carriage, returning to his own in a much happier frame of mind.

He left behind a perplexed Mrs. Buxton. "Who would ever have thought the Viscount Quires would be in trade?"

"He is not in trade in the conventional way." Stella's voice revealed a strain of annoyance. "It is gossip in which he deals, cousin, and unfortunately I have need of it. For the moment."

"But your reputation might suffer, might it not, to be seen going about with him?"

"Quite the opposite," said her mistress. "Society dotes upon him. Also, do not forget that he is an eligible bachelor and although I am certain he will never marry, his presence may serve to remind Broadmoor that I am not without other suitors."

In fact, she had been concerned when the marquess failed to call on her that morning. Had he abandoned his suit so quickly?

When she had been out in society before her marriage, it was with the knowledgeable help of her mother, who had since passed on. Now Stella was beginning to realise that wending one's way in the world, even as a wealthy widow, was not so easy as it seemed.

Yes, she needed a source of information. If he could be trusted not to reveal her private thoughts and statements, Lord Quires might well make a suitable ally.

"Damn foolish idea," opined Sir Lindsay, glaring at the disconsolate Mr. Lenham across a glass of claret in Sir Lindsay's study. "Cannot help the fact that Miss Mary Beth Williams was not in to you this morning, and don't look to me to remedy the matter. Quires said it would be best to encounter her accidentally a few times before you went calling again, and if you plan to ignore his advice, you'll get no help from me. If there's anyone knows how things work where women are concerned, it's Quires."

"Odd that he's unmarried then." Lenham knew the comment was churlish, but it fitted his mood.

"It's only the man who knows his way around women who can stay clear of them," said Sir Lindsay.

"Did you call upon Lady Sarah this morning?"

The baronet indicated in the negative. "Don't want to give the miss airs. Keep her dangling, that's my plan."

"That's precisely why I made my suggestion," said Lenham, returning to the topic that Sir Lindsay had termed a "damn foolish idea." "Do you know that Lady Sarah will be accompanying the Williams cousins to Vauxhall tonight?"

"I cannot see why that should interest me."

"It will give you the opportunity to pretend to flirt with Miss Kitty Williams, as I proposed. Can you not see how that will trouble Lady Sarah?"

Sir Lindsay was forced to concede the point. "But it will also give you the chance to further your own suit with that heiress of yours, or do you think me too daft to notice?"

Lenham shrugged. "If we can kill two birds with one stone, where's the harm in it?"

"Hmmph." Sir Lindsay was not much given to trifling with ladies, although he had to admit that he had enjoyed himself devilishly on the previous day. Lady Rowdon's colour had gone from ashen to green to grey to ashen again as he blithered on about his lack of anxiety over her daughter.

Not that the baronet held any grievance against Lady Sarah herself. He still regarded her as a biddable young miss, eminently suitable to marry, breed, and be sent off to his country home. It was her conniving parents he intended to distress, although he did wish the damsel would show a trifle more appreciation of his person.

Lenham's plan was not without its strengths. Sir Lindsay spared a brief concern for Miss Kitty Williams, but concluded she would not become overly attached, for it was clear that she sought the attention of the marquess.

Broadmoor. Now there was another matter. Deuced if he hadn't seemed to enjoy himself with Lady Sarah! Couldn't be that he'd had a change of heart where she was concerned, could it?

"What do you think of Broadmoor?" he asked Lenham as the butler refilled their glasses and a footman built up the fire. No matter what the weather, the high-ceilinged rooms felt eternally cold and drafty.

"Handsome chap." Lenham brimmed with admiration. "Dressed bang up to the mark, and has a certain air . . ."

"You mistake my meaning," growled the baronet. "Do you think he intends to offer for Lady Sarah?"

Lenham considered. "I think you can be easy on that account. It would be natural, given his character, for him to treat her coldly, yet he seems without any rancour at all. Therefore, he must be feigning."

Sir Lindsay smiled upon his younger friend, his earlier disgruntlement forgotten. "You may yet teach Quires a thing or two. You've the knack for it. Heaven knows, I never had."

But what Lenham really wanted was his Mary Beth and, he told himself happily, it looked as if he were going to get another chance at winning her.

Lord Broadmoor had considered long and carefully what costume to wear to the masquerade, and decided it would be a good joke to go as a black-caped villain of the sort featured in melodramas and romance novels.

For one thing, black looked dashing with his dark colouring, giving him an air of menace and seduction that could only enhance his reputation with the *ton*. For another thing, it would be great sport to surprise Lady Sarah in some dark corner and see how she responded.

"The scarlet lining is a splendid touch," he told his valet, McGaugh, as he donned the thing. "If I am not a success at Vauxhall, I might run about London frightening small children into good behaviour."

"Ay, an' that'll do it," said McGaugh dourly. The valet, who had served him through years of battle, regarded frivolous entertainments with a cold eye.

Lord Broadmoor had received numerous invitations to join parties going to Vauxhall, but had decided to arrive independently. Once there, he would be able to visit more freely from table to table.

This business of winning Lady Sarah was going better than expected, he thought cheerfully as he descended the stairs of the grand house—much too large for a bachelor—and was on his way.

The night was balmy, and Lord Broadmoor reflected over the previous day's encounter as he drove. Lady Rowdon had smoothed his way, making sure he had plentiful opportunities to speak privately with Sarah.

As for the chit herself, she had responded warmly enough, although that was to be expected, since she was clearly trying to attach him. Odd way to go about it though, openly asking where he would be and telling him bluntly that she planned to throw herself in his path.

The marquess shivered as if feeling a chill breeze, although the night was still, as he remembered her aspect after he released her wrist, when she confessed that she dreamt of fighting off creditors.

What a fool she was, to concern herself about her parents when they had so little concern of her! thought Broadmoor, steering for Westminster Bridge; he had chosen to go to Vauxhall by land rather than water. Why should the chit, who would never want for money as Sir Lindsay's wife, worry about a father who gambled away their money and a mother who did nothing but scheme?

It shook his image of Lady Sarah a bit, to realise how she worried about her family. Was she then not a cold, calculating wench after all? Nonsense; of course she was.

How dreamily she had gazed into Broadmoor's eyes when first they met, at a house party. She had welcomed his suit, even kissing him with unseemly passion once in her family's garden. Then, when he offered for her, she refused him as if he meant nothing to her. And that, he reminded himself grimly, had been well before the Rowdons lost their blunt.

The memory of that kiss lingered in the marquess's mind. What a bloody waste, that she should marry Sir Lindsay, that puffed-up fellow with his garish clothes. She gave no sign of feeling any of the emotions for him that she had displayed during her courtship by Captain Kenneth Link.

Could he rouse the same passion in her again? he wondered. If it had been counterfeit, he had been too love-besotted to notice four years ago, but now he could be more objective.

And if it were not false, if she had perhaps begun to have feelings toward him? In that case, he reflected with satisfaction, his plan was well under way. He would have his revenge full force before retiring from the field.

=9=

PREPARING FOR THE masquerade was not easy for Lady Sarah, since she had no abigail to assist her.

None of the Rowdon servants had been paid in more than a year. The upper servants—Cook, Henderson, Lady Rowdon's dresser, the coachman—stayed on out of loyalty, along with two young footmen who were Henderson's nephews, but most of the other servants had long since fled. Nor could Sarah blame them; their wages were low enough even when paid, and they needed money as much as anyone.

Nevertheless, her preparations were most difficult this evening. Since Lady Rowdon was also going out, to Lady Cowper's, her dresser could not assist.

Moreover, Lady Sarah's choice of costumes had been limited by material at hand. A rummage through the attics had brought forth a silvery gown of her grandmother's day, an elaborate piece of silk brocade with great panniers and a peach underskirt looped with embroidered butterfiles.

Not only was the dress difficult to fasten, but she must fix her hair in an elaborate style, with sausage curls heavily powdered and interwoven with curled feathers found in an old trunk. A black half-mask completed the ensemble.

It was only a few minutes before nine, when the Williams cousins were to call for her, and Sarah had scarcely finished applying the requisite beauty patches to her cheek and forehead. She was certainly glad she'd not been born a few generations earlier, for she could not imagine lacing and powdering and patching oneself this way every day.

Lady Rowdon came in to take a look at her and proclaimed her costume superb. "I should be hard put to recognise you!" she said. "The bodice is perhaps cut a bit low, but that never hurt a lady in any gentleman's eyes, and Lord Broadmoor is a red-blooded specimen if ever I saw one."

"That is how I thought also," said Sarah. Her mother nodded an approval she would never have given had she known that Sarah was bent on seduction rather than mere allure.

I wish I knew how one went about seducing a man, or even what it meant, thought Sarah. She had given some thought to ways in which she might arrange an introduction to Harriette Wilson, but gave up for lack of time.

The Williams's carriage arrived at ten minutes past the hour, and Sarah donned a grey shawl against the night air. She descended the stairs with some difficulty, owing to her high heels and voluminous skirts, but it was all made worthwhile by the envious looks she received as she was handed into the carriage.

"How very cunning of you." The compliment issued reluctantly from Kitty, who was garbed as a faery princess with little wings sprouting from her shoulders. "However did you contrive to have the dress made in such a short time?"

"It is the genuine article, from the attic," Sarah admitted. "I am glad to know it does not look old."

"It is so daring!" said Mary Beth, done up as an apple-cheeked milkmaid. "So very worldly, Sarah. Oh, I cannot wait to get there! This is my first visit to Vauxhall, you know."

The girls prattled on as the carriage rolled to the Whitehall stairs, where they transferred into a wherry—a long, thin boat pointed at both ends—and thence across the water.

Ahead of them stretched the gardens, the trees hung with magical coloured lanterns that warmed the night and glowed across the Thames with yellows, reds, and blues. "Oh, Kitty, you have chosen the right costume, for this is a faeryland indeed!" breathed Mary Beth.

"Take care," warned Sarah. "For all the beauty of the place, many of the walks are remote and quite dangerous. Ladies foolish enough to stroll there unaccompanied have been attacked by ruffians and . . . and badly hurt."

"Can anyone come to the gardens, then?" asked Mary Beth in amazement.

The two older girls nodded.

"Anyone at all?" Mary Beth appeared quite delighted when they once again indicated the affirmative. She glanced at the elderly great-aunt who was accompanying them as chaperone; that lady was already dozing and clearly would present no encumbrance to their enjoyment.

"Sarah is right; do not go anywhere alone," cautioned Kitty. "We are not jesting, Mary Beth. Stay with us or with gentlemen who are known to you."

"You two think that because it is my first season, I am easily frightened," sniffed the younger girl. "I am not so timid as all that, and I think you are deliberately making sport of me. Ruffians would be afraid to accost a lady."

"Perhaps, but not a milkmaid," said Kitty, indicating her cousin's costume.

The conversation came to an end as the wherry docked with a thump and the boatmen came to lift them to the shore. Mary Beth giggled during the entire procedure, while her great-aunt snorted and wheezed, and Sarah began to wonder at the Williams's lack of foresight in not providing a more competent chaperone.

Her concerns were put aside as they strolled to the brilliantly lighted Rotunda, where jugglers and magicians performed to the accompaniment of musicians in cocked hats. Nearby they found a table with a clear view of the sky, where later that night fireworks were to blossom.

Here they held some discussion as to how next to proceed. The elderly great-aunt, awakened by her journey from the dock, suggested a visit to the supper room but the girls, all having dined earlier at home, balked and said they should prefer to stroll about the crescent adjoining the Rotunda.

They were allowed to go without chaperonage, this being a safe enough area and the great-aunt being too ancient to do much walking. Delighted at their freedom, the three strolled arm in arm, with Sarah in the center, trying to recognize people they knew in the costumes of pirates and nuns, monks and figures from mythology.

"Do you mean some of them are truly from Covent Garden, and not ladies and gentlemen at all?" demanded Mary Beth. "Oh, do you suppose we could meet some of them? Ask them what it's like to be them?"

This was an idea with some appeal for Sarah, but she was forced to abandon it, for she did not dare reveal to her two companions and sometime rivals the nature of her plans.

"Do look at the marionettes, Mary Beth," said Kitty. "Are they not remarkably well made?"

"You have not the least interest in marionettes, Kitty, no more than I have; you are merely trying to distract me," said her cousin. "You must find something of greater novelty if you wish to draw me off."

"There are quite a few people gathering yonder." Sarah pointed ahead. "I wonder what they're looking at."

The three of them sauntered over. "Look! Ropes!" Mary Beth pointed upwards, high above their heads, to where lines had been strung between masts. "Whatever can those be for?"

The question was quickly answered by a puff of smoke and the announcement that Madame Saqui and her family were about to perform.

Sarah watched in fascination as a dark-haired woman stepped out upon the highest rope, quite confidently, as if unaware that at any moment she might plunge to her death. Blue flame leaped out behind her, producing an eerie effect, as if she were more spirit than human.

The woman, who wore a plumed helmet and a short, fringed dress, bowed to the people below. Then, to Sarah's amazement, Madame Saqui began to dance on the ropes.

Gasps of astonishment rose from the crowd and there was scattered applause, tempered by fear that the woman would lose her balance.

The amazement increased as she was joined on the two other ropes by a man—her husband, someone said—and a small child, also dancing.

For perhaps a quarter of an hour the antics continued, until Sarah felt sure all three must plummet to destruction. Then, in a shower of brilliantly coloured Chinese fire, the three descended, and were rewarded by thunderous applause.

"Magnificent!" Kitty, like Sarah, was still staring at the empty ropes as if expecting some further magic. Gradually they realised that the music had changed to a waltz and people were dancing.

"I suppose we should return . . ." Kitty looked about her. "Mary Beth? Sarah, did you notice where Mary Beth has gone?"

The minx had slipped away while they were absorbed in the performance, and finding her in this crowd and the enormous gardens was a near-impossibility.

"Surely she hasn't gone far." Sarah tried to disguise her worry. "We did warn her, and although she's naïve enough to wander away, surely she won't venture into any of the walks."

Kitty drummed one foot upon the grass impatiently. "Just like her, to wreck our evening by making us look for her while she goes off and amuses herself! Well, Auntie won't be any help. We can send the footman to search."

"But we should look also," said Sarah. "I couldn't enjoy myself, sitting there chatting with people, wondering all the while if she were in danger. Why don't you go and get the footman, and I'll look about a bit? I promise I'll not stray from the crescent myself, and no doubt I'll have found her by the time you return."

"Oh, very well." Kitty gave her auburn curls a shake that also sent her gauze faery wings to bouncing. "I'll give that chit a piece of my mind when we find her, make no mistake."

Despite her annoyance, Kitty truly had intended to go directly to her great-aunt's table and summon the footman. But she found pushing through the crowd a difficult business, with dancers swirling around her laughing, some of them going so far as to reach out and rattle her wings gleefully.

It was all Mary Beth's fault, and Kitty was wishing, not for the first time, that her parents had not insisted the girl have a London season. After all, with her money and her tolerable looks—for Kitty found her cousin a bit insipid—Mary Beth could have done quite well for herself in the country.

The sparkling, delicate faery crown atop Kitty's head was knocked askew by a boisterous fellow in a clown suit, who might even have been a genuine clown from the entertainments, merrily foxed on cheap wine. Kitty pressed on, although beginning to doubt the wisdom of having separated from Lady Sarah. However, on second thought, that absent-minded miss would scarcely have been any help and would probably have impeded her progress.

The Rotunda provided a readily visible landmark, and Kitty saw quickly that she was not making any headway. Indeed, the jostling of the crowd was carrying her farther than ever away from her great-aunt, and she began to feel the twinges of real fear.

A villainous-looking fellow in a black cape bowed low before her. "May I have the honour of this dance?" he asked, eyes glittering behind his mask.

"Indeed, you may not!" Kitty did her best to stare at him haughtily, but her heart was pounding so loud she could scarcely hear. "Get out of my way!"

The fellow looked at her blankly for a moment and then began to chuckle. So he was in his cups, was he? Kitty turned to dash away but her foot slipped on the grass and she all but tumbled to the ground.

"Stay, Miss Williams!" Her panic at being grabbed by the villain ebbed as she heard her name.

"Do I know you, sir?" she demanded.

The mask was whisked away, revealing the face of none other than the Marquess of Broadmoor. "I beg your pardon, Miss Williams; I did not mean to frighten you," he said. "You are not hurt, I trust?"

She clasped her hands before her, trying to recall what she had said to him and whether it might have given offense. "No, indeed not." She managed a brittle laugh. "I cannot think how I missed recognising you, for you are half a head taller than any other man."

What a rare opportunity this was to be alone with him, she thought. For once, there was no Mary Beth to dimple and blush and chatter of first seasons, and no Lady Sarah to gaze at him dreamy-eyed.

"In fact," Kitty continued, "I feel well enough to agree to that dance you requested."

The marquess bowed again and placed one hand at her waist, the other held out so she might set her hand upon it. She searched for some topic of interest, some way to intrigue him, as they swung out into the throng of merrymakers.

"You are attending with your cousin and Lady Sarah, I believe?" said his lordship before she could begin.

"Oh, yes." She must steer the conversation another way. One hint that Sarah was wandering about unaccompanied and no doubt he would be off like a shot in search of her. "Have you come with a party also?"

"I preferred to come alone," said the marquess. "By accepting no invitations, I give preference to no one and therefore avoid offending the others."

"La, I am of the opposite bent, for I accept all invitations," trilled Kitty. "You know Lady Jersey, of course. Well, she and I . . ."

Her spirits recovered, she chattered on of the latest news and fashions. Neither Sarah nor Mary Beth could match her on those topics, which she felt certain must be of great interest to the marquess. Surely he would see that a man of his stature required a wife who was current with society, not some nit like Lady Sarah, whose family hovered on the brink of disgrace.

They circulated about the area as they waltzed, and from the corner of her eye Kitty was able to identify a number of people whom she knew. There was Lady Mansfield, dressed as a Spanish lady in a black mantilla, sitting with Lord Quires; she must call upon them later that evening, for the viscount always knew the latest gossip. Also, Kitty wished to learn if Lord Broadmoor had paid any more calls on the attractive widow, although why he should favour anyone so old was beyond her imagining.

Another turn, and she spotted Sir Lindsay Manx, seated at a table with a look of annoyance upon his face as he watched the crowd. Why did he put up with Lady Sarah's antics? Surely a man of such high fashion, with a title and a respectable estate, need not hang about for that pallid little thing.

Even as she continued to regale the marquess with one titbit after another, she turned her attention to the other dancers. Why, there was Mr. Lenham, fresh-faced and animated as he conversed with his partner. Then they turned, and Kitty recognized the young lady.

"Why, there's Mary Beth!" she said. "That scamp, wait until I lay hands upon her!"

"What has she done?" The marquess followed her gaze but appeared to see nothing amiss.

"Lady Sarah and I were watching Madame Saqui perform and Mary Beth gave us the slip, although we had both warned her of the dangers of wandering about unaccompanied," said Kitty, her anger loosening her tongue. "I was just on my way to fetch the footman to go and look for her."

"Then where is Lady Sarah?" asked the marquess.

Kitty gazed up at him guiltily. "Walking about the crescent, looking for her. There is no harm in it. She said she would not go far, and she has been here many times before, so it is not as if she didn't know her way. No doubt she's already espied Mary Beth and gone back to sit with Auntie."

Broadmoor stopped dancing and glared down at her. "Fools, the both of you! You yourself were pushed about and could have been in difficulty had I been a real villain, and with her penchant for daydreaming, heaven knows where Sarah has ended up!"

He caught Kitty by the elbow and escorted her firmly to the table she pointed out to him. Why oh why had she not kept silent? she wondered, at the same time taking note of the fact that in his concern he had called Sarah by her first name, without her title.

Sarah was not at the table, and Kitty heaved a small sigh as she watched the marquess stride away. Her hopes of attaching him were fading rapidly.

Kitty had scarcely disappeared from sight before Sarah began to regret her impulsive decision to search for Mary Beth alone. The flickering light from the lanterns cast eerie shadows across the faces of the costumed dancers, giving them a menacing appearance.

But she did not want to wait for the footman. Now that the dancing had started, it could take some minutes to cross to the Rotunda, and who knew what might happen to that idiotic young girl in the meantime?

The most efficient course, Sarah decided, would be to prowl about the peripheries of the crescent. In that way, she might get a look at the dancers and also peer down the secluded walkways leading out into the gardens.

In her elaborate costume, she avoided recognition by the few people she saw who were known to her, and was glad. Those she spotted were of the sort more likely to probe for news than to render any real assistance.

At first she trembled and clutched her reticule tightly whenever a drunken male leered at her in passing, but she had no trouble shaking them off. The imposing powdered hairstyle and old-fashioned dress lent her a commanding air, and Sarah began to enjoy herself.

"Be off, rogue!" she shouted at one would-be attacker, clicking her fan at him threateningly. Unsteady from drink, he took a step backward, slipped, and fell onto his buttocks as she thrust her way past him.

From her bosom, Lady Sarah pulled a short, jeweled dagger that gleamed in the moonlight. "I have no fear of you!" she told the villain in the black cape. "Be gone!"

He eyed the dagger balefully. "You have got the best of me this time, my dear, but never fear, I shall be back."

"And I shall be ready for you, whenever you return!" she called, replacing the dagger in her clothing.

"Ouch!" Sarah looked down at her bosom in distress. The fan, rather than sliding meekly out of sight, was poking her breast unpleasantly. Silly girl. She smiled at her own folly, adjusted the fan inside her bodice—for in truth she was tired of carrying it—and continued her search, staring boldly down the dark lanes that vanished between the trees.

The band finished a waltz and struck up a reel. During the moment of silence between the dances, she heard a short cry from somewhere off in the darkness.

"Mary Beth?" Without a thought for her own safety, Sarah hurried down one of the paths toward the sound.

═ 10 ═

THE SCENE BEFORE Sarah's eyes might have come straight from one of her daydreams. A large man in rough clothing, with an odour that reached her even across the open space, was clutching a slender girl by the wrists, forcing her down onto the ground.

Sarah could not see the girl plainly, but from her garb, which resembled that of a milkmaid, it could only be Mary Beth.

"I've paid well for ye, me sweetling!" the man was snarling. "And I'll not be robbed of me pleasure!"

"Oh, please let me go, please!" the girl begged, her voice thin with fright.

"Unhand that woman!" cried Lady Sarah, whipping her fan from her bosom.

"Eh?" The man turned toward her, displaying a broad and hideously pock-marked face. "And who be this tart, got up like some toff?"

"If you do not release that woman, I shall set the law on you," declared Lady Sarah as the girl gaped up at her open-mouthed.

"Ain't no Bow Street runners at Vauxhall," sneered the villain. "Be ye one of these doxies? I'll take ye instead of her, right enough." He started toward her.

"Be off, or I'll run you through!" She pointed her fan at him challengingly.

"Run me through?" he scoffed. "Ye must be daft, or foxed." One heavy, scarred hand reached for her bare shoulder.

"My father is the Earl of Rowdon, and if you lay a hand on me, you shall hang for it," declared Lady Sarah.

"Eh? Father an earl?" The ruffian surveyed her with a dubious look, then shrugged. "Look here, I've no reason to risk me neck for a bit o' fun. I'm an honest man, not a thief. I've paid for that girl, fair and square."

"Nonsense," said Lady Sarah. "You were cheated. That girl is my good friend, dressed as a milkmaid for the masquerade. Some man has hoodwinked you, sir."

He regarded her through slitted eyes. "If this is some trick o' yours, to get me money and then cheat me of me pleasure . . ."

"How much did you pay for her?"

"Five shillings, miss." He shifted uncomfortably from one foot to the other, apparently becoming persuaded by her accent and manner that she was indeed one of the gentry.

"Five shillings? I pay that much for a yard of silk!" Sarah was truly shocked, that a girl should be sold so cheaply. She extracted the coins from her purse and handed them to him, repressing a shudder as his hand brushed against hers. "Now go and find yourself some other entertainment."

The man grunted and took himself off.

"Next time, will you listen to Kitty and me?" Sarah demanded, turning to the girl.

It was not Mary Beth.

The two young women stood staring at each other in mutual assessment. Sarah saw before her a thin, bright-eyed lass of perhaps sixteen years, her red hair loose and unkempt and her nose sprinkled with freckles that bespoke a life in the sun, on a farm rather than in town.

From the girl's expression, there was no doubt she had never in her life seen such an imposing lady. The elaborate dress and powdered hairstyle that had struck Sarah as absurd were to her the height of grandeur.

"Who are you?" asked Sarah, recovering herself.

"My name is Jennie, my lady." The girl bobbed in a sort of curtsey.

"Are you really a doxy?" This pathetic young thing bore no resemblance at all to the elegant Harriette Wilson who rode through Hyde Park.

Jennie hung her head. "I'm ashamed to say I am, my lady."

"Indeed." Sarah indicated a bench at the side of the clearing. "Let us sit down and you can tell me about it."

She dusted the seat with her handkerchief before settling herself, while Jennie perched gingerly on the far edge.

"Not much to tell, my lady," said the girl. "Same's a thousand other girls. You know how the price of corn has dropped these last few years, and the Corn Law ain't helped much. My family be farmers in Worcester, but there's ten of us and we was starving, so I come to London to seek my fortune."

"All by yourself?" Sarah knew vaguely that country girls were not so well cossetted and protected as ladies of quality, but she had never imagined a family letting their daughter walk such a distance unaccompanied.

"Oh, yes." Jennie nodded vigorously. "Tweren't no help for it, and I'd no shoes left on my feet when I arrived. So when a woman offered me help, I was grateful for it."

"And?" prompted Sarah.

"And she took me to her house, and fed me; then she shut me up in the back room and a man came." A shudder wracked the thin body at the memory. "She'd sold me, and paid extra he did, for me being a virgin. Oh, beg pardon, my lady, I shouldn't be speaking of such things in your presence."

It was rapidly becoming clear to Sarah that there was a world of difference between Fashionable Impures, who were in command of their fate, and hapless lasses like Jennie.

"Nonsense," she told the girl. "Tell me how you came to be in the clutches of that despicable man I found you with."

"He were telling the truth," she said in a low voice. "One o' Mrs. Shamford's chums—that were her name, the woman what took me in—he brought me here, and sold me to that man for his pleasure. And I couldn't take it no more, my lady. I'd rather die." Tears rolled down her cheeks.

"I should think so!" Lady Sarah was thinking rapidly. She had not enough money with her to pay this girl's fare back to Worcester, and if she did, what use would that be, with the family starving? "I'll tell you what. Would you like a position as my abigail?"

Jennie looked up wide-eyed, as if she had been offered a chance to go to the moon. "You'd hire me as your maid, my lady? Knowing what I've been?"

"Well, there are certain drawbacks," admitted Lady Sarah. "Frankly, my family too is rather down on its luck at the moment, and we shan't be able to pay you just yet. But if my plans work out, I shall be in a position to do so within the next month or two, and in the meantime I can promise you plenty to eat and warm clothes and no men coming round to bother you."

"That sounds wonderful!" Jennie gazed at her with adoration.

"I'm here with some other ladies, and I doubt they would approve of my bringing you back in the carriage," said Sarah, trying to think things through. "If I gave you a few shillings and my direction, could you find your way there? I don't want you falling into anyone's hands, now."

"I won't," promised Jennie. "I can give them the slip; would have done so before, but where was I to go?"

"Here, then." Sarah handed her some coins.

"That's too much," protested the girl. "I'll only need enough for a barge across the river."

"You are to take a hackney," rebuked Sarah. "I'll not have you walking across London at this hour. When you arrive, whatever the hour, knock at the kitchen door until someone comes. Then tell them Lady Sarah said you are to be admitted and fed and brought to me directly I return home."

"Thank you, oh, thank you." The girl curtseyed and looked as if she would have kissed Sarah's hand, but thought the better of it and darted away.

Meeting Jennie had strengthened Sarah's resolve to carry out her plans. If she failed to tempt the marquess into setting her up as his mistress, she would have to choose between marrying Sir Lindsay and sinking into dire poverty, perhaps ending up much as Jennie had. The memory of the man's pock-marked face and foul odour wrenched at her stomach.

A good thing for Jennie she had come looking for Mary Beth . . . Mary Beth! She might already have fallen into the hands of another such ruffian!

Sarah stood up, her mouth set grimly, and marched back the way she had come. Let anyone menace her friend, and she would teach him a thing or two.

"Mary Beth?" she called, no longer afraid to let her voice be heard. "Mary Beth, where are you?"

"Perhaps I may be of some assistance." The mocking masculine voice was followed by a black-caped figure that strode into her path, the face covered by a black mask.

"I think not," said Lady Sarah. "Stand out of my way, you villain."

"Never." With a swift motion, the man caught her by the waist and pulled her close, bending to press a kiss upon her lips.

She struggled, but he only held her tighter. The intimacy of his mouth upon hers unexpectedly reminded her of the moonlit night when Captain Kenneth Link had held her in his arms.

She melted against him, savouring the sweetness of his touch, longing to speak of their love but not daring to be the first to do so. Then he uttered the words she longed to hear . . .

"Now that's what a man likes to find wandering about Vauxhall, a buxom lass who's willing to please."

The stranger's voice startled her, and Lady Sarah drew back in horror. "Do not touch me again!"

"You didn't seem to dislike it," he said. "Let me try it once more, and see if you still wish me to stop."

As he moved toward her, she searched desperately for some weapon. The sharp heels on her slippers! Quickly she bent down to wrench off one of the shoes. To her horror, she lost her balance, hopped one-legged for a desperate moment, and then thumped down in a heap.

"What on earth were you trying to do, Sarah?" Shaking with laughter, the man extended a hand to help her up. Confused, she reached up and snatched away the mask.

"Kenneth!"

"The very same." He pulled her to her feet. "What were you trying to accomplish by that manoeuvre?"

"I was attempting to remove my shoe, to attack you with it," she informed him with what dignity she could summon, then abandoned the attempt as she remembered Jennie.

"Oh, Kenneth, you will not believe what has happened to me! I saved a hapless young girl from a villain, I really did." She sparkled up at him, eager to share her story.

"Come and tell me about it." He circled her waist with his arms and gazed at her attentively.

"I was looking for Mary Beth and I thought I saw her, in her milkmaid's costume," said Sarah in a great rush. "This horrid man with a pock-marked face was manhandling her and I drew my fan and chased him off! Only it wasn't Mary Beth after all."

"I think you have been having one of your dreams." The marquis smiled indulgently.

"No, truly, it happened!"

"And then you were accosted by a veritable knave, who took you in his arms like this." He suited action to words, gathering her close and resuming their long and tender kiss.

Sarah knew she should demur, but that would not further her goal of being set up as his mistress. Instead, she relaxed her body and pressed against him, finding the sensation not at all unpleasant.

Broadmoor supported her with one arm as he pressed her backwards, so that she was leaning and his lips could trace the delicate whiteness of her throat and the round orbs that were the tops of her breasts, daringly revealed in the low-cut dress.

A strange thrill ran through Sarah, and a weakness as if she had drunk too much wine. She no longer had any thought of resistance, but wanted to urge him further.

A deep groan issued from the marquess's throat, and then he stopped kissing her. "What in heaven's name am I doing?" he asked hoarsely, straightening her up and turning away as if to gain control of himself.

"I think you were seducing me, weren't you?" asked Sarah, who hoped she had not misunderstood.

"Have you no shame?" the marquess snapped at her. "Do you know what might have happened?"

Sarah wished she could imagine how Harriette Wilson would respond to a situation such as this, but she doubted that any of Harriette's suitors ever stopped and upbraided her for her lack of modesty.

"I suppose I might have been ruined," she said, hoping that Broadmoor would seize upon her lack of distress as an indication that he was welcome to finish the job.

She thought for a moment that he had taken her meaning, but then his muscles tensed and he said coldly, "I believe we should return to the others."

"Are you angry?" She had to scamper to keep up with his long strides as they walked toward the Rotunda. "It was not *your* virtue that was at stake, after all."

"Not my virtue, but my honour."

She puzzled over that one for a few long steps. His grim countenance and harshly spoken words made no sense, unless . . . he suspected her of attempting to trap him into matrimony.

For indeed, had he ravished her, she realised now, he would have been duty-bound to marry her. However much a young man might take his pleasure with married ladies and harlots, he did not go about deflowering young maidens of good family.

The entire idea of Broadmoor's setting her up as his mistress had been a mad notion, she saw now. Only an inveterate dreamer like herself would have given it more than a passing reflection. Now she had destroyed any chance she had with him, putting herself in the light of a wench so calculating that she would stoop to immoral conduct and blackmail to secure a wealthy marriage.

"It was not at all as it must seem," she managed to say. "Kenneth—Lord Broadmoor—you must believe me. I had the strangest notion that you might . . ."

"I believed you once, Lady Sarah, four years ago, and that was a grave error." The marquess did not alter his rapid pace. "Although not so grave an error as it might have been, had you consented to be my wife before I learned what sort of woman you really are."

"But I'm not the sort of woman I really am!" protested Sarah. "I'm not like that at all." Which, she saw too late, made not the least shred of sense.

"We shall speak of this no further." Broadmoor returned her to the table where Kitty and Mary Beth sat chatting with Mr. Lenham and Sir Lindsay. Declining their offer to join them, Broadmoor produced a cold bow and departed.

"I'm so sorry if I troubled you," said Mary Beth. "You were not in any danger, were you, Sarah?"

She shook her head. No danger at all, save of having her heart break into tiny pieces and be trampled beneath the dancers.

"Sir Lindsay was telling me of a new jewellers, in Bond Street," said Kitty. "They have the most cunning bracelet, of gold shaped like a snake, that winds up your arm and has rubies for eyes. We must go and see it."

She resumed her conversation with Sir Lindsay, who, Sarah noticed with alarm, looked far more animated than he ever had in her own presence.

If she lost him as well as Broadmoor, she might soon find herself sharing Jennie's hideous fate. With an inward shudder and a heavy heart, Sarah set herself to joining in the chatter.

She danced several times with the baronet, but he also favoured Kitty with a waltz and a cotillion. To round off the disastrous evening, Sarah had to watch the marquess make himself quite at home at Lady Mansfield's table and dance with her exclusively for the rest of the evening. A darkness settled in her heart that even the brilliant fireworks failed to dispel.

=== 11 ===

THE EARL OF Rowdon had been gambling deep. His vouchers were no longer taken at White's or Watier's, but he was still accepted at Brooks's Club in St. James's Street.

There among the Corinthian pilasters he had made an evening of it that Sunday night, until all but a few players were departed, leaving him ten thousand pounds the poorer.

"A game of hazard, perhaps?" Lord Rowdon was in his cups and vaguely recalled that the gentleman he was addressing, Lord Quires, rarely gambled, but he could not shake the sense that his luck was bound to change if only he were given another chance.

"Do not take it amiss, but perhaps it would be best for you to return home," said the viscount. "It is near three in the morning and your wife may be worried."

The earl waved his hand vaguely. "She never worries about me. Let her worry about our daughter; she's the one who's made a pretty mess of things."

Lord Quires had been about to take his leave, for he was not fond of dealing with inebriated gentlemen, but here was a matter to pique his interest.

"A mess of things?" he asked, gesturing to his manservant, Finley, to bring the earl another glass of wine.

"Can't seem to find herself a rich husband," said Rowdon, accepting the wine without acknowledgement. "Had one I'd picked out, but he ain't good enough for her mother."

"It has been my observation that Lord Broadmoor shows Lady Sarah considerable attention," said the viscount, who had been wondering for the past four-and-twenty hours why the marquess

95

had abandoned the girl at Vauxhall and spent the rest of the evening at Lady Mansfield's table in a foul mood.

"He's got it in his head she's a mercenary sort and he'll have none of it, or so she tells me," sputtered the earl. "Can't think why the fellow cares; everybody else marries for money, don't they? I know I did."

Quires was finding himself more and more repelled by Rowdon and considered taking himself off. Gathering gossip was a matter of artfulness, not of wallowing in a sewer, and he was beginning to think this whole business reeked.

"You make it sound as if you were trying to sell your daughter to the highest bidder." His tone of distaste passed unnoticed. "Surely that is not what you intend."

"Surely it is," replied the earl in a loud voice. "I would sell my daughter to a wild savage with arrows stuck through his ears if he would clear my debts and set me up for life."

Quires glanced about uncomfortably and was relieved to notice they were alone in the room, save for Finley. "Surely she is as good as betrothed to Sir Lindsay," he said, hoping to end the conversation on a more civilised note.

"No, no, he's taken a liking to . . . now what is her name? Kitty, they said. That was it, Kitty." Rowdon glared at his newly emptied glass as if it had personally betrayed him.

Poor Lady Sarah, thought Quires, although it was against his policy to feel much sympathy for anyone whose doings provided prime tittle-tattle.

He excused himself, then called Finley over and said in a low voice, "Have a chat with Sir Lindsay's man and see what you can learn about this business of Kitty Williams. Have you had any more luck with Broadmoor's valet—what's his name?"

"McGaugh," said Finley. "Tight-lipped Scotsman he is, can't get anywhere with him. Lady Sarah's got a new abigail, odd sort of creature called Jennie. P'raps she ain't averse to making a bit on the side."

Good man, Finley, thought Quires as he sent the valet to procure him a hackney. He never took his own carriage on one of his visits to the females of Covent Garden; wouldn't do to get himself gossiped about, after all.

That Wednesday night at Almack's was not at all like the previous one for Lady Sarah. Then she had emerged triumphant, at least in society's eyes. Now she watched wistfully as Lord Broadmoor paid open court to Lady Mansfield and Sir Lindsay waltzed twice with Kitty Williams.

"You've lost them both!" growled Lady Rowdon in her daughter's ear. "All of London is laughing at you, and now we shall be ruined."

Sarah stared down at the floor miserably. I shall be like Jennie, and what will become of her as well? she thought. If only Sir Lindsay would renew his offer now, I would accept him without hesitation.

The memory of the marquess's arms about her at Vauxhall and the thrill of their kisses was too painful to dwell upon. Her heart ached, as it had these past four years whenever she thought of him; best to put the matter behind her and try to win back what might yet be attainable.

However, Sir Lindsay seemed to take particular glee in her unhappiness. He danced with her only once and smirked the entire time.

"Are you not enjoying yourself, Lady Sarah?" he asked as he handed her about in the quadrille.

"I have missed your attentions," she said honestly.

"You did not esteem them so highly a week ago."

"I am sorry if I have given offense." She forced herself to concentrate on the steps of the dance. "But if your heart has been given to another, then perhaps I speak out of turn."

"Enough contrition might yet carry the day." Sir Lindsay produced a broad handkerchief, into which he blew noisily. "The experience of being dangled on a hook, like a fish, is not a pleasant one, is it, Lady Sarah?"

She shot him a startled glance. He was tormenting her on purpose then, to punish her. It revealed a mean streak in the baronet that she had not suspected; still, she must confess he had reason to be angry.

"No, it is not pleasant," she agreed. "And I do truly regret my impulsiveness. May I therefore hope for a renewal of our friendship?"

"You may hope for it." His lips curled smugly. "But whether your hopes will come to fruition, that is a matter yet to be seen."

Sarah managed to rein in her temper during the remainder of the dance, but inside she burned with fury. He had forced her to humble herself before him, only to amuse himself. How could her parents wish her to marry this man? She must, if he would have her; but how her heart rebelled at the thought.

Lord Broadmoor, across the room, was bending low over Lady Mansfield's hand and murmuring something to her. Unable to watch further, Sarah finally persuaded her mother to take her home.

Lady Rowdon sank back in the carriage, her hand to her brow. "How all this distresses me," she said. "I feel a collapse coming on at any time. We shall be cast out into the streets unless you contrive to save us, Sarah. You must bring the marquess round, or the baronet at the least."

Sarah found herself reminded of how poor little Jennie had been sold for money, and thought bitterly that her own fate was not much different. Then she reproached herself. How could she think so uncharitably of her own parents, who faced such disaster and must depend upon her?

"That's a long face, my lady," said Jennie later that night as she assisted Sarah out of her clothes. "Bad luck with the gentlemen?"

"You mustn't worry," said Sarah, removing a sapphire bracelet that she had inherited from her grandmother. "I promise that no matter what happens to my family, I'll do my best to keep you from harm."

"It's not me I worry about." Jennie slipped a nightdress over Sarah's head. "Nor even you, my lady, though it do bother me to see you unhappy."

"What does worry you, then?" Sarah took a seat at her dressing table.

"The other girls." Jennie began to brush out her mistress's hair.

"What other girls?"

"The ones at Mrs. Shamford's," said Jennie.

It had not occurred to Sarah before that there were others still in Jennie's horrifying circumstance, but of course there must be. How naïve of her, not to consider that London was full of country girls led, or forced, into sin.

She could not help them all. Indeed, she did not know how long she could go on helping Jennie, although perhaps with a letter recommending her, the girl might get a place in some other household.

"Did you know these other girls very well?" she asked. "Did they all hate the sort of life they led as much as you did?"

"Not all." Jennie's hazel eyes looked thoughtful. "But the ones who liked it, they didn't stay long, for they could make more blunt in one of them bagnios, if they had the looks for it. Some of them even got set up by wealthy gentlemen, but there weren't many that lucky. And a few had a taste for, well, unnatural practices, my lady, and they could turn a pretty penny, they could."

Sarah decided it would be wiser not to ask what unnatural practices were.

"What of the others, the ones who didn't like it and can't leave?" Preoccupied as she was with her own troubles, she nevertheless could not tear her mind from the memory of little Jennie writhing in the grip of that hideous pock-marked man.

"Mostly they don't live too long," said Jennie matter-of-factly. "A kindness it is, too. They die of disease, or in childbirth, or some bloke what's badly dipped takes a cudgel to their heads. One girl while I was there . . . well, never you mind about that, miss."

Sarah bit her lip. After all, this was her bedtime, and she had no wish to spend the night in bad dreams. But somehow she felt that to refuse to hear the story was to condemn some poor girl to anonymity. "Come, Jennie, out with it."

The younger girl sighed. "All right, if you say so, my lady. Tweren't more than thirteen she were, and the first day, well, Mrs. Shamford brought in two fellows, both at once, big red-faced brutes they was. That night Beulah—that were her name—she hanged herself with a sheet. Dirty old sheet it were, too."

Sarah shuddered violently. "Oh, Jennie, this is horrible. We must do something for those girls."

"You can't bring them all here," Jennie noted sensibly.

"Don't some of them have homes they could go to?" asked Sarah. "Surely they'd be better off back on farms than being beaten and sold to strange men in London."

"The ones that want to get away most, they'd take any chance," said Jennie. "But I know how it was with me—I never saw a penny of that money, never had a stitch but what I was wearing and no shoes except when they took me out a-purpose. I wouldn't have got five miles by myself."

"If they had a little money, even a few shillings, do you think that would help?"

"It might." Jennie nodded dubiously. "But one would have to get it to them, my lady, and I'm not going back there where they can lay hands on me. Mrs. Shamford and her pals, they'd half-kill anyone they caught encouraging their girls to run off. And if you don't mind my saying so, you can't spare the money."

"Oh, yes I can." Her own problems could wait, Sarah decided, pulling her head free of Jennie's absent-minded brushing and rummaging through the drawers of her dressing table.

She heaped up a small pile of jewelry: her sapphire bracelet, a small gold necklace with a jade locket, her pearl earrings, another bracelet set with turquoise stones, a silver buckle and the most precious of all, a hair clasp wrought of filigree gold with a small ruby at the center, which had been a gift from her father for her eighteenth birthday. Her mother had decreed that these few baubles might be kept, for appearing with no jewels at all would certainly stir talk.

"You cannot mean to sell them!" gasped Jennie. "Your lady mother will never permit it, Lady Sarah. And you cannot go about in society without them, even I know that much."

"We have no engagement until Monday, when we go to a card party at Lady Mansfield's," an invitation that had been issued before Sarah's fall from grace. "That gives us enough time to have them copied in paste, and then who will know the difference?"

Jennie stared at her in wonder. "You would actually do this, my lady, when you might need the money yourself soon enough? I do beg your pardon for speaking frankly, but I've no wish to see your tender heart lead you into trouble."

"I'm certainly not in any trouble that can compare with that poor little girl you told me of." Sarah gathered the jewels into a small velvet bag. "I shall give you the name of a jeweller's in St. James's Street who can have them made up, and will purchase the items besides. I do not need to tell you, I suppose, that no one must know of this."

"Indeed not." Jennie looked almost affronted. "It's honoured I am, that your ladyship would trust me with your most precious possessions, and I'll not play you false. Indeed, my lady, I've a crown or two of my own I'll be donating to the cause."

Sarah turned around in surprise. "Where did you come by that, Jennie? I know we've not paid you."

The abigail grinned mischievously. "It's Finley, Lord Quire's man. He come round sniffing for gossip and paid me well if I'd keep my ears open for him. Of course, I'll only tell him what you want me to, but I've no objection to taking his money."

"Oh, you are a sly one!" laughed Sarah.

Despite her merriment, she was not heedless of the risk she would run. For it had become clear to her that she must take the money to the girls herself.

The evil old crone blocked the doorway, pointing a crooked finger at Lady Sarah. "You think to steal my doxies? I'll make you one of them instead!" A clawlike hand reached out and grasped Lady Sarah's arm.

"Fortunate for you that I would not harm an old lady," she retorted, wrenching away the hand and pulling the startled woman from the doorway. "Jennie, gather the innocents; we must leave at once!"

"You're having one of your fancies again, ain't you, my lady?" said Jennie, helping her mistress into bed. "I'm afraid this is nothing a well-brought-up young miss like you could ever imagine."

"We'll just have to do our best then, won't we?" came the answer.

Lying awake after Jennie had departed with the candles, Sarah found her thoughts straying back to Lord Broadmoor as he had appeared earlier that night at Almack's, strikingly handsome in a dark blue coat of Bath superfine, a swanskin waistcoat with stripes in blue and silver, and grey breeches.

Every movement of his lithe form was engraved on her mind: how he bowed over Lady Jersey's hand, how he bent his head to listen to Lady Lieven, how he waltzed with Lady Mansfield. A trail of fiery pain followed their whirling path as they danced through her heart.

She remembered his revulsion that previous Saturday night, when he believed she was trying to trap him into marriage. Why was their friendship so full of misunderstandings? Four years ago loyalty to her father had barred her from explaining herself, but this time she was trying to be honest, yet in spite of it seemed never to be able to persuade him of her sincerity.

The trouble was this selfish longing of hers for a perfect happiness, which could not exist: to have her Kenneth back again. She must, she concluded, content herself with the happiness of others. If she could secure that for her parents, for Jennie, and for the other girls at Mrs. Shamford's, surely that would be enough.

Her mind eased slightly by the prospect of self-sacrifice. She fell asleep at last.

═ 12 ═

By The Time the guests began arriving for the evening card party, Lady Mansfield was heartily glad to see them. The preceding dinner with a few close friends, while it had gone smoothly on the surface, had in her estimation been a disaster.

The problem as ever was the Marquess of Broadmoor, thought Stella as she stood in the front hall to greet her visitors. True, he had accepted her invitation, and his presence had lured such trumps as Lady Jersey and Lady Lieven. In addition, he had sat on Stella's right and attended her politely through the meal.

Yet his mind was distracted. There were none of the deep gazes of a genuine admirer, none of the subtle innuendoes that implied real sentiment. Instead, she had the feeling he was play-acting with her.

No need to ask where his thoughts were. Lady Mansfield had seen his stormy frown as he strode away from Lady Sarah at Vauxhall. Nor had she failed to notice, at Almack's, how one might perceive Lady Sarah's whereabouts at any moment from Lord Broadmoor's, for he was ever in the most distant part of the assembly rooms, evidence that he remained fully aware of her presence despite his apparent indifference.

Things certainly did not look promising.

I wish I had not invited the Rowdons tonight, Stella thought. Well, at the time Sarah was all the rage and it seemed the most likely way to attract Lord Broadmoor, and there's no helping it now.

"Everyone is commenting on his attentions to you," murmured Lord Quires, who had made himself useful at dinner by regaling the guests with the latest news.

"His thoughts are elsewhere," Lady Mansfield replied, sotto voce.

"A mere two weeks more and the Rowdons must leave their home, unless Lady Sarah finds herself a husband," he reminded her. "I think she will soon consent to be Sir Lindsay's bride."

"If he will have her, in view of his latest *affaire du coeur*." Stella smiled at the Williams family as they entered, relaxing again when they disappeared into the Yellow Saloon, where tables had been set up for cards. Normally she would have greeted them there, but tonight she felt too restless to sit still and had asked Lady Jersey to play hostess within while she took up her post in the hall. Patience Buxton, unfortunately, was too scatter-brained to manage things, even for a quarter hour.

"You are referring, I presume, to Miss Kitty Williams, that sharp-faced girl we saw just now?" said Quires. "I think you need have no worries on that score."

"Why is that?" More and more, Lady Mansfield was finding the viscount's assistance indispensable. She wished he did not so often depart at an early hour, and would have suspected him of keeping a mistress had it not been for the fact that he had a horror of becoming a subject of gossip.

"His servants say it is merely a ploy to punish Lord and Lady Rowdon for preferring the marquess, and to keep Lady Sarah uncertain until the last minute," said Quires. "He still intends to make her his wife, and I should think the time for that cannot be far off."

"I am delighted to hear it." Lady Rowdon and her daughter having arrived, Lady Mansfield broke off to welcome them in her friendliest manner. The girl was looking far too cheerful for one who was all but scorned by society and whose family faced financial ruin; whatever was making her eyes sparkle that way with excitement—or was it determination?

Perhaps it was merely fever, thought Stella with a touch of spite as the Rowdons moved on to the card room.

"Did you notice?" whispered Quires. "Lady Sarah's necklace is paste."

"I could not tell."

"One learns to spot these things, when one wants to get at the truth about people," assured her companion. "Things must be desperate indeed, for the original piece cannot have been worth much."

Then why, wondered Stella, was Lady Sarah smiling?

Lord Broadmoor was wondering the same thing. He expected some sign of pallor or grimness, but the young woman who nodded to him politely seemed far too robust.

She certainly cannot be pining away for love, he thought, and she does not appear overly concerned about being thrown out into the street. Perhaps she has already accepted Sir Lindsay.

Why this notion sent a pang through his chest, the marquess could not be certain. After all, he had seen through the scheming minx, had he not?

Despite his fury at her treatment of him four years earlier, he would never have suspected her of such low deviousness as she had displayed at Vauxhall.

To attempt to seduce him so that she might force him into marriage, that was a nasty business indeed. Well, he had found her out in time, thank heaven.

Seating himself for a game of whist, his lordship felt nevertheless a touch uneasy. Despite having been put on his guard long ago, he continued to succumb, or nearly so, to her charms at every encounter.

He had warmed to her that first night at Almack's, flirted outrageously at her home, and kissed her with great pleasure at Vauxhall. Perhaps it was time to abandon the battle entirely and retreat while his forces were still intact; she was much too formidable a foe.

No! he thought, slamming down his cards with such vehemence that the other players stared at him. Lady Sarah could not defeat him so easily. Now that he was thoroughly cured of her, and need no longer fear being taken in, it was time to concentrate on manoeuvres that would help complete his revenge.

At the first opportunity he excused himself and joined Sarah at her table. Briefly he noted a distressed glance from Lady Mansfield; well, she would be rewarded for her patience when he made his proposal, and it would not be more than a few weeks away.

Seated with Sarah were Lenham and Mary Beth Williams, who paid scant attention to their cards as they held hands under the table and made sheep's eyes at each other, with the result that Sarah was winning steadily. She continued her lucky streak, taking five shillings from the marquess.

"What do you plan to do with all your money?" asked Broadmoor, and noted with puzzlement Sarah's startled reaction.

"My money?" she said.

"Your winnings." He gestured at the pile of shillings beside her. "Shall you purchase some new jewels, do you think?"

Now why the devil was she staring at him so? "Oh, not jewels, I don't think," she managed at last, so distracted that she lost the hand.

"I do beg your pardon," said the marquess. "I did not mean to upset you. The words were only spoken in jest." How was he to make her dote upon him, when he could not even discern what she was about?

Lenham was murmuring what appeared to be words of love in his sweetheart's ear. Mary Beth giggled, then clapped one hand over her mouth. "I do beg your pardon." Then she giggled again. "I am so glad Kitty and Aunt Williams are not sitting with us, for they would surely rebuke me, and Mr. Lenham is so amusing." She poked that gentlemen in the side and he beamed at her.

The marquess followed Lady Sarah's gaze to where Kitty sat on a sofa, chatting briskly with Sir Lindsay Manx. Sarah had gone pale, then set her mouth firmly and excused herself after the next hand.

His attention gone entirely from cards, the marquess also stood up, circling by the refreshment table that he might keep an eye on Sarah.

She took a chair near the baronet and Kitty and appeared to listen intently to their conversation, once in a while murmuring something Broadmoor could not hear.

It infuriated him that she should go pale over the baronet, yet not seem to mind his own indifference at all. So her affection for him had all been a sham! But he refused to let her escape so easily. He crossed the room and took a seat near the small group.

"I do not envy you men, that you may not wear feathers as we ladies do!" Kitty was chirping to Sir Lindsay. "Have you been to Botibol's in Oxford Street? The ostrich feathers are quite splendid. How I should like to see an ostrich someday!"

"Peculiar-looking things, I understand," replied Sir Lindsay. "Such as one might see in a bad dream, when one has the stomach-ache. I'd bloody well—excuse my language, please—dashed well hate to run across one when I was badly dipped!"

"I hear that Byron has visited Waterloo." Kitty prattled on, heedlessly changing the subject. "Surely he will write something most poetic about it, don't you think, Lord Broadmoor?"

"The story of that battle has already been written, in blood," snapped the marquess. "It does not need some shallow sentiment from a young man whose behaviour makes him unfit for polite company."

"Must agree with you there," said Sir Lindsay. "But you can't expect ladies to understand about war and hardship and suffering and all that."

"Do you not think women suffer also?" Lady Sarah's soft voice joined unexpectedly in the conversation, for she had uttered not a word previously since Broadmoor sat down. "Perhaps not on a battlefield, but in other ways."

"I do believe Lady Sarah is being profound." Lady Mansfield, who had slipped up unnoticed, spoke from where she stood behind Lord Broadmoor's chair. "The pain of childbirth . . . but they say it is soon forgotten, my dear."

"That was not what I meant." To the marquess's surprise, the girl drew herself up earnestly and said, "Can you imagine how dreadful the suffering must be that would make a child of thirteen hang herself with a sheet?"

"I do not think this is a fit topic for our ears, do you, Lady Sarah?" cautioned their hostess, taking the seat Broadmoor vacated for her. "Pray do not continue."

"But women *are* suffering, right here in London, and how can we sit back and chatter of fashions, and do nothing to help them?"

"I see nothing wrong with discussing fashions," sniffed Kitty. "It is a topic of interest to any well-bred young lady, and many gentlemen as well."

Sir Lindsay cleared his throat. "I believe Lady Sarah has been swept away by her tender heart. She is always moved by the plight of others, and means no harm, eh?"

At this, Sarah glanced about in some confusion, as if newly awakened from one of her dreams. "Oh . . . yes, I do beg your pardon, Kitty, Lady Mansfield. No offense was intended, I assure you. It is only that I have heard the most distressing tales . . . well, no matter."

"And you would do anything to aid someone in trouble, especially someone you loved, is that not true?" The marquess spoke with heavy double meaning.

"I suppose it is." Sarah threw her chin up in an elfin gesture. Lord Broadmoor had an image of a small child defiantly confronting a bully.

"Surely not *anything*," probed Lady Mansfield.

"I can think of nothing I would not do, to save those I care for," said Lady Sarah.

Lord Quires came up beside Lady Mansfield. "Such an intense conversation," he observed. "Tell me, what have I missed?"

"Nothing of importance," said Sarah. "Sir Lindsay, will you not join me for a game of whist?"

The baronet accepted readily, smiling to himself, no doubt at being thus noticed above the marquess.

Broadmoor subdued his anger quickly. In scarcely more than two weeks, this matter would be ended. Somehow he must contrive to win the field before then. Clearly, his initial plans had not been sufficiently detailed. What was needed was some new twist . . .

"Now that you have opened the house in Grosvenor Square, surely you plan to entertain, Broadmoor," said Quires. "All the ladies are hoping for a grand ball."

The devil take it, at times he could swear that man read his thoughts. But it was a good idea, no denying it.

"As a matter of fact, I am having one." Lord Broadmoor had won Wellington's respect on the battlefield for the quickness with which he arrived at decisions, and almost always good ones. "Saturday after next. You shall all be receiving invitations, of course."

Kitty recovered from her annoyance at the baronet's desertion to clap her hands joyfully. "How splendid!"

"We shall all look forward to it eagerly," said Lady Mansfield.

"What? What are we to look forward to?" Mrs. Buxton had ambled over, her face bright with amiable curiosity.

"Lord Broadmoor is giving a ball," said Lady Mansfield. "It will be the highlight of the season."

"Hmph." The elderly companion did not appear impressed. "What I want to know is, why is Lady Sarah sitting with Sir Lindsay when she is betrothed to you, Lieutenant Link?"

"Oh, cousin!" cried her mistress. "You have got it all muddled again."

A guilty look spread across Mrs. Buxton's broad face. "Oh, I do beg your pardon. My memory does play tricks on me. I meant to say, Captain Link."

Quires tried unsuccessfully to hide his amusement behind his hand.

"Come with me, Patience, and I shall explain it all to you again," said Lady Mansfield, spiriting her companion away.

The marquess excused himself a short time later, not bothering to make his farewells to Lady Sarah, who was deep in conversation with Sir Lindsay.

Quires's suggestion had started Broadmoor's thoughts churning. Yes, he would have a ball, and he would arrange for McGaugh to give word to Quires's man that the marquess would have an important announcement to make that evening, along with hints that the announcement concerned a wedding with Lady Sarah.

Word would soon be all over London. Broadmoor had no doubt that Lady Sarah herself would hear of it and key her hopes accordingly.

Then, the morning of the ball, he would pay Lady Mansfield a visit and offer for her. If she refused, he would find some other announcement to make; but if she accepted, and surely she would, his revenge would be completed before all of London society.

Cracking the whip over the backs of his team from his perch high on the phaeton, Broadmoor unexpectedly recalled Sarah's words. "Can you imagine how dreadful the suffering must be that would make a child of thirteen hang herself with a sheet?"

What could she have been thinking of? He shook his head as he urged the horses forward. One of her strange imaginings, no doubt. The other night, she had told him of besting some villain, as though it had really happened.

Perhaps, under the stress, Lady Sarah was losing her mind. Disturbed, the marquess slowed his team to a walk, frowning.

It must be some further plot of hers to snare him, for it seemed the chit did little else than scheme and calculate her actions. She implied, of course, that it was for her parents' sake, but the marquess had no doubt her main lookout was for herself.

Whatever had made Lady Sarah smile at the beginning of the evening, he doubted very much she would feel merry after a week from Saturday.

= 13 =

SARAH WAS CERTAINLY not smiling as she rode home beside her mother in the creaky Rowdon carriage.

The relief that had spread through her when Jennie had returned at the last moment before the card party with the paste jewels and the payment for the real ones, and the delight she had felt at the prospect of freeing those poor girls from virtual slavery, were rapidly giving way to stomach-burning nervousness.

What if she did not succeed? But she would never give up, not with those poor girls depending on her.

"I shall not fail you," Lady Sarah told the wide-eyed prisoners who lay on the dungeon floor, heavy chains about their ankles. "My sword will not cut metal, and so I must devise another plan and return another day."

"We have faith in you," they chorused . . .

"The marquess made a point of sitting beside you, even when you left the card table," Lady Rowdon was saying with satisfaction. "His offer cannot be long in coming."

"Oh, mother, it will be an eternity in coming." Sarah could not keep the bitterness from her voice. The man was infuriating, but she did love him, and losing him hurt dreadfully.

"I don't know where you came by your pessimistic outlook," chirped her mother. "Where would your father and I be if we had not always the hope of a better future?"

That was true enough, and thinking of their blameless, hard lives, Sarah resolved to try to be more cheerful in their company. "At least Sir Lindsay appeared receptive to me again. He was almost rude last Wednesday while we danced, and I began to fear all hope was lost."

Lady Rowdon shrugged. "He is well enough, I suppose, if Broadmoor cannot be brought to heel. Blast your father! I do not see why he cannot stall matters a bit longer. What a shame if you are forced to wed to less advantage than you might, purely for press of time."

Much as she hated to depress her mother's spirits, Sarah felt she must take a hard-headed view of their situation. "I believe we should invite Sir Lindsay to tea," she said. "Then I shall have the opportunity to tell him that I accept his offer."

"You run ahead of yourself." Lady Rowdon pulled her cape closer about her shoulders, for the hot bricks wrapped in blankets that Lady Mansfield had provided were already losing their warmth in the cool evening air. "Ah, good, we are arrived."

If Anna Rowdon thought she had ended that conversation, she was soon disabused of the notion, for the earl was waiting up, and in no pleasant mood.

"Well?" he demanded when she and Sarah came into the library to bid him good night. "What news have you?"

"All looks promising," replied his wife. "Sarah, run along to bed."

"Not yet." A look from her father held her motionless. "Your mother tells me endlessly that Lord Broadmoor is on the point of offering for you, yet you say the opposite, and I have received no letter from him requesting an interview with me. Has he spoken to you on the subject?"

Sarah shook her head timidly. She always found her father a little frightening late at night, especially when he had been drinking, as she now suspected that he had.

"And what of Sir Lindsay? Have you chased him off altogether?" His voice had a harshness to it that she had seldom heard.

"No, Father," she said. "He was quite friendly with me tonight, and took my part in a discussion. I was suggesting to Mother that we invite him to tea, so that I might agree to accept his offer." And be finished with the matter, she thought.

"Then it shall be done," commanded her father. "Now leave me."

"Not yet." Lady Rowdon stood her ground. "Do you want to trade a future of comfort, even luxury, for an amount scarcely sufficient to clear our present debts?"

"I agreed to take a gamble, but the odds are mounting against us and the stakes are high," said her husband. "I say it is time to call in the cards."

"That is precisely the trouble with you," snapped Lady Rowdon. "You take a risk and then, when the moment comes to hold fast, you fold. Had you more genuine courage, no doubt you should have more luck as well."

For a silent moment, the two glared at each other in what appeared to Sarah to be a battle of the wills. It troubled her, for after all what use was money if her parents grew to despise each other?

"Can we not find some compromise?" she asked.

Lady Rowdon heaved a deep sigh. "Very well. I shall invite the baronet to tea—Sunday after next."

"Sunday after next?" protested Lord Rowdon. "That is almost two weeks from now. It gives us only a few days' grace before the wolves close in."

"It is enough," said his wife. "They will leave us be, when they learn of the marriage settlement."

"Yes, but why wait until then?" The earl eyed her suspiciously.

"On Saturday week the marquess is giving a ball," said Lady Rowdon. "Lady Mansfield spoke of it this evening. Surely if he intends to ask for Sarah's hand, he will give some indication by then, for he will make much of her at the ball. If matters do not progress sufficiently, why, she can agree to marry Sir Lindsay the next day."

Sarah twisted her hands together. She did not think she could bear the delay. How painful it would be, watching the marquess dance with Lady Mansfield, no doubt flirting just enough with Sarah to keep everyone else guessing. But she had divined the truth: He only wished to keep her hoping, as he believed she had once done with him, to punish her.

Well, once she was betrothed, her mother would cease to insist on attending balls. The marriage no doubt would follow shortly, and Sir Lindsay had already made it plain that his idea of a wife's role was to retire to the country and raise children while he went about his business in town, a prospect that suited Sarah very well.

"There's many a slip 'twixt cup and lip," said Lord Rowdon. "We may lose the baronet before then."

"Nonsense." Lady Rowdon beamed, seeing that she had carried the day. "Sarah has done exceedingly well; she quite enchanted both gentlemen tonight, I'm sure of it. She need only go on as she has begun, and all will end happily."

"We have come this far; I suppose we might as well see it through," said Lord Rowdon. "But I shall hold you to task, madam, if we lose both fish . . . er, gentlemen."

Much distressed, Sarah bid her parents good evening and went up to bed. Or rather, to her bedroom, for she had no intention of going to bed tonight.

She detested the thought of herself as bait to hook Lord Broadmoor or Sir Lindsay. But for the moment she must concentrate on a more immediate problem.

"We'll have to delay at least an hour," she whispered to Jennie, who was waiting up for her. "They're still downstairs, both of them."

The abigail nodded. "Best you take off that ball gown and put on your night things. Your mother might come up."

Sarah did as she suggested, all the while telling Jennie of the evening's events. "I wish I could persuade my mother that my case with Lord Broadmoor is hopeless."

"Hard for me to say, not having met the man," said Jennie, brushing out Sarah's hair. "If you like, my lady, I'll see what I can learn from Finley."

"Finley? Oh, Lord Quires's man. Well, try not to be too bold, Jennie. I suppose in return you can tell him about the invitation to Sir Lindsay for tea."

"It will soon get about to everyone," warned Jennie.

"All the better. If Mother should prove right—although I'm sure she isn't—and Lord Broadmoor has a *tendre* for me, that will make it clear he must take action before then."

The abigail, meanwhile, was tucking a pile of coins in a gilt reticule. Sarah added her newly won shillings.

Lady Rowdon did not come in. What seemed like hours later, the house settled down with the creak of bedsprings from her parents' rooms.

Quietly, Sarah shed her nightgown and put on the costume she had worn to Vauxhall, while Jennie powdered and curled her hair and fetched high-heeled slippers.

Sarah's first intention had been to go plainly dressed, so that she might avoid attention, but Jennie had prevailed. The fancy dress might be a generation out of date, but it was grand and imposing, and the powdered hair made Sarah look older than her three-and-twenty years.

Altogether, she made such an impressive effect, Jennie said, that Mrs. Shamford would be far more likely to yield to her than if she came looking like the merest slip of a girl.

"Are you sure you want to go ahead with this, my lady?" Jennie whispered as Sarah wrapped a glittering golden cloak round herself to heighten the effect. "You've no idea what danger you will be in."

"We agreed on this long ago," said Sarah firmly. "It must be done."

"Perhaps we should go tomorrow, in daylight." Jennie rubbed her hands against her apron worriedly.

"Mother would never allow it, as you well know. You are merely giving in to fear. Now come!"

They tiptoed down the back stairs and out to the mews. The footmen being Henderson's nephews, there was no trusting them not to blab, although their company would have been most welcome.

It was Sarah's intention instead to persuade the coachman to accompany them, and buy his silence. The futility of this plan became apparent as they approached the stable and heard a male voice singing drunkenly.

The two young women peered round the door into the tack room to see a man sprawled on a pile of straw with an almost empty bottle of whiskey in one hand. Fortunately he did not see them, and they retreated hurriedly to the garden.

That, thought Sarah, was only to be expected when one could not pay one's servants properly and must employ a coachman no one else would have.

"Well, that's that," said Jennie with a touch of relief. "We cannot go tonight, for I doubt he can walk, let alone hitch up the horses and drive us to Covent Garden."

Sarah shook her head fiercely. "I may never have the courage again. Come on; with what we would have paid him, we can hire ourselves a hackney."

"If we can find one," muttered Jennie ominously.

It took perhaps three quarters of an hour to find themselves an empty hackney, and then the driver looked at them strangely when told the direction. But he did not argue with the coins Sarah handed him.

Jennie was becoming more and more unsettled. What devil had driven her to agree to this plan? She should never have told Sarah about the other girls at all, knowing her mistress's soft heart.

Not that she didn't relish the prospect of freeing some other hapless lasses from that hellhole, but she knew only too well how easily Mrs. Shamford's man could set upon the pair of them.

Although she might be forced back into that hideous life, it was not for herself that Jennie worried during that uncomfortable ride into her past. It was for Sarah.

Come morning, the young lady would be missed, and sought for; within a few days, she would be found, and rescued. But she would be ruined beyond all hope, and her family with her. What a cruel world it was, thought Jennie, that would cast out a virtuous girl for being ravished by a villain, when her only sin was to have tried to help those less fortunate than herself.

She peeked sideways at her mistress and felt a rush of pride. How very grand she looked in that shimmering dress and cloak! Such a fine lady had never before set foot on Mrs. Shamford's premises, and Jennie knew from their first meeting that Lady Sarah possessed unusual daring.

And, truth to tell, Jennie's dreams had been much troubled since her own escape, with memories of Rose and Daisy and Mary and the other girls she had left behind on that lucky night at Vauxhall.

She looked out the window and shuddered. The wide streets and stately houses of Mayfair were giving way to the narrow, crowded lanes of the poorer areas of London.

The stink of rotting garbage thickened the air about them, and Lady Sarah touched a perfumed handkerchief to her nose.

"I do beg pardon, my lady," said Jennie, feeling personally responsible for the foul condition of the streets.

"However did you bear it for so long?" asked her mistress.

"One gets used to it, after a while."

The hour was late, and they saw few people abroad until they reached the area near the Royal Opera House. Here one heard drunken voices in song—the coachman would have fitted in seamlessly—and saw cheaply dressed women rollicking arm in arm with disheveled men.

Jennie's eye picked out two or three expensively dressed fellows, young bucks enjoying a night of revelry. They would awaken the next day to find themselves stripped to their unmentionables, minus clothes, pocket watch, stickpin, and snuff case, not to mention any money they might have been carrying.

The hackney drew up at last in front of a four-storey building. Jennie shivered as she took in the familiar battered exterior of weathered brick, the paint long peeled away.

"It's not too late, my lady." She turned to Lady Sarah, and saw that familiar faraway expression. "This is not one of your dreams, Lady Sarah, and I fear it will prove the undoing of both of us."

"Nonsense." Clearly emboldened by her latest fantasy, Lady Sarah swept grandly from the hackney as though it were a coach-and-four, and Jennie could only follow behind.

Ignoring the garbage strewn everywhere, her mistress strode through the doorway of that miserable dwelling, then hesitated and turned. "What do we do now?" she asked.

"Wait here. Out of sight of the street—behind the staircase, if you please." Aware that they might be apprehended at any moment, Jennie raced up the stairs.

Left alone, Sarah found herself trembling inside the thin cloak. Her heightened senses caught every nasty odour from outside, every far-off shriek and cry. How could anyone tolerate such evil surroundings? Yet surely one could, if one must.

She shepherded her weeping mother up the narrow stairs. "I cannot bear it!" moaned Lady Rowdon. "Arthur in prison, and now us, forced to live here."

"I have been here before, Mother—do not ask when—and I assure you, one does become accustomed to it."

But did one, really?

Footsteps creaked across the floor upstairs. What was Jennie doing?

Muffled voices, then someone coming lightly down the stairs. It would not do to be seen cowering in corners! Sarah drew herself up proudly and stepped forth.

Amazement showed on the dirty face of the thin young girl who confronted her. "Jennie weren't fibbing," she gasped, holding out her hands as if Sarah's brilliant cloak were a warming flame. "Ye be a real lady!"

More thumping sounds on the stairs, and four more girls came down, their clothes ragged and hanging from their emaciated frames. None wore shoes.

"Here." Sarah pulled the coins from her purse. "Will you take these and buy yourself suitable clothing, and go back to your families? Or go away from here, anywhere that you will be safe?"

"Aye," they chorused softly. Sarah distributed the money.

"Take care," she murmured. "You don't want to be spotted on the streets."

"Never fear about that," answered one saucily, her voice sibilant between the gaps in her teeth. "This chicken ain't likely to be plucked twice!"

The girls vanished out the door. Sarah wondered how much of the money would be spent for liquor, and how many of the girls would truly find a better way of life. But even if only one of them were saved, it would all be worth it.

Without warning, a great clamour erupted above, full of shrieking and scuffling. Jennie had been caught!

Sarah lifted her voluminous skirts and dashed upstairs. "Jennie!"

"Run for it, my lady!" came the familiar voice. "They're on to us!"

At the top of the stairs, Sarah found herself on a narrow landing with closed doors all round. The noise was coming from the next floor up, so she took a deep breath and continued on.

She emerged to see Jennie struggling in the grip of a fat, toothless woman and a tall, muscular man with a patch over one eye. He was grasping at the girl's body in a way that filled Sarah with fury.

"Let her go, you knave!" she commanded. "How dare you lay hands on a servant to the Earl of Rowdon?"

"And who be this fancy lady?" The old crone regarded her suspiciously. "Why be ye stealing me girls away in the middle of the night?"

"Because you have trapped them here in a life of unspeakable depravity. I have given them their freedom!" Sarah drew herself up, wishing she were taller.

Leaving Jennie squirming in the grip of the one-eyed man, Mrs. Shamford—for it must be she—advanced toward Sarah, reaching out boldly to finger the material of her cloak.

"We'll get a pretty penny for this one, I warrant!" she chuckled. "Harry, me lad, lock up that other baggage and come 'ere."

To Sarah's horror, the man named Harry shoved Jennie into an adjoining room and locked the door from the outside.

"Let her loose!" Sarah stepped forward purposefully, brushing away the old woman's hand. "She is in my employ."

A firm grip closed over Sarah's arms, accompanied by the rancid smell of the man. She shrieked and twisted away, feeling her carefully powdered curls fly in disarray and scatter powder over her. Sarah coughed, unable to resist as the man grasped her tightly about the waist. She heard an evil, lewd laugh—whether from the man or the woman, she could not tell.

119

Jennie was pounding at the door that imprisoned her, scream-
ing at the top of her lungs. Surely someone must hear!

But there was no one in this part of town who would help,
even if they did hear. Suddenly Sarah realised how very foolish
she had been.

"Come on now, me fine lady." Mrs. Shamford opened the
door of another room. "Put her in here, Harry. We'll soon find
a buyer that'll pay well enough . . ."

"Whatever is the meaning of all this commotion?" The refined
masculine accents floated down from the upper storey.

"Nothing ye need worry about," called Mrs. Shamford in a
wheedling tone.

"Oh, please!" The words stuck in Sarah's throat, coming out
little above a whisper. "You must help me!"

"Eh? What's that?" Someone was coming down the stairs.

"Here's a lucky chance," muttered Harry, dispelling her rising
hopes. "This gent has a fine taste. I'll wager he'll pay gold sov-
ereigns for this beauty."

Fear swelled inside Sarah, almost choking her. Was this new
arrival to be her saviour, or her ravisher?

"Such a lot of fuss," came the voice again. A pair of shiny
leather evening shoes stepped into sight as their owner descended the open staircase at a leisurely pace. "I've no desire
to be caught in a brawl, Mrs. Shamford, and if this is how you
plan to run your establishment, I'll not be coming back in future."

"Nay, sir, wait an' see what a lovely surprise we have for ye!"
she said.

Well-tailored trousers, a broad figure encased in coat and vest
of subdued tones, and then . . .

"Lord Quires!" said Lady Sarah.

As for the viscount, he could only stare.

=== 14 ===

"LET ME GO!" Sarah seized the opportunity to free herself from the evil Harry and move closer to Lord Quires, who was still speechless. "I beg you to escort me home, my lord. These villains have attempted—well, I cannot even speak the words."

"Lies, all of it," protested Mrs. Shamford, her narrow slitted eyes darting back and forth as if seeking some plausible excuse. "Twere she who come here, interfering . . ."

"Freeing innocent girls who were kept enslaved," said Sarah.

"Oh, come now." Lord Quires had regained command of his tongue. "That is somewhat of an exaggeration I think, Lady Sarah."

"No, indeed it is not." Only then did it occur to her what the viscount had been doing upstairs and why he would not wish to believe that the girls whose favours he apparently enjoyed were in fact exploited and degraded.

"And it does not explain what you are doing here in this outlandish costume, which I believe you wore at Vauxhall for the masquerade," continued his lordship. "Is it your custom, Lady Sarah, to run about the scurvier parts of London late at night dressed as . . . as . . ."

"A harlot!" crowed Mrs. Shamford, having hit upon an explanation.

"I am not!"

"Lord Quires." Mrs. Shamford turned to that gentleman. "I put it to you plain. This lady come to me seeking employment."

Sarah gasped, overcome by the woman's pure effrontery.

"Says something about needing money—didn't ask what for." Sarah could tell the woman was inventing shamelessly, but she could see Lord Quires register the fact that her family did indeed need money. She hadn't missed his glance at her necklace earlier that evening, at Lady Mansfield's; no doubt he had spotted it as paste.

"My lord, you can hardly believe my parents would permit such a thing," Sarah returned.

"But you are known to be tender-hearted and much concerned about their financial difficulties." Lord Quires looked reflective.

"Hardly of such low character as to stoop to this! And wait, I have a witness. Harry, open that door."

After a glance at Mrs. Shamford for permission, the one-eyed man released an infuriated Jennie, who had been taking in the conversation through the keyhole.

"Lady Sarah speaks the truth," she told Lord Quires. "She sold all her jewelry and we come here to give the money to the girls so's they could return home, or go off wherever they wanted 'stead of being held here without even shoes."

"A likely story!" trumpeted Mrs. Shamford. "She's the very proof of what I say, me lord. This doxy, Jennie, was one o' me own, lately gone into service, I gather, for this bit o' baggage who claims to be a lady.

"Now why would she be taking her in, I ask you, save she be intending to follow the same profession? And I take you to say her family's hard up, and she's worried about them; then what call has she to be selling her jewellery to help some strumpets she's not even seen before? I'd not believe a word of it, me lord."

"This is incredible." Sarah pinched herself on the wrist to be sure she had not slipped into one of her dreams. "Such absurdities! I cannot think you credit them, my lord. I rescued Jennie at Vauxhall, quite by accident, and was moved by her tales of the horrid life she led here."

"Well, no matter," said the viscount. "Why you are here is your own business, Lady Sarah, and far be it from me to pass judgement one way or t'other. Be advised, Mrs. Shamford, that this young lady is the daughter of an earl and not someone for you to be trifling with."

"No, indeed, me lord." The old crone bobbed slightly, saving for Sarah a sideways look of unmitigated malice.

The viscount took Sarah's arm and escorted her down the stairs, with Jennie trailing behind. Sarah wished she did not have the uncomfortable feeling he half-believed Mrs. Shamford.

Harry had dashed down before them and stood waiting in the street with a hackney, tipping his battered hat as Lord Quires handed him a coin. From the fact that no word had been said between the two men about securing a carriage, Sarah gathered that the viscount's behaviour fell into a routine. That meant he visited the place frequently.

"I'd no idea you knew him," whispered Jennie while Lord Quires was giving the Rowdons' direction to the driver. "Had his lordship one time myself, you see."

"Oh, Jennie, no!",

The girl shrugged. "He weren't so bad. Leastways he didn't smell so bad as the others."

Quires returned to join them in the carriage and spent the journey to Mayfair lecturing Sarah about the dangers of young girls wandering about town at night.

"Please give me your word that you'll not tell my parents," she said, and then had another, more horrible thought. With his penchant for spreading talk all over town, Lord Quires could destroy her reputation and with it her family's hopes.

"And I trust that your honour as a gentleman will prevent your saying anything of this . . . this unfortunate escapade to anyone else," she added.

Lord Quires looked displeased.

"Naturally, I would not wish to blacken your name," he said.

"Then may I have your word on it?"

He tugged at his neckcloth, already tied crookedly in a manner indicating the viscount had dressed in a hurry. "That is not necessary, surely, Lady Sarah?"

"Oh, but it is," she said.

Lord Quires gave her a long, considering look before nodding. "You have my word that I'll not make idle gossip of your conduct tonight. Nor will I tell your parents, since apparently no harm has been done. By the way, what *was* the idea of that peculiar costume?"

"Splendid, ain't it?" Jennie had cheered up considerably and now bounced against the squabs, apparently beginning to enjoy herself despite the chill of the late night that seeped into the seedy carriage.

"The idea," said Lady Sarah, "was to appear grand and imposing, neither of which I am thought to be in my ordinary attire. Jennie believed this would do the trick."

The carriage stopped in front of the modest Rowdon residence. "I take it you'll not be wanting me to see you inside," said Quires.

Sarah smiled for the first time in some hours. "No, thank you. We shall see ourselves in at the back. I cannot thank you enough for your assistance this evening, my lord. I must confess things were not turning out as we'd planned."

He bowed politely and waited until the two of them disappeared through the side gait before departing.

"It were a narrow squeak, but we done it!" Jennie could scarcely keep her voice to a whisper as she helped Lady Sarah remove the offending dress, safely back in her room.

"Oh, yes, we done it . . . did it," said Sarah grimly. "Now if only Lord Quires can be trusted. What did he promise?"

"Not to make it idle gossip." Jennie shook out the gown and tucked it inside the wardrobe.

"That's it." Sarah nodded slowly. "Idle gossip. And then drew off my attention before I could swear him to keep entirely silent on the subject. We must trust to his good character, Jennie, and after tonight, I'm not sure he has very much of one."

Lord Broadmoor's attentions to Lady Sarah at the card party had somewhat restored her to the good graces of society, and she was not allowed to sleep past noon the next morning.

"Your lady mother says she expects visitors at any moment and you're to be up and dressed," said Jennie, throwing wide the damask curtains to the morning sunshine.

Sarah sat up, feeling stiff in every muscle, no doubt from the uncomfortable ride in the hackney. She opened her mouth to protest that she was too tired, then realised Jennie must have been up and at her duties since early morning.

"Very well," she said.

Lady Rowdon was not wrong, but the visitors were not the ones she had hoped for. It was the Williams cousins who arrived first, followed not a quarter of an hour later by Mr. Lenham. Sarah had a strong suspicion that the coincidence was not mere happenstance.

The conversation remained general until Lady Rowdon excused herself to attend to other matters, leaving the young people to chat among themselves. She left instructions with Henderson to inform her should any more guests arrive.

"I presume you have heard that Lord Broadmoor plans to give a ball," Kitty said, perching on a settee near Sarah. "Have you received your invitation?"

"I don't believe so," she said. "Have you?"

"Not yet," Kitty admitted. "Perhaps they have not been sent. He only mentioned the ball last night as if he had just thought of it."

"I did not hear him mention it." What was Kitty's point? Sarah wondered.

"You and Sir Lindsay had gone to play cards," continued her visitor. "He was speaking to Lady Mansfield, Lord Quires, and me."

"Then I am certain that by now all London knows of it." Sarah hoped the mildness of her tone would disguise the irony of the comment, and apparently it did, for Kitty appeared to take no heed.

"Here is something all London does not know." She bent forward confidingly. "There is to be a grand announcement at the ball."

"Oh? And what is that to be?"

Kitty looked disappointed. "I was hoping that you might know."

"I'm afraid I do not. How do you know there is to be an announcement?" said Sarah.

"The usual way." Kitty took in her blank expression. "Do you not use your abigail to obtain tittle-tattle? Everyone does it."

Sarah remembered Jennie's comments about Quires's man, Finley, attempting to purchase information from her. "Oh, yes, sometimes I do, but she was . . . otherwise occupied last night."

"You must promise me that if you should learn more about this announcement, you will tell me before anyone else," said Kitty. "Especially Lord Quires. I cannot bear him, the way he goes about pretending that he knows everything before anyone else. One of these days I will show him up, indeed I will."

Their conversation was interrupted by Mr. Lenham, whose voice rose as he told Mary Beth, "I will not accept it! And neither must you!"

"Begging your pardon, may I ask what is the matter?" Sarah looked from Mary Beth's tear-stained face to her lover's angry one.

Before either of them could speak, Kitty leaped into the breach. "It is Father," she said. "He has refused Mr. Lenham's request for Mary Beth's hand."

"He believes that because I am poor, I seek her only for her wealth." Mr. Lenham's voice was laced with contempt, and he spoke more forcefully than Sarah had ever heard him before. "It was true that at one time I might have been considered a fortune hunter, for what man in my position would not be, but in truth my heart is engaged and I will not give up the woman I love."

Mary Beth's wide blue eyes stared at him admiringly. With a stroke of pain, Sarah remembered her own rejection of Kenneth Link's proposal, on the same grounds, but in that case her family's welfare had been at stake.

If I had Mary Beth's inheritance, I should never have given him up, she thought. No matter what perils I faced.

Locked in the tower, Lady Sarah began knotting the sheets together. Her maidservant peered out the window. "It is a long way to the ground, my lady," she cautioned. "And your father will beat you if you are caught."

"I am not afraid," said Lady Sarah. "On to Gretna Green!"

"Gretna Green?" repeated Mary Beth, and Sarah perceived that she must have spoken the words aloud. "Do you mean that we should elope?"

126

All three of her companions were staring at Sarah. "I suppose so," she said hesitantly. "What other recourse is there?"

"How romantic!" Her tears gone, Mary Beth heaved an exaggerated sigh. "But can we not go somewhere closer than Scotland?"

"Don't be a goose!" said her cousin. "In Scotland they will marry the two of you without Father's permission, so of course you must go there."

"The thing must be planned carefully." Sarah was beginning to wonder if she had made a serious error. So many things might go wrong. "If Mary Beth and Mr. Lenham were to start out alone and be apprehended, Mary Beth's reputation could be ruined. *Would* be ruined, without question, had they already passed a night at an inn."

"We shall stay in separate rooms of course." Mary Beth looked at her as though she had taken leave of her senses.

"That will not signify," said Kitty. "You are a green young miss indeed, cousin. Separate rooms or no, you cannot go unchaperoned. Therefore, I shall go with you."

Sarah felt as if perhaps she should offer to go as well, but she did not dare leave London just now with the creditors almost at her parents' doorstep.

Still, she wished the enterprise well. Her own life had been blighted by the need to reject Kenneth's offer; she fervently hoped no other woman would ever have to suffer as she had, and so she turned her mind to helping Mary Beth. "You must disguise where you have gone, or you may be caught," she said.

"That can be arranged." Kitty was clearly beginning to enjoy her role. "A word to the right servant, and my parents will learn that we have gone off in the opposite direction."

Mary Beth clapped her hands in excitement. "We must go soon! I can hardly contain myself."

"We must be back in time for Lord Broadmoor's ball," agreed Kitty. "Today is Tuesday. By the time we see to our packing, and Mr. Lenham arranges for the carriage, it will be Thursday."

"But on Thursday we go to Astley's Royal Amphitheatre," said Mary Beth. "I cannot miss that."

"You can certainly go later, when you are married," reproved Kitty. "Honestly, Mary Beth, one would think we were planning a picnic rather than your marriage."

"I have it," said Mr. Lenham. "We shall make our escape in the early morning hours Friday. You will all have made your appearance at Astley's and gone to bed late, and your parents will most likely be too tired to suspect anything."

"That's it!" said Mary Beth. "How exciting it sounds! Kitty, what shall I wear?"

The arrival of other guests—a middle-aged couple and their elderly mother—drew Lady Rowdon back to the room, and the Williams party shortly made their excuses.

On the ride home, Kitty's mind was reviewing the planned elopement, seeking a way to derive some benefit from it for herself.

It came to her all of a sudden, how she might secure an advantageous match by persuading one particular gentleman to accompany the runaways—without telling him that she too would be going along.

She would send a note round to Mr. Lenham that very afternoon, omitting certain details of her plan, and had no doubt the thing would be arranged without difficulty.

=== 15 ===

THE INVITATION To Lord Broadmoor's ball arrived Wednesday, with a note to Lady Rowdon that read, "I particularly hope that your family can attend."

"You see, I was right all along!" crowed Anna. "He does plan to declare his intentions that night."

"Or to make us think that he does," said Sarah grimly.

"Nonsense," replied her mother. "And in any event Sir Lindsay has accepted our invitation to come to tea the next day, so if Lord Broadmoor has played us false, you can then become betrothed to the baronet instead."

So Sir Lindsay had agreed to come. Sarah could not help reflecting on his animation Monday night while speaking with Kitty at the card party, yet he had come away willingly enough to play cards with Sarah. She could not puzzle him out.

"Very well," she said. "I am glad that at least I have only another week and a half before this business is settled, for I must say, it is wearing to the nerves."

"Do not speak of nerves to me, young lady!" cried her mother. "I am the one who suffers, not you."

Sarah reflected on this for a moment as she worked at her embroidery, sitting in the small, comfortable salon at the back of the house where a litter of yarns, fashion journals, and scraps of cloth testified that the two ladies were taking their ease without fear of public intrusion.

"Why did you marry Father?" she asked at last.

"Why?" Lady Rowdon looked startled. "Because it was a splendid match, of course. He was so handsome and wealthy— we were well off at the time, you know."

Sarah tried not to think of how different her life might have been, had that money not been lost through dishonest estates managers and investments gone awry. "Did you love him?" she ventured.

"Love him?" Anna examined a bonnet that she was trimming with feathers. "Of course I did. And as much as he vexes me, I suppose I always will."

Lady Sarah stared glumly down at her hands, trying to imagine her life twenty years from now. Married to Sir Lindsay, left to rusticate in the countryside—but there would be children, of course, who would more than compensate for whatever she had lost.

And by her marriage to the baronet, she would make certain that none of them would ever have to give up what they loved most for lack of funds.

"She refused to say anything further." Finley was serving up the morning's news along with Lord Quires's coffee.

"Only that you are to station yourself in the alley behind the Williams house at two o'clock Friday morning," mused the viscount. "That abigail is not having sport with you, do you think, my man?"

The valet shook his head. "She seemed deadly serious, my lord, and the wench knows I'll not tolerate being made a fool of."

"Then be there you must," said his lordship. "You shall be well rewarded for the inconvenience, of course, and have the rest of the day free—after you have told me what you've seen, naturally."

"Very good, my lord." Finley took himself off.

Damned valuable man, that, thought Quires with satisfaction. Now whatever could the Williams cousins be about? It must be something the abigail did not dare spill in advance, for fear of word reaching someone's ears, most likely those of the Williams parents.

How he should enjoy having the drop on that uppity Kitty Williams!

Finley returned in a moment with the post. On the top of the stack was an invitation to Lord Broadmoor's ball.

"Ah, very good. Remind me to send round an answer this afternoon, will you? There's a good chap." The viscount glanced without interest at the other letters and circulars. Nothing of note, he saw from the franking. "That was a deuced good bit of information you got from Broadmoor's man, about the announcement to be made at the ball. Can you not pump him a bit more as to the nature of it?"

"I do not think he knew the nature of it." Finley hesitated before speaking further. "My lord, there is something I feel I must say."

"Yes, yes, out with it."

"I have been having a rather excessive amount of luck these past few days, getting information." The valet stood stiffly, hands behind his back.

"Excessive amount of luck? A rather odd bit of phrasing." Idly, the viscount opened another letter, an invitation to a breakfast at the home of an ambitious and wealthy cit who sought to rub elbows with the *haut ton.*

"Yes, my lord," said Finley. "It has occurred to me that one might do well to examine this information with a bit of scepticism, if you'll pardon my presumption."

Quires eyed him balefully. Presumption was indeed the word for it! "Do you mean to suggest that Lady Sarah's abigail, that hackabout little chit, and Lord Broadmoor's stern Scotsman, and Miss Williams's maid are all in some sort of collusion to mislead us?"

"Not precisely, my lord."

"Has any of their gossip proved untrue?"

"No, my lord." Finley cleared his throat. "I meant only to put you on your guard, my lord."

"Finley, you are an excellent servant and I fully appreciate the work you do for me, but you must trust me when it comes to evaluating gossip," said Quires, pouring himself a second cup of coffee.

"Very good, my lord."

But the viscount was not finished. "One can sense when information is not quite right. I do not dispute the need for caution when, as it seems, one is suddenly inundated with titbits from servants who have heretofore kept their silence."

Finley, having seen the futility of speaking, merely waited patiently.

"However, there are mitigating circumstances," Quires continued. "Matters are coming to a head between Lady Sarah and Lord Broadmoor. Other matches also may be made during the next few weeks, and then there is the matter of this announcement. Perhaps it concerns someone other than Lady Sarah. So you see, there is a great deal of activity, and therefore a great deal more than usual for servants to gossip about."

"I take your meaning, my lord," said Finley, and bowed himself away, silenced but patently unconvinced.

There was no reasoning with the man. Well, his inclination to be mistrustful was a useful trait, thought Quires. But it was clear to the viscount that what was happening was what he had always hoped for. His carefully laid snares, in the households of those who aroused his curiosity, were finally catching rabbits.

Above all, he prided himself on the development of a friendship, albeit a wary one, with Lady Mansfield. There was a woman he could genuinely admire and who made no attempt to compete with him in his chosen field.

In fact, he decided, he would visit her that very day. Perhaps Lord Broadmoor would even come to see her. Frankly, Quires did not think the marquess showed sufficient appreciation. Much as he liked the currents Broadmoor was sending through society, he could wish that gentleman had the taste to see that the baroness stood far above any and all rivals, especially the peculiar Lady Sarah.

He set aside the rest of the letters and rose to begin his day.

Preparing for a ball was not Lord Broadmoor's idea of enjoyment. However did women tolerate this business? he wondered, especially considering how often some ladies entertained. Once a year was more than sufficient for him.

There were additional servants to be hired, and lists to be gone over with the housekeeper—what to serve at supper, where to put the orchestra, whether it would be necessary to rent additional crystal and silver, how many tubs of flowers to order. The entire house smelled of beeswax and soap as the immense and long-unused second-floor ballroom was cleaned and set to rights.

At the same time, the marquess must interweave his campaign of retribution against Lady Sarah with his need to stay current with business affairs and the workings of the House of Lords, where he was only beginning to learn his way about.

With so little time, he had barely been able to write personal notes to her and to Lady Mansfield, encouraging them to attend, and most likely stirring their hopes.

McGaugh, against his Scotsman's recalcitrant nature, had aided his master by trading information with Quires's man, and had learned that both ladies were to attend Astley's the next night. Busy as he was, Broadmoor knew he would have to go also; at least it would take less time than seeing them individually.

On Thursday afternoon, he went to order a new top hat at Lock's in St. James's Street, his old one having been sorely tried when it flew from his head while he was driving, landing under the horses.

He entered to find Sir Lindsay there before him. The two acknowledged each others' presence with easy civility despite their purported rivalry.

"Getting a new hat, eh?" asked the baronet.

The marquess nodded. "My top hat met with a sorry fate on the road."

"I've had that happen, more than once." Sir Lindsay nodded affably to an acquaintance who passed outside the open door of the shop. "Picking up my new beaver—would have sent my man, but I was passing by. I'll need it tonight, that's for certain."

Not at Astley's, he wouldn't, thought Broadmoor. The baronet must be planning to go for a drive, rather a long one, but where would he be going at night? Nor did Sir Lindsay strike him as the sort of fellow to leave London in the middle of the season.

"Going to Gretna Green?" He meant it as a joke, but Sir Lindsay paled. Good heavens, he wasn't running off with Lady Sarah? Broadmoor felt his heart perform some odd manoeuvres.

"Gossip! I've never seen this town so full of gossip as it's been this year!" said his companion. "Word's got out already, has it? The devil take that Lenham!"

"Lenham?" inquired the marquess, puzzled.

"It's only a favour to him," grumbled the baronet. "Hasn't got his own carriage, you know."

The shop clerk returned at that moment with Sir Lindsay's high-crowned beaver hat, and the conversation ended as the baronet said farewell and decamped. Strange goings-on, thought the marquess, but he felt reassured at the information that Sir Lindsay was not the gentleman eloping.

Mr. Lenham was the one going off, and with who else but the Williams heiress, the chit who was always prattling about this being her first season. He wished them luck, although he suspected they hadn't a farthing's worth of sense between the two of them.

It was a day for encounters, Broadmoor saw when he emerged from Lock's and espied Lord Quires coming out of a nearby jeweller's shop.

There followed a ritual exchange of good mornings. The marquess, aware of the viscount's penchant for loose talk, refrained from mentioning anything of what Sir Lindsay had said. No use having the elopement bruited about all over London before the couple was safely off.

"Looking forward to your ball." Quires spoke above the clop and creak of passing traffic. "Someone was mentioning an announcement you're to make. Anything to that rumour?"

"Could be," said the marquis. "Who told you there was to be an announcement, do you remember?"

"Afraid not." Quires looked apologetic—and sly, thought Broadmoor. "Look here, I know you must be busy, what with one thing and another, but we did say we'd have dinner together soon and I wanted to invite you to my club."

"I'd be delighted, but my schedule is rather full up this week," said the marquess. "Next week be all right?"

Quires appeared to be searching his memory. "Thursday?" he said at last.

Broadmoor nodded and the arrangements were made. He looked forward to the dinner, if not the conversation, for the food at Watier's was reputed to be superior.

Broadmoor's path toward his waiting phaeton was briefly interrupted as a slender, dark-haired woman brushed past, leading a small girl by the hand.

For a moment he imagined it to be Lady Sarah, until a closer look at her back revealed that she was somewhat taller and broader through the shoulders.

He climbed up into his seat, reflecting that had Lady Sarah accepted his suit four years before, the little girl might have been theirs. What would it have been like, to have been her husband?

But it had all been a hum; she was not in love with him, and therefore their marriage, had it taken place, would have been miserably unhappy. How fortunate for him that he had learned the truth, even though he had spent some wretched months as a result, he told himself as he guided the horses through the crowded street.

He thought again of Sir Lindsay, jovially strutting from Lock's with his new beaver hat. McGaugh had brought back the information that the baronet was to take tea with the Rowdons the day after the ball.

One had to admire Lady Sarah for her skill at strategy, thought Broadmoor. Even while scheming to win the richer prize, the minx was keeping her other suitor in reserve. Poor Sir Lindsay, good-natured chap that he was, could only be seen as a hare ruthlessly hunted to ground by a cunning fox.

Lord Broadmoor tried hard to feel sorry for Sir Lindsay, cozened into spending the rest of his life married to Lady Sarah. But he found it a very difficult task indeed.

══ 16 ══

A MOST UNFORTUNATE—though hardly tragic—thing happened in the Viscount Vincent Quires's dressing-room as he was preparing to go to Astley's that night. It was all his sister's fault, really.

His sister, Lady Beatrice, a spinster who lived with her younger, married brother, prided herself on her fine embroidery. Each Christmas she could be counted on to present Lord Quires with some useless pillowcover or other knicknack entirely out of place in the apartments of a bachelor. Two years ago, it had been a hassock in the shape of a toadstool, its top covered with bilious-looking embroidered mushrooms.

The trouble was, one could not simply pitch Lady Beatrice's work into the street or hide it properly in the attic, as she always searched it out when she came to visit. Lord Quires, not wishing his friends to think him a man of such monstrous taste as to accumulate these items, hid them away in his dressing-room.

Thus it happened that Finley, while assisting his master in preparing for the evening's entertainment, tripped over the offending stool and sprained his ankle. Not a serious injury; Finley assured him it would be right enough in a day or two.

But there could be no question of sending the man out in the wee hours of the morning to spy upon the Williams cousins. Therefore, Lord Quires concluded, with feelings of malice toward Lady Beatrice, he would have to do the honours himself.

This prospect cast a damper upon the rest of the evening, which would otherwise have delighted him, combining as it did a visit to the handsomest pleasure haunt in London with a chance to observe his favorite subjects.

The weather boded ill for the journey to Lambeth, with a fine mist beginning to fall, and Lord Quires was not his usual self as he descended and allowed himself to be ushered inside.

Although principally interested in people, Lord Quires had made a point of refining his powers of observation concerning details of decoration as well. They could often yield hints as to the taste or financial condition of their possessors, as in the case of Lady Sarah's paste necklace. So it was that he made a brief but thorough survey of the amphitheatre.

The interior was filled with ships' masts and spars, its canvas ceiling lashed together with ropes and stretched on fir poles. The viscount examined the great chandelier for signs of grime or other neglect, but the fifty patent lamps sparkled brightly.

The huge stage appeared freshly painted, and the galleries were nearly filled. He concluded that Astley's retained its desirability as a place for a gentleman of rank to be seen.

The feats of horsemanship in the sawdust ring, which were the chief attraction, had not yet begun. Quires ascended leisurely toward his box, nodding to various acquaintances as he went.

Under other circumstances, this would have been a delightful evening. As in a quadrille, with its intricate dance steps, ladies and gentlemen flirted and retreated, exchanged meaningful looks, and gossiped behind their hands.

Lord Broadmoor joined Quires and Lady Mansfield for a time, exchanging banalities about the excellent riding by John Astley and his daughter-in-law Hannah. The marquess also visited Lady Rowdon and her daughter, but although Quires could not hear the conversation, it was clear that the presence of the countess precluded any but the most formal exchanges. Sarah, as usually, appeared to have her head in the clouds half the time.

Kitty and Mary Beth were on hand also, with Kitty's parents, and Quires saw nothing exceptional in their behaviour. He wished fervently for a clew as to the night's proceedings, for he had no desire to stand about in what bade fair to become a rainstorm. But Mr. Lenham, who might have had some information, was not even present, nor was his friend, Sir Lindsay.

The absence of that gentleman, needed to play his role in the drama of Lady Sarah, also helped to put the viscount out of sorts. The deuce take it, if only he hadn't bothered to come at all, he wouldn't have been dressing, and Finley . . . well, no use dwelling on that. It was entirely Beatrice's fault, and no doubt he would have to endure yet another of her hideous gifts with a semblance of good grace next Christmas.

The entertainments finished several hours before Lord Quires was to take up his appointed post, but he had no time to spare. It was a matter of many minutes to extricate his carriage from the crowd; then he must return home and change his clothing.

He inquired after Finley, whom the housekeeper declared was still soaking his ankle in a hot tub and consoling himself with a shot of whiskey in his tea.

This image of domestic comfort contrasted unpleasantly with the chilly rain that greeted Lord Quires on his exit from the house. He summoned himself a hackney, for it would not do to be seen clattering about in one of his own conveyances, which might be recognised.

Wretched weather for this time of year, thought the viscount sourly as he paid off the driver and stationed himself in an inconspicuous spot in the mews that gave a good view of the Williams's stables. Might as well be November as April.

Opening his black umbrella against the increasingly heavy rain, Quires set himself to wait.

"You needn't take your entire wardrobe!" Kitty shook her head at her cousin's folly. "We'll be back in a few days, you know."

Mary Beth peered at her innocently from behind a pink satin ballgown embroidered with roses, which she was holding up before the mirror. "I shouldn't want to look common, Kitty. Suppose we are invited somewhere in Gretna Green?"

"There isn't anywhere to *be* invited, so far as I know," hissed the older girl, whose own portmanteau had been packed for over an hour. "I'd better make the selection, or we'll never get off in time."

Packing was more difficult than one might think, for they had concluded it would be too dangerous to let their abigails in on the secret, even the one entrusted to pass information to Finley. She might suspect, but it would be to her own advantage not to know too much; that way, she could honestly tell Kitty's parents she'd known nothing of the scheme.

Kitty chose several sensible gowns to pack into Mary Beth's valise, but even these must be carefully folded to avoid wrinkling, for there would be no dresser along to iron them. Then there were the cosmetics and jewels—Mary Beth insisted on taking far too many—and the ribbons, shoes, reticules, and other paraphernalia.

Only a heated argument, conducted in whispers to avoid waking anyone, dissuaded Mary Beth from taking along an enormous Pamela bonnet. Kitty could envision it streaming behind Sir Lindsay's carriage, tied to the doorpost for want of any other space for it.

Mary Beth persisted in giggling as they cloaked themselves warmly against the rain and crept downstairs. Every step on the back stairs creaked and groaned, as in the fearsome houses of Fanny Burney's novels. Had it not been for her own stake in this venture, Kitty might well have changed her mind and let her silly cousin fend for herself. As it was, she felt certain that only the aid of some unsuspected patron saint saved them from detection.

Once they reached the back door, her fears began to ease and her spirits soared with thoughts of the events to come. What a brilliant idea it had been, having Mr. Lenham convince Sir Lindsay to drive them! Of course, the baronet hadn't been informed who the lady was that would chaperone Mary Beth, or he might have had second thoughts.

Once en route to Gretna Green, Sir Lindsay would easily be persuaded to make the elopement a double one and marry her—for Kitty, being of a practical bent, had abandoned the hope of snaring the marquess for herself and had turned her sights to a more accessible catch.

After all, she reasoned, why should she not take as her husband the eminently eligible Sir Lindsay, with his comfortable station and his exquisite tastes, so well suited to her own? Ensconced as his wife, she no doubt would soon rule over London society.

Lady Sarah would be greatly put out, especially if the marquess settled on Lady Mansfield. But while she bore Sarah no ill will, neither did Kitty intend to sacrifice her own prospects. In fact, it had become clear to her that Sarah lacked an appreciation of Sir Lindsay's finer qualities.

Should the baronet demur, Kitty would play her trump card: the likelihood that Quires was already spreading gossip about a double elopement. Once she explained that she had spotted his valet watching as they drove away—naturally omitting any mention of her own role in alerting him—the baronet would feel duty-bound to marry her and save her reputation.

All in all, she reflected happily, her plan could not fail.

"They're not here yet," muttered Mary Beth. "Let's go inside the stable and get dry."

"Very well." The grooms would surely be asleep by now, Kitty calculated. However, despite her dislike of the water that slanted beneath her umbrella, she lagged behind her cousin until she spotted a portly figure half-hidden behind a corner of the garden fence.

Lord Quires himself! The man must have been consumed by curiosity. Not wishing to draw attention to her awareness of his presence, she turned and hurried after Mary Beth, chuckling to herself.

It was only a few moments later that her ears picked up the sound of horses snorting and a carriage wheeling into the alley. She and Mary Beth waited beneath the eaves until the equipage drew to a halt.

Mr. Lenham and the coachman leaped down to assist them with the valises. Kitty recognised the barouche as belonging to Sir Lindsay, but where was he?

"Have you not brought your friend?" she demanded of Mr. Lenham in a voice tight with apprehension.

"He was to drive us himself," he returned as he handed Mary Beth into the carriage. "But he said his health would not permit it in this rain, so he sent his coachman."

"But he might have ridden inside with us." Kitty hoped her voice did not betray her desperation.

"To what end?" Mr. Lenham helped her up, then climbed inside himself. "We have you as chaperone. Oh, do not think ill of Sir Lindsay; he missed the entertainment at Astley's expressly to make sure the carriage was on hand and everything in place for me, and in hopes that the rain would let up, but as you see, it has not. He has even lent his new beaver hat to his coachman, to keep him warm, and promised to lie low for a day or so lest anyone inquire as to my whereabouts."

"Oh, blast," muttered Kitty ungraciously as the carriage rolled forward. She could, she supposed, call a halt to the entire venture right then, but whatever explanation could she give? Mary Beth and Mr. Lenham would be furious. Worst of all, she had provided Quires as a witness, and word of these strange doings would reach her parents in any event.

Not only must she make herself the subject of idle talk and speculation; not only must she open herself to punishment for her part in aiding Mary Beth's elopement; not only must she endure a cold and uncomfortable ride all the way to Scotland and back; but she had left Lady Sarah a clear field with Sir Lindsay for at least four days.

Oh, blast Lord Quires anyway! thought Kitty viciously as they headed north, away from London.

Thank goodness he had not been forced to wait long, reflected the viscount as he made his way back to the street and began looking about for a hackney.

What a splendid night this had turned out to be, after all! Mary Beth Williams eloping with Mr. Lenham was a trifling bit of gossip, scarcely worth a special call on Lady Jersey or Lady Lieven.

But his eye had caught what Finley might have missed in the rain: Sir Lindsay's crest on the door of the barouche.

Without it, even Quires would not have identified the figure of the man in the driver's seat, so bundled up was he in a greatcoat. True, it might have been a coachman, but the viscount's keen eye had noticed that fine beaver hat, still resplendent despite the rain. It could only have come from Lock's, and servants did not purchase their hats at Lock's.

What a juicy item this would be—Lady Sarah's suitor gone off with Kitty Williams! Quires wished now that he had brought his own carriage, so that he might have followed them and made certain they were on the road to Gretna Green, but no matter. Where else did one creep off to at this hour of the morning, in dead secret?

He rubbed his gloved hands together in delight, nearly dropping the umbrella.

A hackney came by at last. About to give the driver his address, Quires thought the better of it. In his present elated mood he had no wish to go quietly to bed, and it was far too late to pay a social call.

Instead, he gave the driver an address in Covent Garden. When one wanted to celebrate, what better place was there, in spite of Lady Sarah's nonsensical proclamations about girls being exploited and enslaved? The wenches were always happy to make a few shillings.

So caught up was he in the matter of the Williams cousins that Lord Quires had all but forgotten the question of what to do with that other interesting bit of news, concerning Lady Sarah's visit to Mrs. Shamford's establishment.

He had promised not to make idle gossip of it, and indeed he would not. Yet it went against the grain to leave such a juicy titbit untold.

Perhaps it would serve him well at some future time. He would keep it in reserve, thought the viscount as he descended at his destination and paid off the driver.

Well pleased with his night's work, he sauntered inside the building and up the stairs, already loosening his cravat in anticipation of what lay ahead.

=== 17 ===

THE WONDERFUL TALE of the Williams cousins, which represented unquestionably the high point of Lord Quires's adventures in news-gathering, had to wait until Saturday, and while part of the blame might rest with his sister, he was compelled to admit that most of it lay on his own shoulders.

One would expect a gentleman of his experience in life to realise that getting drenched in the rain was a perilous enough occurrence without choosing to spend the next few hours stripped to the buff in an unheated room, however much heat one might be generating oneself.

The result, as could have been predicted, was a severe chill, enough to keep him laid up all of Friday. As a result, he missed a dinner given by Lady Jersey and was forced to wait until Saturday afternoon, when he felt sufficiently recovered to attend a breakfast at the home of Lady Cowper.

Lord Quires had not slept well the previous evening, for fear word of Sir Lindsay's absence and that of the two young ladies might already have spread. However, Finley made inquiries Saturday morning, and apparently Kitty's parents were keeping quiet on the subject.

In a fever of anticipation, Quires dressed carefully in a biscuit-coloured coat and pantaloons with a light blue waistcoat and French top boots, Fortunately, the rain had ended, giving way to an almost unnatural clarity of sunlight for which he had no doubt Lady Cowper would claim personal credit.

But no mind. Undoubtedly his latest news would establish him head and shoulders above Lady Jersey and the others as the master of *on-dits*. The thought of the thorough trouncing he was delivering to that upstart Kitty Williams on all counts made the business the more delicious.

As breakfasts were held in the afternoon, it was almost four o'clock when Lord Quires arrived at Lady Cowper's. He found most of his acquaintance there before him, dining out of doors on quail and roast turkey, ham fritters and veal pie, fruit tarts and syllabubs laced with rum.

He nodded to the ladies Lieven, Jersey, Cowper, and Castlereagh, bowed to the Princess Esterhazy, smiled warmly at the Marquess of Broadmoor, and wondered where the devil Lady Sarah had got to.

He joined Lady Mansfield at her table, and was soon informed that the Rowdons had not been invited.

"They are not, you know, really good *ton*," explained their hostess, who was seated with them.

"But Lady Sarah appears in the way of making an advantageous marriage," noted Lady Mansfield. "Do you not think she might take exception to being snubbed?"

"Sir Lindsay is not so highly placed as to elevate her above me," returned Lady Cowper. "Furthermore, I have only recently had Lord and Lady Rowdon to dine here, so they cannot make too much fuss—if, indeed, Sir Lindsay can be brought to marry her after the chase she has led him. By the bye, I wonder where he can be, for I have not seen him today."

"Perhaps he was ill with the same ailment that afflicted you, Lord Quires," said Lady Mansfield. "He was not at Lady Jersey's last night."

The Marquess of Broadmoor having approached their table and bowed to the ladies, the viscount saw his opportunity and took it.

"Sir Lindsay is not ill," he said in his most casual manner. "He has eloped."

A stunned silence fell over the table. Broadmoor's startled expression and the agitation apparent in his suddenly clenched fists were all Quires could have hoped.

"I would not have credited it," gasped Lady Cowper at last. "So Lady Sarah has captured her quarry after all!"

"I did not say he had eloped with Lady Sarah." Quires could not repress the shadow of a smile.

"With whom, then?" said Lady Mansfield, who retained as ever her impeccably calm manner.

"Miss Kitty Williams."

Stares of astonishment all round.

"Are you quite certain?" asked Broadmoor. "Surely her parents can have had no objection to the man, so there was no need for secrecy."

"To your first question, indeed I am certain, having seen them depart with my own eyes." The viscount tried not to look too smug. "As for that other matter, I hasten to explain: It was a double elopement."

Lady Jersey and several others had gathered round the table, having noted the stir being created there and the fact that it was Quires at the center of it.

"We are discussing the elopement of Sir Lindsay Manx with Miss Kitty Williams," Quires informed them. "They departed about two o'clock in the morning yesterday, in Sir Lindsay's carriage, along with Miss Mary Beth Williams and Sir Lindsay's good friend, Mr. Franklin Lenham."

This last detail appeared to allay many doubts. "I can well believe the Williamses would object to *him*," sniffed Lady Jersey. "He is the merest fortune hunter."

"I do believe he truly cares for the chit," said Broadmoor quietly.

Lady Jersey hastened away, no doubt to spread the word among the other guests. Quires sat serenely, beaming at how neatly he had pulled off this triumph.

He was not too preoccupied, however, to note that Broadmoor was gazing restlessly about the grounds, apparently not having heard that the Rowdons had been excluded. Lady Mansfield looked thoughtful.

His business accomplished, Lord Quires requested a passing footman to bring him a plate of food. Nothing gave him so sharp an appetite as besting all his rivals at the game of gossip.

Had he known what Sally Jersey was about, Quires might not have felt so complacent.

It being clear that she had been soundly defeated at her favourite sport, that lady determined to waste no more time. With her vast experience, she knew that whoever has the lastest word becomes the center of attention, and that yesterday's gossip is no more esteemed than yesterday's fish.

So she departed shortly, pleading a previous engagement, and went to call on Anna Rowdon.

She was informed upon her arrival that the countess had taken to her bed with a headache, a fact that did not surprise Lady Jersey. She chould well imagine Anna Rowdon's reaction to learning that she had been put aside by Lady Cowper.

"Tell her that it is Lady Jersey and that I have important news for her," she ordered the butler, who bowed and escorted her into the drawing-room to wait.

Lady Sarah joined her a minute later. "I do beg your pardon, Lady Jersey," said the girl. "My mother is dressing and will be with you soon."

Lady Jersey, whose eminence in society carried with it the right to be as bold as she liked, openly scrutinised the young woman before her. In the company of others Sarah tended to fade into the wall hangings, but on closer inspection one could not deny a certain delicate beauty.

"May I offer you some tea, or ratafia?"

Lady Jersey shook her head. "I will not be staying long." However, she did bestow herself upon a sofa, and Sarah perched timidly on a chair opposite.

The chit certainly had no conversation. She sat with her eyes cast down, as if she had forgotten anyone else were present. Whatever had Lord Broadmoor seen in her? In any case, Lady Jersey felt quite certain, as did the rest of London society, that his current flirtation with her would never lead to marriage.

Anna Rowdon joined them a few minutes later, her once-beautiful face haggard and her morning gown of amber striped silk clearly, to her visitor's discerning eye, of last year's style.

"Lady Jersey," she began. "We are delighted to see you."

Sally did not believe in roundaboutation. "I have just been informed, by the most unimpeachable source, that Sir Lindsay

Manx has eloped with Miss Kitty Williams, and I thought you would wish to be informed of it."

Lady Rowdon paled and groped about for a chair, finally sinking onto one without ever taking her eyes from Lady Jersey's face. "Eloped? Sir Lindsay?"

Sarah's expression was more difficult to read. "I wish them every happiness," was all she said.

"It is well known that he was *your* suitor," snapped Lady Jersey. "Have you nothing more to say for yourself? He has as good as broken an engagement, I believe."

"There was no betrothal," said Lady Sarah. Was the chit merely too insipid to realise that she teetered on the brink of disgrace, or was she more clever than Lady Jersey had imagined? "Sir Lindsay was free to marry whom he chose."

Lady Rowdon appeared to have recovered herself somewhat. "It is not as though my daughter lacks for suitors."

"If you are referring to the Marquess of Broadmoor, all London knows that he has been an admirer of Lady Mansfield for years." Lady Jersey rose to her feet as if to leave, but she was determined to provoke some more overt response that she could relate to her friends. "Sir Lindsay's defection appears to leave your family in an unenviable situation."

To her amazement, Lady Rowdon's mousy daughter stood abruptly and confronted her. "I must ask that you cease tormenting my mother. I hardly think the object of gathering gossip for idle tongues justifies your subjecting an ailing woman to needless pain." Sarah's light green eyes gleamed with a fury that rendered her quite formidable.

Lady Jersey stared at her speechless for a moment before replying, "You have mistaken my meaning, young woman, but I will overlook it as owing to your distressed state. I take my leave of you now, Lady Rowdon."

And off she went, back to Lady Cowper's breakfast to tell of the shock with which her news had been greeted. Yet her triumph was somewhat blunted by the nagging sensation of having been well and truly put in her place.

No sooner had the Rowdons seen her back than Anna turned on her daughter. "You should not have spoken so! All London will hear of it."

"I hope they do," said Sarah. "It was for your sake I spoke, Mother. Are you all right? I shall help you up to bed, and bring you some negus."

"Bed?" Her mother clasped one hand dramatically over her heart. "Did you not hear what she said? Sir Lindsay is gone, stolen away from you by that scheming Kitty Williams! Now you must bring the marquess up to the mark, or we shall be ruined!"

So concerned had Sarah been over her mother's reaction that the impact of Lady Jersey's news only now struck her full force. Kitty had played her false, had used her own idea of an elopement for Mary Beth to take away her suitor.

Not that she mourned for her own sake the loss of a man she could not love, but she was only too aware how slim was the possibility of Broadmoor's offering for her. With Sir Lindsay gone as well, what was to become of her family?

The abbreviated visit of Lady Jersey had not gone unnoticed by the earl, whose library window overlooked the street. He summoned the two females to his room and extracted the news from them.

"You let him get away!" To Sarah's distress, her father's wrath was turned full force on her. "Do you know to what lengths I went to secure an eligible suitor for you? Blasted fool of a girl!"

Sarah stared at him blankly. Surely she had misheard him.

"Now, Arthur." Lady Rowdon leaped into the breach. "There is still the marquess, you know, and he has expressly indicated that he wishes us to attend his ball. It is only a week away."

"He has always been a long shot," snarled her husband. "Do you think me unaware that you have been dropped by Lady Cowper? Do you think a man of his standing would wish to ally himself with a girl who has been so openly snubbed by society?"

"All is not hopeless," pleaded Lady Rowdon.

"I have done my best." Sarah felt her voice catch in her throat. "I have always done as you instructed, Father."

"Do not attempt to lay this blunder on my shoulders!" roared the earl. "You are an ungrateful wretch of a daughter. Now we are to be cast out upon the street, and all through your bungling!"

"That's not fair!" Hot tears burned at Sarah's eyes. "Four years ago I gave up the man I loved for you, at your insistence, and look what has come of it! I am not the one who bungled; it was you, both of you."

Her statement thudded dully into the silent room.

"Need I point out that it was only to ensure your future that I made the investments that have brought us to our knees?" There was something akin to pleading in her father's eyes, and it came to her that his anger stemmed from dismay at his own powerlessness.

"Oh, Mother, Father, I am sorry." Overcome by pain and love for these two people who had sacrificed so much for her, Sarah fell to her knees, sobbing. "I did not know what I was saying. It is just that I am so worried about what will become of us all. Please say that you forgive me."

Before they could reply, Henderson knocked at the door. She barely managed to scramble to her feet and avert her tear-streaked face before he entered.

"The Marquess of Broadmoor has come to take Lady Sarah driving in the park," said the butler.

═ 18 ═

FROM LADY SARAH'S red-rimmed eyes and wan countenance, Broadmoor gathered that she had already heard the news of Sir Lindsay. Did she mourn the man for himself, or merely for what he represented?

Oddly, although he should have rejoiced in her suffering, he felt a wrench of pain at her woebegone appearance.

As he handed the girl up into his phaeton, he noted how extraordinarily light she seemed. Had she lost weight in the past few weeks, or was that merely a trick of the imagination? He might have girded her waist with his two hands . . . but to think of that was to aid his own enemy.

"I take it the gossip mongers have been here before me," he said as they traversed the road to Hyde Park.

"Lady Jersey came to call." Sarah's voice sounded muffled. "I'm afraid I was rather rude to her."

"Good for you. She only came to take away word of your reaction."

"I know." Despite the necessity of keeping close rein on his spirited team, Broadmoor noted that her hands were clasped tightly in her lap. "People can be terribly cruel."

Although he himself had been the victim of cruelty from Lady Sarah, the marquess could not help wishing to speak harsh words to Sally Jersey for inflicting pain on this small, brave spirit. His reaction alarmed him, and he suppressed it ruthlessly.

"Your mother is unwell?" he asked instead. "I observed that you were not at Lady Cowper's."

"We were not invited," she said.

As ever, her blunt honesty caught him off guard. She should have made some excuse, anything but admit that her family had been snubbed. At times like this, he began to doubt the deviousness of her character.

"I find it difficult to imagine Sir Lindsay running off to Gretna Green." The marquess returned to the subject that interested him most, and watched for her reaction as they clopped through the gates and into the park.

"It was all my idea, in a way," sighed Sarah, her eyes darker than usual, no doubt from weeping.

"You can scarcely expect me to believe you proposed that your suitor run off with Miss Williams. Or was it you who were supposed to make the trip to Scotland?" He could not keep the rough edge from his voice.

"Oh, don't be difficult!" Her chin rose and she bestowed a quelling look upon him. "You know neither of those things is true. It was I who suggested that Mary Beth and Mr. Lenham elope, since her parents would not permit the match."

"Surely you cannot have wished to further a marriage between a wealthy young lady and a mere fortune hunter."

"I wished to further a match between two people in love," Sarah retorted. "The state of their pocketbooks is no concern of mine."

Again he had to stop himself from making reference to the very different attitude she had shown in regulating her own life. "So it appears your advice had unexpected repercussions."

"I do hope they will be happy." What a puzzling chit she was; one might almost have thought she meant it. Any other young woman in her situation would have been railing and wishing her successful rival ill.

"Then I gather that your heart is not exactly broken into a thousand pieces?"

"No, but if that man in the calash does not take care, my body may be broken into a thousand pieces very shortly."

Lord Broadmoor guided the horses away from the reckless calash and into the Serpentine. He was forced to nod and lift his hat to a number of acquaintances, but none being of the elite, who were all at Lady Cowper's, he was spared the necessity of engaging in conversation with them.

"What will you do now, since your suitor is run off?" he asked.

"For one thing, I am going riding with *you*." She yielded up a saucy grin. "Now what would Lady Jersey think of that? Do you know, she told us in so many words that you are going to marry Lady Mansfield."

"Lady Jersey has a loose tongue, and unfortunately neither end of it is attached to her brain." He cursed silently. The object, after all, was to build up Lady Sarah's hopes, and Lady Jersey was certainly not helping.

On the other hand, with Sir Lindsay out of the picture, where else could Sarah turn? He felt a twinge of pity for the chit. In fact, her circumstance and her appealing presence almost made him doubt the justice of his own tactics. What was the charm she exerted that nearly made him forget the wrong she had done him?

"Do you know what they are saying about you?" she went on. "It is said that you plan to make some sort of announcement at your ball, and of course everyone thinks that it concerns matrimony."

"And you think it does not?"

"I think that you are no fool, my lord," she said. "Kitty is not the only one of us who knows the uses of providing particular bits of information to a servant named Finley. You are playing at some game, unless I miss my guess."

She was straying too close to the truth. "Whether there will be an announcement or not depends on whether there is one to make," the marquess said. "I can assure you that I am not the type to play at games."

"One must draw some conclusion from the fact that you appear to be courting both me and Lady Mansfield," said Sarah. "Can it be that you do not know your own mind? Or perhaps you wish to mislead society as to your true intent. Or perhaps you wish to mislead one of us."

"That is arrant nonsense!" He cracked his whip in the air, urging the horses forward as a diversion while he collected his thoughts. She must not suspect what he was about, or all would be ruined.

"My inheritance, my high station, are all new to me," he said when the team had settled again to a steady pace. "I do not know what qualities I want in a wife, for she must assist me in both my private and my public life. I have not wished to be hasty, but neither have I much time to devote to courting, for my other duties are considerable. Yes, it is my hope to arrive at some decision by Saturday next, and make some announcement at the ball. Until my decision is made, I shall keep my own counsel."

"For all that Lord Quires and Lady Jersey pride themselves on their expertise at gossip, you are their master, for you are calling the plays and keeping your cards close to your chest," said Sarah. "Oh, pray excuse my odd turn of phrase; I fear I have borrowed my father's favourite form of speech."

"He views life as a gamble, then? Not surprising, given his proclivities." Drat the wench. The cynical talk of a gambler, issuing from her innocent little mouth, had the endearing effect of a small child parroting an adult's knowledgeable conversation. She always knew how to penetrate his defenses; it could not be purely accidental.

"Oh, Father does not gamble deep," Sarah assured him. "He does play at cards, of course; all gentlemen do that. It is only that he likes to speak that way."

It seemed impossible that she did not know the truth. And surely she could not think to fool the marquess, for he knew what all London knew about her father. Whatever did the girl intend?

A gleaming carriage, surrounded by horsemen, passed nearby, the breeze carrying the mingled voices of the men and the tinkling response of the auburn-haired beauty inside.

"Harriette Wilson!" cried Sarah. "Do you think she looks happy?"

"What an odd question," said the marquess. "I assume that she is, but it is not a matter to which I give much thought."

"There is such a great contrast between her life and those of others . . . less fortunate." Sarah's eyes took on that familiar faraway look.

"Where are you now?" he asked. "Fighting off cutthroats again?"

"Oh," she smiled wistfully, "I was thinking on an adventure that I had."

"Respectable young women are not supposed to have adventures." He remembered how, at Vauxhall, she had spoken of besting a villain as though it had really happened. "You are not beginning to believe in those daydreams of yours, I hope?"

"Perhaps I am not so extremely respectable as I ought to be," said Sarah hesitantly. "Does one not have an obligation to help others, even if it means a sacrifice on one's own part?"

A strange turn to the conversation. "I cannot say, for I suppose it would depend on the circumstance. Why, what has happened?"

"Well," she said, "it is rather a long story . . . Lord Broadmoor! Look over there! Does not that man look remarkably like Sir Lindsay?"

The marquess followed her gaze to the curricle in question. "Either that is the baronet, or he has hired someone who strongly resembles him to drive about in one of his carriages," he said, heading the horses in that direction.

It took some minutes of threading through the crowd of carriages to reach Sir Lindsay. What an interesting turn of events this was, thought the marquess. He glanced at Lady Sarah and was annoyed to see her glowing with good cheer, as if a great burden had been lifted from her shoulders. She might at least be a bit angry with her errant suitor!

"Sir Lindsay! I am so very glad to see you!" she called as they drew abreast.

"Eh? To be sure." He nodded politely to Broadmoor. "Glad to see you also."

"Do you know that Lord Quires has it you've run off to Gretna Green with Kitty Williams?" said Sarah. "You must be an excessively fast horseman, to have returned so soon."

"Gone to Gretna Green? Bother and nonsense." The baronet snorted rudely. "He's got it all turned round. It's Lenham who's gone off, with Mary Beth Williams, and in my barouche. I'd have driven them myself, but for the rain. Nothing to do with Kitty Williams."

"Quires claims he saw you himself," said Broadmoor, becoming more and more curious, for he knew of the viscount's reputation for accuracy. "Says he distinctly saw you, the two girls and Lenham going off in your carriage."

"Must have seen my coachman, wearing my beaver—the one you saw me pick up at Lock's. I gave it to him, against the rain. Would have gone myself otherwise." Sir Lindsay scratched his head. "But what the devil was Kitty Williams doing with them?"

"Chaperoning, I suppose," suggested Sarah.

"So it would appear," said the baronet. "But then, where does Quires come in?" The three of them mulled this point for some seconds as the horses walked alongside each other through the park.

"One of the Williams's maids must have told his man Finley," said Sarah.

The challenge of solving this riddle had a certain appeal to the marquess, and he was pleased with himself for being able to add, "But you say it was pouring rain. Quires would scarcely have gone himself, merely to see Mary Beth Williams run off with Mr. Lenham. I've no doubt Finley could have served as well for such a mild bit of tittle-tattle. And he couldn't have expected to see you and Kitty Williams, Sir Lindsay, for you weren't eloping."

The baronet's face slowly turned a deep purple, a fascinating process. "Oh, couldn't he? He could indeed, if someone had told him we *were* eloping."

"Kitty?" Sarah gasped at such duplicity. Either she was truly startled or an amazing actress, thought Broadmoor.

"That scheming little minx!" Sir Lindsay slammed his fist against his seat, startling the horses. "Trying to trick me into marrying her! And Quires's busybody ways would have accomplished it for her, too, were it not for the rain. Well, I've been lying low since they left, for fear of letting slip where they'd gone before the marriage could take place, but if you'll excuse me, I'm off to Lady Cowper's to set matters straight."

The two readily assented, and watched him urge his horses away.

Sarah sank back, her heart lighter than it had felt in ages. Just when she had thought all was lost, all was restored.

"You look pleased, to have your suitor back," observed the marquess, also turning his horses toward the park entrance. "If Miss Williams fancied herself your rival, I suspect that through her own folly she has succeeded in removing herself from the competition."

"Such contriving," said Lady Sarah. "How did she manage it? I could never keep it all clear. I am sure I would make a muddle of things."

"You give yourself too little credit," said the marquess.

Sarah noticed all of a sudden that birds were singing in the park and the sun was warming her shoulders and the top of her head. Removed from the brink of possible disaster, and aware as she was of the marquess sitting beside her, she felt her soul swell with happiness.

She turned to look at him hungrily, enjoying the way his eyes narrowed slightly in the sunlight, the commanding sureness with which he handled the ribbons. Perhaps it was true, what he had said about not knowing which woman he would marry. Perhaps there was still some hope for her.

"I will love Lady Sarah until the day I die," declared the marquess.

"That day is today." The villain lunged forward, but Broadmoor deftly stepped aside and dealt him a blow with the flat of his sword. The rascal lost his balance and took a header over the edge of the cliff, vanishing with a last, despairing cry.

"You have saved me!" Lady Sarah ran to Lord Broadmoor and gazed up at him adoringly. "Oh, look, your shoulder! He has cut you." Shyly, she reached out.

How firm he felt as her hand caressed the silky fabric of his jacket...

Slowly, Sarah became aware that the sensation was real. She looked up and met his eyes.

"Dreaming?" he said.

156

She nodded. "Can I pretend that I am still?" Yielding to impulse, she laid her cheek against his shoulder, jouncing against him lightly as the phaeton rolled into the street.

If only he could forgive her; but perhaps he already had. She never would have expected him to call upon her this way. She tried to ignore a voice deep within that cautioned against raising her hopes too high.

They were nearing the Rowdon house, and she withdrew to her side of the seat, feeling the freshening breeze tug at her jaunty chip straw hat. Then she remembered the hideous scene that had taken place in her father's study, and her spirits plummeted.

The marquess assisted her down without further conversation, and saw her to the door with a bow.

"I shall look forward to seeing you again soon," he said formally. "Please give my respects to Lord and Lady Rowdon."

"I shall." If only she could go away with him now, and never come back to this house full of tension and anger. But what a disloyal thought that was!

"Thank you for your company," Broadmoor added as he turned away.

"It was my pleasure."

She felt very small, watching him go. Would she really see him again, before the ball? How strange to think that her fate, all her future happiness, would be decided in the next week.

Her mother met her inside the door. "Has he gone already? He has not asked to see your father?"

"No," Sarah said, then brightened. "But it was all a hum about Sir Lindsay. We saw him in the park, and he has not run off with Kitty after all."

"The devil take Sally Jersey!"

"It was Lord Quires who erred." Sarah followed her mother to the library. "He mistook the coachman for Sir Lindsay. The baronet says he believed Kitty planned to trap him into marriage."

The matter was quickly laid before the earl, whose countenance lost some of its sullenness. "A dashed good thing, too," he muttered. "All right, gel, I'll forgive you for your cheek. But you'll have one of the two brought to heel by next week, or I'll not be so generous."

Slowly climbing the stairs to her bedchamber for a nap before dinner, Sarah wondered what it would have been like had her parents not sacrificed for her all these years, nor pinned their hopes upon her, nor loved her so much.

She thought she might have preferred it.

=== 19 ===

THE SCENE THAT ensued at Lady Cowper's breakfast following the arrival of Sir Lindsay Manx was so painful that Lord Quires cancelled all engagements for the next few days and took to his rooms, speaking to no one but Finley.

His public humiliation was not at all allayed by the look of dismay on the face of Lady Jersey, who had enjoyed a moment of triumph by regaling the gathering with the tale of how Lady Rowdon had nearly swooned away. They had both been brought low, but Quires most of all, and the fault was entirely that of the odious Miss Kitty Williams.

The viscount was sorely tempted to give up London altogether for the season and take himself off to the country, but for two considerations. The first was Sir Lindsay himself, who also laid the blame upon Miss Williams and, after an initial fit of pique, fully forgave Lord Quires.

The second consideration was Lady Mansfield.

"I would be lost without your help, Lord Quires," she confided when he summoned the courage to call upon her the following Wednesday. "I have missed your visits, and although you made an error on Saturday through no fault of your own, I do not forget how many times you have been right."

"Thank you, my lady." His admiration of her restrained demeanour and inimitable blonde beauty had not eroded one whit despite the frequency with which he found himself in her company. "Nevertheless, I believe you have a clear field with Lord Broadmoor, and there is no purpose in delaying my departure from town."

"I cannot agree with you." She offered him a plate of macaroons, and he accepted several. She turned as if to offer some to her companion, but Mrs. Buxton was clearly sound asleep in her wing chair. "Do you not recall how it was that Sir Lindsay learned of the mistake?"

Quires searched his memory. "I had not given it much thought. Broadmoor, wasn't it?"

Lady Mansfield nodded. "Out riding with Lady Sarah. He went directly to her house as soon as he heard the news."

"This leads you to believe he holds her in some affection?" said the viscount. "I rather think it merely idle curiosity."

"Curiosity perhaps, but nothing Broadmoor does is idle," she said, a slight tension about the mouth betraying her worry. "Some weeks ago, when you encountered him here, I believe the two of you made plans to dine together. Have you done so?"

"Tomorrow night, but it was my intention to cry off." Quires had delayed cancelling until the last moment, for despite his open wound at the mention of gossip, he had to concede that dinner with the marquess offered unparalleled opportunities.

"Please do not." When Lady M. fixed those earnest grey eyes on him, it was nigh impossible to refuse. "I am not so green as to think he will confide in you, but I hope some good may come of it. At least you can speak well of me. I do not suggest you speak ill of Lady Sarah, of course, although if there were some item . . . No, no, I am sure it would have come out by now, and furthermore, what can a milk-and-water miss like her have done to reflect badly on herself?"

"What, indeed?" Quires gritted his teeth, remembering the promise he had made to Lady Sarah. He would not make idle gossip of the story. But could the vouchsafing of vital information to a prospective bridegroom be called idle? "Well, I shall proceed with the dinner, at any rate, for your sake, my dear."

"I am deeply appreciative." For that soft look of gratitude, Quires thought he would have walked through fire.

So it was that he welcomed the Marquess of Broadmoor to dinner at Watier's on Thursday night, having arranged a splendid meal of tenderones of veal, broiled mushrooms and partridge, fillets of salmon with caper sauce, braised onions and carrots, salad, and, for dessert, French fruits and nougat cake.

The gentlemen discoursed upon the horses at Tattersall's, the boxing at Gentleman Jackson's, their mutual dislike of cock fights and bull baiting, and their mutual admiration for the acting of Mrs. Siddons before her retirement four years earlier.

"None like her today," said Quires, wondering how to broach the subject of Lady Sarah's questionable conduct.

"What do you think of Edmund Kean?" asked the marquess. "There are some who prefer his interpretations of Shakespeare to those of Kemble, but I am not among them."

"He is a man of great passion—off the stage as well as on, or so I am told." Quires helped himself to another glazed fruit, surreptitiously studying the man opposite him. Surely Lady Mansfield must be in error; he could not possibly prefer Lady Sarah to her.

"They say he holds a grudge against the world for the many years he spent ignored and ill paid as a traveling player," observed Lord Broadmoor.

"I did not know you were so well informed upon the subject."

"To be frank with you, I am more interested in the performances of players than in the petty doings of the *ton*," the marquess admitted. "I can well understand why Kean prefers the taverns around Drury Lane to dining at Holland House."

The viscount saw his opportunity and edged toward it gracefully. "I myself am somewhat fond of visiting the area around Covent Garden on occasion. I prefer it to the entanglements of mistress or wife."

"One does run a certain risk, however." The marquess, whose attention had been straying as he studied the other diners, returned his gaze to his companion. "One can be rather roughly treated, I understand."

"I am in the habit of patronising one particular establishment, which is glad enough of my business to make sure I am not interfered with," Quires told him. He must choose his words carefully, he knew, to avoid overstating the case and inspiring the marquess to defend Lady Sarah. "Females of delicate breeding, however, can meet with serious danger indeed."

The marquess looked at him oddly. "Surely females of good breeding do not even know such places exist."

"So I had thought." The rest was going to be easy. "You can imagine my surprise, then, when I encountered Lady Sarah Rowdon there only last week."

"Lady Sarah?" Astonishment, scrutiny, a trace of doubt.

"With her abigail, a curious sort of girl named Jennie," said Quires.

"They were perhaps making a visit of charity," suggested the marquess. "Accompanied by a footman, no doubt? Although I do think it rather peculiar of her parents to permit her to go there at all."

"I am sure they knew nothing of it." Lord Quires leaned forward, lowering his voice. "In point of fact, Broadmoor, it was in the early hours of the morning and they had come by hackney, just the two of them."

"Pardon me, but I find this difficult to credit."

"I was upstairs with a doxy when I heard a commotion on the landing and went down to investigate." Quires sat back, warming to his tale. "What did I see but Lady Sarah, all got up in that old-fashioned costume she had worn to Vauxhall, with her hair powdered and the bosom cut low, as you will recall."

The marquess was listening intently, he noted with gratification.

"She was in heated conversation with the woman who runs the establishment, Mrs. Shamford, and the rough sort of chap who works for her. The long and short of it, Broadmoor, is that Lady Sarah told me that her maid had formerly worked in that house and had persuaded her that the other girls were being held there against their will, and that she had come to give them funds and set them free."

"Why in the middle of the night?" demanded Broadmoor. "Why in secret, then, and in that strange costume?"

"So I asked, and she gave me a story about believing the costume would protect her, that it would intimidate everyone into thinking her a grand lady. Well, I cannot say I fully believed her, but I did not believe Mrs. Shamford's tale either."

Oh, how smoothly he had opened that door! Quires congratulated himself.

"What did she say?"

"Some rubbish about Lady Sarah seeking employment there, saying she needed the money. I do not credit it, of course, although the circumstances were rather odd." There, he had done it.

"Seeking employment? As a prostitute? That does sound like one of her shatter-brained ideas," said the marquess with a touch of anger.

"Surely the chit would never go so far as to carry it out," soothed Quires. "Naturally, I insisted on escorting her and her abigail home. To the best of my knowledge, they have not returned there."

He would have given a great deal to have been able to read minds at that moment, for Broadmoor quickly recovered his customary cool expression and changed the subject to other matters. A short time later they amicably parted company.

I have done my best for Lady M., thought the viscount. If Lord Broadmoor discounts this, well, the man must be top-over-tail in love.

In fact, the marquess's seeming indifference concealed a great deal of agitation.

He could not help remembering Lady Sarah's curiosity about Harriette Wilson, and her remarks on Saturday as they rode through the park. What was it she had said? "Perhaps I am not so extremely respectable as I ought to be." Yes, and she had said something else after that, about having an obligation to help others, even if it entailed a sacrifice on one's own part.

Sacrifice? Indulgence, more likely! How could he have let himself forget, for even one moment, her disgraceful behaviour at Vauxhall, pressing herself against him and returning his embrace while he remained masked and unknown to her? Then, after discovering his identity, she had blatantly attempted to seduce him.

Even so, he found it hard to imagine her in a Covent Garden hell-hole. Yet . . . Why *had* she gone there in that outrageous and almost lewd costume? She would scarcely be distributing money to doxies, when her own family stood deep in debt. It seemed unlikely she possessed any funds at all, beyond the few paltry shillings she had won at cards at Lady Mansfield's.

Then there was the matter of the statement by—what was the woman's name?—Mrs. Shamford. Had Lady Sarah gone there in all innocence, Mrs. Shamford could not have known that her family needed money, yet apparently she *had* known.

The vision of Lady Sarah, decked out like a strumpet and haggling loudly with Mrs. Shamford, did not fit the young woman he knew. But he had thought four years ago that he knew her, only to be played false.

He had been a simpleton, to let himself begin to yield again to her charms. The woman was hollow, made of sham and lies.

But there was even more to consider. If Sarah had truly lain with men for money, then she was unfit for polite company, too sunk in depravity even to cross the threshhold of his house at the ball two nights hence.

He could not ban her from the premises on so little evidence, for he knew his actions would destroy her reputation irrevocably. He must in all fairness confront her with Quires's accusation and allow her to speak for herself.

Was she clever enough to twist the facts to her own account? Lord Broadmoor thought not. He was on the alert for her tricks, and once he had confirmation for himself, he could proceed as he knew was right.

Yes, he would pay a call on Lady Sarah the next day. And he very much doubted he would ever see her again after that.

While Lord Quires and Lord Broadmoor were having dinner that Thursday night, Lady Sarah and her mother had gone to the opera. The event proved a trying one for Lady Rowdon.

She was forced to sit quietly by as that odious Kitty Williams and her cousin, the new Mrs. Lenham, paraded themselves about, boasting of their escapades en route to Gretna Green.

What made it well-nigh intolerable was the way they were lionized by the *ton*, with Lady Jersey and Lady Lieven hanging upon their every syllable. Instead of displaying outrage at the way Kitty had tricked Lord Quires and attempted to entrap Sir Lindsay, everyone thought it great sport.

Furthermore, the members of the beau monde scarcely nodded to the Rowdons and hardly anyone visited their box, with the result that for long stretches at a time Anna Rowdon was forced to pay attention to the performance.

"I should think they would be ashamed, and hide their faces!" she declared to Sarah during one interval as they observed the cousins preening in their box across the theatre. "What can Kitty's parents be thinking of?"

"I do not believe there is any real harm in her." Drat the girl's meekness! She should be angry; it was her suitor nearly lost, after all! "Merely an excess of high spirits. I must confess, Mother, that she and Sir Lindsay rub on rather well together. I have hardly anything to say to the man, and he looks dreadfully bored in my company."

"You are exactly the kind of wife he requires," corrected her mother. "As for her, well, I do not see how she can be held respectable. She is certainly two-faced, pretending all along to be your friend only so that she could cheat you of your beau."

"I hardly think it was as premeditated as all that." Why, the girl seemed almost cheerful about the whole thing! "There, look, they are leaving their box and coming this way."

"Why are you in such high spirits, may I ask? You have not had good news of the marquess? For that would be above all things, if you could bring him round. After all, he did take you riding last Saturday."

"It may be that he himself will not know whom he wishes to marry until the last possible moment," said Sarah.

"You must come up with some plan to trick him, as you did at Almack's that first night," prompted Lady Rowdon.

"I did not . . . well, never mind. Believe me, mother, if I could devise a way to win his heart, I would do so."

To Anna's surprise, Miss Williams and Mr. and Mrs. Lenham joined them a few minutes later, full of tittle-tattle and squeals of delight. Kitty assured them her part in the elopement had been all in fun, and she had never seriously intended to wed

Sir Lindsay, and Sarah responded that of course they were still friends.

Scarcely able to restrain an outburst, Lady Rowdon withdrew to the far side of their box and left the young people to chatter together.

Her temper was not at all improved by overhearing a conversation from the next box, which was occupied by two young blades.

They were boasting to each other about how much they had won at gambling, and genially insulting each others' skills at the card table. She prepared to ignore them, when she heard a mention of her husband's name and was immediately at full attention.

"It is no use playing with him," one was saying. "He cannot meet the debts already owed, let alone the thousand pounds you won from him Wednesday."

Lady Rowdon glanced fearfully at Sarah, but fortunately the girl was deep in conversation with her companions and had not heard.

"Oh, he'll get that daughter of his married off to someone or other, and then he'll make good on it." The other fellow paused to offer some snuff, then observed, "I'm to meet him again tonight. He says he'll win it all back again. What a quiz the fellow is!"

So Arthur was still gambling, although he'd promised to desist. She must endure snubs and slights, while he went on his merry way!

Despite her assurances to Sarah about Lord Broadmoor, Lady Rowdon harboured strong doubts that he would ever come up to scratch. As for Sir Lindsay, he bid fair to renew his offer, but the settlement he had proposed with the Rowdons was not so generous as to accommodate Arthur's continued gaming.

She would have it out with her husband, once and for all. If he were gambling tonight, then perhaps the confrontation must wait until the morrow, but she would not rest until he swore never to pick up a hand of cards again.

If not . . . would she ever have the strength to leave him? She thought of him as he had been when they married, handsome and loving. No, she admitted silently, she would never leave him, but tomorrow she would give him a piece of her mind.

The music began again, and their visitors took their leave. But Lady Rowdon did not hear a single note of the opera for the rest of the evening.

═ 20 ═

LADY SARAH'S APPARENT cheerfulness at the opera stemmed not from any real optimism but from a sense that the future was out of her hands, and so she might as well take what enjoyment she could from the present.

It was not lost on her that Broadmoor's ball was two nights hence, that she had last seen him Saturday, and that her chances of being chosen by him were becoming slimmer with each passing day.

On Friday afternoon, after no one at all had come to pay their respects that day, she retreated to the garden. The fragrance of the first spring roses bolstered her spirits somewhat. Surely there were roses at Sir Lindsay's country home. If not, she would see that they were planted at once.

Sir Lindsay's country home. That had a pleasant sound to it, and no doubt it would be a pleasant place, particularly when Sir Lindsay was not about.

"Mama!" The children rushed up to Lady Sarah eagerly, leaving their nanny behind. "Tell us about the adventures that you had in London! Tell us how you rescued the poor girls from slavery, and tell us about Jennie . . ."

Jennie. Would she like the quiet life in the country? No doubt she would become accustomed to it, although Sarah had noted how much her maid enjoyed lively conversation and interesting company. She frequently related tales garnered from the other servants, and had even struck up a mild sort of friendship with Quires's man Finley, who was a source of unending diversion.

Jennie also appeared to have kept current with at least one of the girls they rescued, for she had happily informed Sarah that the young woman was safely back home with her family and being courted by a young farmer.

"Lady Sarah?" Henderson, looking stiff and steadfast as ever in his black butler's garb, appeared through the French doors. "The Marquess of Broadmoor is calling. Shall I send him out, or will you see him in the drawing room?"

If they met indoors they would need a chaperone, and Sarah had no desire for her mother's company just now. "I will receive him here, if you please," she said.

"Very good, my lady."

Would she ever stop feeling so stunned at the sight of Broadmoor, at the barely restrained power of his body and the proud tilt of his head? He strode determinedly along the walk toward her, and only at the last moment did Sarah notice the fury glimmering in his eyes.

"I have a matter of extreme importance and delicacy to discuss with you." From his icy tone it was evident that the matter was not marriage.

"Please be seated." Sarah sank down upon a marble bench and the marquess unbent just enough to fit his form to a bench opposite her. "Yes?"

"I understand that you and your maid paid a visit, late at night, to an indecent establishment in the vicinity of Covent Garden, and that the proprietress thereof accused you of soliciting employment with her."

The light in the garden seemed to change, to become denser and harsher. Several birds had the bad taste to continue singing.

"You have been talking with Quires. What else did he say?" Her words sounded flat to her own ears.

"That you were got up like a strumpet in the costume you wore to Vauxhall, that you claimed to be distributing funds you could not possibly possess, that you came without footman or carriage. Is that enough, or shall I go on?"

"And from this you conclude that I have compromised myself and my family beyond redemption," she said. "I must say, I appreciate your having the courtesy to lay this manner before me in person."

"Do you not leap to your own defense?" He was watching her closely.

"Did Lord Quires also tell you that I was wearing a paste necklace that night at Lady Mansfield's card party?" Her own calmness surprised her. All her hopes, of any sort, and those of her parents rested solely on the outcome of this interview. There was a kind of serenity in coming face to face with one's doom at last.

"Paste? No. I cannot see how that signifies." Strange that she should be aware how handsome he was, in his anger.

"I am sure he noticed it." Sarah swallowed and went on. "As for where I obtained the money to distribute, I sold my jewels and had them copied. They weren't worth a great deal, but it was enough."

"Pray continue."

"You recall that night at Vauxhall, I spoke of vanquishing a villain? That was when I rescued Jennie from a man she had been sold to. I thought at first she was Mary Beth. After I had chased him off—bought him off, really—I hired her as my abigail."

He continued to sit in silence, waiting for more.

"I could not bear the thought of other girls like her, enslaved—and what else can you call it, when they have no money and not even shoes to walk away in? My parents would never have allowed me to go, had they known, so we went in secret. The dress was Jennie's idea; she was much taken with it at Vauxhall."

"What a clever wench you are," said the marquess, but his eyes remained cold. "Can you explain how Mrs. Shamford knew that your family needed money?"

"No," Sarah answered. "I'm not sure she did know. She and her ugly friend were trying to lock me up and sell me to the first gentleman who came along, for daring to interfere with their business. When it turned out that Quires knew me, she had to invent a plausible excuse. It seems that she succeeded."

She knew she had not convinced him. What a strange twist this was, that she, who had always been the mildest and shyest of creatures, had, by trying to do good, made herself appear the vilest of women! And how ironic that this man who had once loved her must believe it!

Lord Broadmoor rose. "I cannot confess myself satisfied with your explanation, Lady Sarah. You will kindly refrain from entering my house, tomorrow night or at any time in future."

She stood also, feeling a crushing weight descend upon her chest. "As you wish. I think there is no point in calling Jennie as my witness, for you will not believe her, and I am sure Mrs. Shamford would support everything Lord Quires has said."

Lord Broadmoor began to walk away, then turned back. "It goes against my nature to expose you publicly without your own admission of guilt, Lady Sarah. Will you not tell me the truth?"

"I have done so," she said. "I went to Mrs. Shamford's to help those poor wenches. I never had any intent of seeking her employ. I would kill myself before I would let myself be used in that manner."

"Then why did you inquire about Harriette Wilson?" he challenged. "You asked me twice about her, and how she came to be what she is, as if you wished to emulate her. Then at Vauxhall you fell into my arms like a wanton. What was the meaning of all that, Lady Sarah? I would like to hear how you explain that away."

"Oh." Embarrassed, Sarah kicked at the bark strewn upon the garden path. "I had an idea, you see, of how to save my family."

"Yes?"

Might as well confess all of it. "I knew you would never marry me, because of the way I had treated you, and I did not really want to marry Sir Lindsay, because I do not love him," she said. "So I thought what a perfect solution it would be if I became your mistress."

He seemed to be choking on something. "My mistress?"

"I had the rather absurd notion that you might consider setting me up and assisting my parents," said Sarah. "That was why I inquired about Harriette Wilson, as I was not and am not entirely sure what qualifications are required to succeed as a mistress.

"That, I am ashamed to admit, is why I fell into your arms at Vauxhall. It was only when I saw how you misinterpreted my actions that I realised I must have been dicked in the nob to think I could carry out such a plan."

Lord Broadmoor was regarding her with something akin to warmth, although perhaps it merely seemed so by contrast with his former hostility. "That does sound just mad enough for you to have done it," he admitted. "What a strange, puzzling chit you are, Sarah."

"I wonder now at my folly in going to Mrs. Shamford's," she said. "I could have ruined my life and that of my parents had I not run into Lord Quires, though in truth his loose tongue may have accomplished the same thing. Still, I cannot say I regret it. Jennie tells me she has heard from one of the girls and she is safely home again, out of London."

The marquess continued regarding her strangely. "Were those girls really held against their will?"

"Some of them." A thought occurred to her. "Have you ever been to one of those places?"

"Never."

She shivered. "I cannot say how it would seem from a man's point of view, but I thought it ghastly. Foul odors, filth strewn about, and . . . I could not help remembering that awful man from whom I rescued Jennie. Lord Quires should be deeply ashamed."

Broadmoor stiffened at the mention of that name. "Speaking of Quires, I am ashamed at having played so readily into his hands. The man only wants to stir up trouble so he can have something to gossip about. Lady Sarah, please allow me to apologise for my harsh words to you."

"You were only following your conscience," she said.

The marquis took her hand in his, and Sarah was conscious of nothing but the exquisite sensations shooting through her. "I beg you to forget what I said. You will not hold it against me, and stay away from my ball? It would spoil the evening for me."

"Oh, I think we shall come." She tried to keep her tone light, hoping he wouldn't notice how her heart thumped at his nearness. "My mother would sell me to the gypsies if I tried to keep her away."

His shoulder brushed hers and she turned toward him instinctively, tilting her face up like a flower toward the sun. She could scarcely breathe as he bent down and gently touched his lips to hers.

The kiss deepened, and his arms closed around her. Hungrily, Sarah clung to him, trying to show him through her embrace how much she loved him.

She lost track of the time—was it hours, or merely seconds?—until they drew apart. Not once did she have any desire to escape into a dream. No dream could possibly compare to this.

"Oh." She gazed up at him in some alarm. "I hope you did not mistake my meaning, my lord."

He blinked, as if coming out of a daze. "No, Sarah. It was not at all like Vauxhall."

Shyly, she reached out and stroked the back of his hand. He turned his hand over so that she was touching his palm, and watched intently as her fingers traced the creases in the skin, roughened from driving.

Abruptly, as though he had reached a decision, the marquess drew away. "Forgive me if I leave you now, Sarah, but there are matters I must attend to."

"Of course," she said. "I will see you tomorrow night, then."

"Tomorrow night. If I can live so long, without the sight of you." He bowed, let his eyes play over her one more time, and left.

How very lucky she had been, that he believed in her innocence. But what did this mean, that he had kissed her, and spoken so sweetly in parting?

She remembered her suspicion that he wished to humiliate her before society by engaging her affections and then throwing her over. But he could have destroyed her far more completely by exposing her supposed misdoings at Covent Garden, and instead he came to her openly and honestly for explanation.

There was no deceit in the man, and never had been. Her belief that he sought revenge was base and unworthy. Therefore his last words must also have come from the heart.

He cared for her, perhaps even loved her. Sarah hugged herself joyfully, and began to hope.

As for the marquess, walking into the house that he had once thought never to enter again, he could not but reflect how different this interview was from one that had taken place here four years before.

Then he had loved, and been rejected. Now amazingly, he loved again, and knew she would accept him.

How could he have believed that nonsense of Quires's? Lady Sarah hadn't an ounce of evil in her whole being.

Well, much as the formalities grated, this time he would do the proper thing and approach her father before he asked for Sarah's hand.

The Rowdons retained few servants, Broadmoor noticed, but he knew the house well enough to conduct himself unaided to Lord Rowdon's library.

About to knock on the closed door, he was halted by the sound of voices arguing within. They were clearly those of Sarah's parents.

As Broadmoor was debating whether he ought to retreat and come back that evening, he could not help overhearing the combatants.

"Do you think I enjoy being snubbed by Lady Cowper and patronised by the likes of Kitty Williams?" demanded the female voice. "One would think you could at least refrain from running up more debts!"

Lord Quires might enjoy prying, but Lord Broadmoor did not. He was about to make his exit when he heard Sarah's name and hesitated.

"You promised that Sarah would win over the Marquess of Broadmoor, and I was numbskull enough to believe you!" It was the earl speaking. "She should have accepted Sir Lindsay weeks ago."

"You despair too soon, husband." Did he detect a note of triumph? "She assured me only yesterday that she would use all her wiles upon him."

"Wiles?" snorted the earl. "The girl has no wiles! Half the time she moons about like an imbecile. I should like to see her show a sign of wit, even once."

"There you are wrong." The countess spoke more calmly now. "She tricked all of society, and the marquess as well. That first night at Almack's, we had planned in advance that she should faint into his arms on the dance floor. She proceeded in a slightly different manner, but all the more effective. So I have every reason to believe she can succeed again."

The marquess had heard enough. He hurried away, burning with fury. What a lying, false wench that Sarah was, and how nearly she had carried off her stratagem.

That first night at Almack's, even as he distrusted her, he had discounted the notion that she might have cast herself at him purposely, thinking it too outlandish for anyone to carry off intentionally. Now he saw how extraordinarily skilled she was, and how incredibly close she had come to triumphing.

Well, he would have the final victory. Tonight, when he was certain the earl was not home, Broadmoor would call for him, then leave word with the butler that he planned to return as soon as possible. With luck, the family would assume that preparations for the ball kept him away Saturday, but that a proposal was as good as theirs.

Then, at the ball, before the curious and unsympathetic eyes of the beau monde, he would crush Lady Sarah's hopes forever.

= **21** =

"THEN YOU GO to the country next week, Lord Quires?" Lady Mansfield already knew the answer, but she could not help hoping it might change.

"As early as I can. I must settle a few business affairs first." The viscount set down his empty glass and shook his head when she offered more wine. "Naturally, I retain enough curiosity to want to learn for myself that all has gone as anticipated: Lady Sarah's betrothal to Sir Lindsay, and yours to Lord Broadmoor."

"You do assume too much in that regard." Stella wondered why she no longer felt her former thrill at the prospect of wedding the most handsome and eligible lord in London. Perhaps I am merely weary of the uncertainty, she thought. Thank heaven all will most likely be resolved by tomorrow night, at the ball. "As I mentioned to you, I believe Lord Broadmoor cares more for Lady Sarah than is apparent."

Quires smiled mysteriously. "Do not concern yourself on that account, my dear Lady Mansfield. When he and I dined, I made mention of certain matters . . . well, I will not repeat them here, but I believe Broadmoor may have undergone a change of sentiment. We shall see."

He bowed over her hand and that of Mrs. Buxton, who awoke from one of her frequent naps to smile sweetly at him.

"Such a dear fellow," said the companion, when he had gone. "When are you going to marry him?"

"Not him. Lord Broadmoor. And do not tell me again that he is going to marry Lady Sarah, Patience, for I cannot believe your memory is as faulty as that." Stella watched out the window until Lord Quires's carriage moved away, and wished he were not quitting London so soon.

"I have almost finished." Mrs. Buxton lifted the shapeless garment she was knitting. "I hope to have it ready in time for your wedding."

"And what, pray tell, is it?" Lady Mansfield decided not to press her luck by inquiring which gentleman she was expected to marry.

"Why, a muff, of course." Mrs. Buxton picked up the needles and resumed work. "Have they got your dress ready for the ball yet?"

Her mistress paced restlessly, wondering why she did not take more pleasure in the thought of the silver gauze embroidered with acorns, over white silk. She knew it enhanced her fair colouring and combined sophistication with delicacy. "Yes, it was delivered this morning. Do you hear a carriage? Perhaps Lord Quires has come back; did he leave his gloves, do you suppose?"

She returned to the window, but it was not Lord Quires. The sight of the black and gold phaeton and its impressive occupant inspired in Lady Mansfield a burst of anxiety.

"Oh, Patience, it is the Marquess of Broadmoor," she said. "Do promise you will say nothing to embarrass me."

"I would not dream of it." Mrs. Buxton's assurance did nothing to allay Stella's nervousness.

The butler announced the visitor, and Lord Broadmoor strode into the parlour. Stella noted the rigidity with which he held himself, and the tight working of his jaw. One might think he had come to dispute with her, but on what topic?

"Mrs. Buxton, would you be so kind as to permit me a word in private with Lady Mansfield?" Such a cold voice, yet the tone and words were polite.

The companion assented, clearly perplexed, and Lady Mansfield found herself alone with the marquess. Her highly developed social skills threatened to desert her, and she had to force herself to remember to offer him a seat and some refreshment.

Instead, he lowered himself to one knee. "Please excuse my going directly to the point, Lady Mansfield, but I am here to ask if you would do me the honour of becoming my wife."

A less passionate proposal she could not imagine. Nothing in his speech or manner bespoke love or even admiration.

Why should I expect them? she demanded of herself, feeling oddly deflated. I did not require them in my first marriage.

Recognising that her thoughts were causing an awkward delay, she responded with suitable decorum, "I should be gratified to marry you, Lord Broadmoor."

He climbed to his feet. "May I request that you not make our betrothal public before tomorrow night? It is my plan to make the announcement at the ball, and I should like it to be a surprise. If that is agreeable to you, of course."

"Certainly." A surprise to whom? she wondered.

"I would like to linger in your company, but I fear my preparations for the party call me away," Broadmoor said. "Be assured I will call upon you as soon after the ball as possible so that we may complete our arrangements."

"I understand perfectly."

He took her hand and kissed the back of it in a perfunctory manner.

After he was gone, Lady Mansfield stood at the window trying to sort out her impressions of the curious scene that had just taken place.

Such a strange man he was. Why had he chosen her? There was no pretty speech about her beauty, her fine character, or any other such thing, and certainly no show of warmth.

Well, no matter. She would soon reign over society and over the much larger house in Grosvenor Square. Her husband was comely, considerate, and of high station. It was all a wife could ask.

Still, she wished the marquess had not sworn her to secrecy. She would enjoy her situation more were she able to give Lord Quires the pleasure of learning it before anyone.

The viscount, convinced that Lady Mansfield knew nothing

of what the marquess was to reveal the next night, dispatched Finley to question Lady Sarah's abigail.

The valet, arriving late in the evening, found her in the kitchen, eating a solitary meal of cold chicken and peas.

"Do you not sup with the other servants?" He helped himself to a cup of tea and joined her at the battered table.

Jennie took her time before answering, letting her gaze range over the valet. He could not be called handsome, with a nose that gave evidence of having been broken and one cheek traversed by a scar. But his face had a pleasing aspect nonetheless and his muscular body exercised a decided effect on her pulse.

"It makes them uncomfortable, knowing what I've been," she said. "Don't it bother you? No, I suppose you wouldn't say if it did, for then I mightn't talk to you, eh?"

"Don't bother me, anyway." He looked down at his tea, as if wishing for something stronger, then set the cup back on the table. "Seen a bit o' the rough and tumble in my time, afore my cousin helped me get into service. Serves me good stead, 'times, going about for his lordship."

"So what are you wanting to know now, and what are you paying?"

He grinned. "Always come right to the point, don't you, Jennie? I like that in a wench. All right. My master's wanting to know if your mistress be betrothed to Lord Broadmoor, or any hint that she might be soon. What I pay depends on how good the information is."

Jennie shook her head. She'd noticed her mistress's lift in spirits, but had no intention of passing it on. "No sign of any betrothal, I'm afraid. You off, then?"

"What's the hurry?" Finley stretched his legs before the kitchen fire, and Jennie found herself deliciously aware of the masculine scent of him. "Thought you might get lonesome for a bit o' companionship."

"Did you now?" Before she could think of a smart reply, he caught her off guard by swooping in for a kiss. It didn't last nearly long enough, but she had no intention of saying so.

"Still want me to leave?" he said. She tossed her head, giving no reply. He glanced about the room as if seeking a topic of conversation. "Right cozy place here. Too bad you'll all be out on the street soon."

"No, we won't. Sir Lindsay is coming to tea on Sunday, as I told you last time you came nosing about," she said.

"Your mistress'll be all right then, but Lord Rowdon will soon gamble away whatever he profits from the marriage."

Jennie frowned. "My lady says the problem is bad investments. What's this about gambling?"

"So it's information you want, is it?" Finley chuckled. "It's peculiar how having a pretty woman sit in my lap does loosen my tongue."

Jennie considered for all of five seconds before sliding onto his lap. "That's what you had in mind? Now what's this about gambling?"

"His lordship's notorious for it." The valet helped himself to another, longer kiss.

Rather surprised at how pleasant it felt, for she'd certainly not enjoyed her experiences with men at Mrs. Shamford's, Jennie forced herself to keep her mind on business. "You can't mean to say it's his gaming that's caused all their troubles?"

"Indeed it is." Finley's hand found its way to her thigh, exploring the shape of her leg through the heavy poplin. "Got the facts myself, but no need for it; everyone but his daughter knows what a rogue the man is. Wasted her entire inheritance and now trying to sell her off to the highest bidder. Heard him say it himself, in so many words."

Shocked as she was by these revelations, Jennie felt no haste to run upstairs and enlighten her mistress. Instead, she leaned her head against Finley's neck and allowed his questing hand to slip inside her blouse and fondle her breasts.

"Hey, then, how about we slip round the stables and have a bit o' fun?" he murmured in her ear. "Might be you miss that sort of thing, I'm thinking."

She wanted to deny it heatedly, but could not. Indeed, the sensations she was feeling at the moment bore not the slightest relation to what she had undergone at Mrs. Shamford's.

Nevertheless, she could not betray Lady Sarah's trust in her. "No. I'm done with that." She pushed his hand away and jumped to her feet. "I'm an abigail now and I must behave like one."

"Nothing but a flirt, ain't you?" To her dismay, Finley got to his feet and brushed himself off, as if wishing to be rid of the feel of her. "Might have guessed as much."

"It's not that." She reached out and touched his sleeve. "I would like to, honestly. But if my mistress ever found out, she'd be hurt. And she did save me, you know."

Finley looked her over and then nodded reluctantly. "I suppose I been a bit hasty." He reached in his pocket and pulled out a shilling, which he flipped onto the table.

Jennie bristled. "I won't take money for a bit of a cuddle. I'm not in that line any more."

"Hey, stow it. It's for the information, about Lady Sarah not being betrothed."

"Oh." She pocketed the coin. "You coming round again soon?"

"Not likely. We're off to the country next week, and won't be back until fall." Finley regarded her speculatively. "Though I could come by before we leave, if you like."

"Yes, I would like." Jennie saw no point in denying her disappointment at the news of his upcoming departure. "Yes, I would like that very much."

"All right then." Finley leaned over and claimed another kiss, boldly running his hand over one breast as he did so. "See you."

Jennie's body hummed with his touch for a long time after he was gone, making it difficult to sort out her thoughts.

So the earl was playing his own daughter false. Perhaps Lady Sarah should be told. But what would it accomplish, other than to distress her? Jennie thought.

After all, whatever the cause, the fact was that the Rowdons were in deep trouble, and Sarah would be disgraced with the rest of them unless she was married soon. Better she should be spared any more anguish than necessary.

Her decision made, Jennie went up to help her mistress prepare for bed. Nevertheless, she told herself, loyalty extended only so far. Finley was leaving London, and she intended to give him something to remember before he went.

It was amazing how the sea-green silk ball gown, fastened down the front with tiny white satin rosettes, enhanced the green of her eyes, Sarah thought. She studied herself in the mirror, watching Jennie fix a spray of baby white roses in her hair.

But it was not the dress—purchased with almost a hundred borrowed guineas, at her mother's insistence—that put the glow in her cheeks.

The marquess had not immediately gone to see the earl as Sarah had hoped he might, but he had called again in the evening and promised to return. She waited all day for further word, but no doubt some unanticipated difficulty in preparations for the ball kept Broadmoor away.

Am I being foolish to hope for so much? she asked her reflection as Jennie tortured a curl into place with the aid of an iron from the fire.

No, she answered herself silently. He all but declared himself to me, and he has called on Father. How else could his actions be interpreted?

"You do not think Broadmoor would announce our betrothal tonight, without having asked Father's permission?" she said.

"That would be cheeky, but a bit of high-handedness ain't out of place in a lord, to my way of thinking," replied Jennie. "Romantic, I'd call it."

Sarah closed her eyes for a moment, recalling the sensation of being held close yesterday in the garden. "I could do without the ball, and the money, and everything, you know," she murmured. "He's all I want."

The abigail sounded faintly sad when she said, "Yes, I do know, my lady. None of the rest matters, does it?"

At another time, Sarah might have questioned her further, but now her stomach was skipping about in anticipation and she didn't want to wait a moment longer than necessary before seeing Lord Broadmoor again.

"You've done a splendid job," she told the maid. "Please don't wait up for me, Jennie. We could be quite late."

"We'll see. And good luck, my lady."

"Thank you." Lady Sarah drew a fine Norwich shawl about her shoulders, tucked a painted vellum fan into her reticule, and stepped out for what was sure to be the most wonderful evening of her life.

22

THE HOUSE IN Grosvenor Square, long silent and echoing only with the footsteps of servants and their single master, blazed with light and music as carriages thronged before it. Footmen holding lanterns illuminated the way inside, while from the second storey wafted the strains of the orchestra.

Sarah took it all in with awe as she and her mother descended from their carriage. She could not imagine living in so grand a place. Would she really soon be mistress of it?

They were ushered into the line of guests on the staircase, waiting to be greeted at the top.

"He should have asked you to be his hostess," murmured Lady Rowdon in her daughter's ear. "It does not seem right that you should wait in line with everyone else."

"Oh, Mother!" Such talk made Sarah uncomfortable, as if it were bad luck to count too heavily on what she wanted most.

She looked about them, but none of those immediately adjacent were particular friends of hers. She saw some people studying her with open curiosity. No doubt they too had heard that an announcement was to be made.

I wish this were not all so dramatic, she thought, moving up a step as the crowd advanced. I much preferred being alone with him in the garden.

She supposed she would learn to govern such a household, and prepare such immense entertainments as this, but she would do so for his sake, not for her own vanity.

At the head of the stairs, the marquess was welcoming the guests. Sarah was able to observe him for a few minutes unnoticed. He bowed and spoke civilly to everyone with so much

184

assurance that he might have had the title for years instead of only weeks. How very fine he looked too, elegant and restrained.

"Lady Rowdon. Lady Sarah," Broadmoor greeted them. "I am delighted to see you here. Lady Sarah, will you be so kind as to save me a waltz?"

"Of course," she said.

"I fear my duties as a host preclude my showing you the attentions I would like, but be assured I take great pleasure in your presence here."

If only there were not so many people behind her, she could have gone on gazing into his deep brown eyes for hours. Instead, Sarah merely said, "The pleasure is mine, my lord," and passed along.

The ballroom was far grander than most of those she had seen, with huge candelabras, fresh cloth hangings, and bowers of potted palms.

"One cannot help noticing that the dominant colour is light green." Lady Rowdon smiled complacently. "And that of course is your best colour, Sarah."

"I scarcely think it can be intentional," she said, but the quickening of her heart told her that she hoped it was.

A gawkish young man claimed Sarah's first dance, and she was kept occupied from then on. There was also a reel with Sir Lindsay, who seemed rather distracted, but the vivacity of the dance left no opportunity for conversation.

What shall I be saying to him when he calls tomorrow afternoon? Sarah wondered. Or will he call at all, if the marquess announces . . . what?

The assembly hushed as the marquess stepped up on the orchestra platform.

"My dear friends." His voice resonated through the room. "I have taken a rather unorthodox step tonight. You have heard, perhaps, that I plan to make an announcement, but that is not quite true.

"Rather, I plan to make a request." Several gasps were heard as his lordship dropped to one knee. "Lady Sarah, will you do me the honour of becoming my wife?"

185

"Looking unusually gay tonight, my dear," commented Sir Lindsay. "Eyes sparkling and all that. Enjoying yourself, are you?"

"Immensely," said Lady Sarah.

"Good, good." But his eyes were focused elsewhere. She followed his gaze to Kitty Williams, dancing halfway across the room with what appeared to Sarah to be forced merriment.

Everyone who mattered, and many who did not, was present tonight. The ladies Lieven, Cowper, Jersey, Castlereagh, and Sefton, Mrs. Burrell, the Princess Esterhazy. Even the Prince Regent himself made a brief appearance, looking splendid but fatter than ever.

Sarah took more interest in those she knew better. There was Mary Beth Lenham, dancing with her bridegroom, their faces bright with happiness. Soon Sarah too might know such joy. She thought she would burst with anticipation.

Kitty did not look near so happy, although she was kept busy by her many partners. Not once did she dance with Sir Lindsay. Sarah had no doubt the incident of the elopement still rankled with him.

How could I have thought to marry him? she wondered. For a cold moment, she debated what she would do if the marquess did not propose, and her family's future rested on her wedding Sir Lindsay. She supposed she would have to go through with it—but surely that would not be necessary.

It was even possible that Sir Lindsay would realise by then that he was in love with Kitty, and send regrets instead of paying a call tomorrow.

Sarah pulled her thoughts from the subject and glanced about until another prominent figure caught her eye.

Lady Mansfield. The sight of her chilled Sarah slightly. Perhaps it was the silver dress, ash-blonde hair, and grey eyes that had a frosty effect. Or perhaps it was the knowledge that if anyone might take away her happiness, it was she.

It was impossible to tell from Lady Mansfield's countenance, as she gracefully performed a quadrille with Lord Quires, what she might be thinking. How did she manage to remain so unruffled in every situation? It must be tedious to live with her, Sarah thought uncharitably.

Quires himself had started to approach Sarah several times and then drawn back. He wants to know the gossip but he is afraid I will upbraid him for breaking my confidence about Mrs. Shamford's, she thought. And indeed I would.

An hour passed, seeming like an eon, before Broadmoor presented himself to claim his waltz with Lady Sarah.

"Your ball is a splendid success," she told him, quivering inside with gladness as he placed one hand on her waist and held out the other, upon which she laid her own hand. "I suppose everyone has told you that."

"It means nothing coming from anyone but you." He led her through the turns of the waltz, and she felt hundreds of eyes burning into them as they danced.

Should she mention his visit to Father, or their talk in the garden? Somehow she felt it would be presumptuous. Let him broach the topic if he wished.

"I will take great care not to fall on you this time," she said, and wondered why he started at the words.

Perhaps she had imagined it. "That gown is lovely. In that shade of green, you look entirely at home here. Do you like my decorations?"

So the colours had been chosen on purpose! "I am overwhelmed," she admitted. "What a magnificent house you have, Lord Broadmoor. Who could have imagined it, all those years ago? I'm so happy for you."

"It is I who am happy, to be able to entertain and bring enjoyment to those I care for most," he replied.

She wished he would not speak so formally. There was a remoteness about him that gave her pause. She had to remind herself that he must feel constrained by the presence of so many others, most of them watching his every move.

The dance ended, and he went to claim Lady Mansfield for a quadrille. He was keeping everyone guessing until the last possible moment, she saw.

"I do think he might pay you more attention," muttered Lady Rowdon when her daughter rejoined her. "I told Arthur he should come tonight, but no, he would go to his club. If he were here, Lord Broadmoor could have arranged a few words with him in private, but the man thinks only of himself."

"You are too harsh on Father," said Sarah. "I think he is ashamed of our ill fortune and embarrassed to be seen here before society."

But privately she too was puzzled by her father's conduct. Surely there must be some wondrous attraction at his club, or some obsession, to keep the earl occupied there for most of his waking hours.

Tired from so much dancing, Sarah retreated into the powder room, where a maid assisted in straightening the roses in her hair.

Kitty came in, her face strained until she saw that she was not alone and put on a smile. "Sarah! Everyone is dying to know what this announcement will be." She sat beside Sarah and allowed her own curls to be smoothed into place.

"I wish that I knew," said Sarah. Should she confess about Lord Broadmoor's visit? There could be no harm, now that the moment was so close at hand.

Yet something stayed her, a weasel of doubt that would not be kept at bay. Perhaps no announcement would be made that night, since Father had not yet given his permission. It would be best to bide her time.

"Everyone is sure he is going to marry Lady Mansfield." Kitty slanted a look at her. "I hope he marries you."

Kitty was not usually so generous, and Sarah regarded her in surprise. "Why, that is kind of you."

"Not kind," the other girl admitted. "Then you will not be marrying Sir Lindsay, and perhaps in time he will forgive my rashness. I did not realise then how much I cared for him."

Faced with such candour, Sarah felt a surge of compassion. "I hope that you and I may both be happy." She took Kitty's hand in hers for a moment.

Other ladies came into the room, and the two girls departed. Sarah had been on the point of telling Kitty more about the marquess, but the opportunity passed.

As the hour grew later, a tension could be felt among the assembly. It manifested itself in a growing buzz of conversation, in frequent glances at the marquess and the two ladies concerned, and in frequent mistakes and inattention among the dancers.

Sarah was becoming increasingly nervous. Kenneth had always, to her memory, had a dislike for pomp and ostentation, and his behaviour on this occasion was greatly out of character.

I wish it were all over, and we were dancing in each others' arms and gazing into each others' eyes, she thought. Who could have believed such perfect happiness was still possible for me?

It was almost time for the supper dance. Surely Broadmoor would make his announcement before choosing which woman to escort to supper. However, there was always the possibility he would keep them guessing by choosing a married lady— Sally Jersey, most likely.

Oh, he cannot put it off so long! though Sarah feverishly. She began to think perhaps she should leave without waiting. Things would, after all, be sorted out in the end. Yet she knew she could not bear to be absent, and of course, her mother would never consent.

"I am glad to see you have been popular," Lady Rowdon said in a low voice. "As for me, Lady Lieven gave me only the curtest of nods and Lady Cowper pretended not to see me at all. I cannot wait until you are raised high, and they will seek me out and fawn over me."

Sarah at the moment had very little patience with the snobberies and pettiness of any of the ladies, including her mother, and only by keeping her tongue wedged firmly against her teeth was able to prevent herself from responding sharply.

Her heart lurched as the orchestra smoothed into silence and Lord Broadmoor took the platform.

"My dear friends, it gives me great joy to welcome you to my home this evening," he said, and was greeted by applause and cries of "hear! hear!"

Oh, do get on with it, thought Sarah.

"It has come to my attention that I am expected to make some sort of announcement tonight," he said. "And I would not wish to disappoint my guests."

The room was so quiet, Sarah thought the pounding of her heart must echo like wild drums.

"Therefore I wish to present to you the woman who is to be my wife—the Baroness Mansfield."

Vaguely, Sarah realised that people around her were clapping politely, and that the icy Lady Mansfield was stepping up beside the marquess, smiling coolly at her many well-wishers.

Some part of her brain registered a low moan from Lady Rowdon beside her, and the words, "Why, that blackguard, he has done this on purpose to bring us low."

At that moment, her sole thought was that she must not collapse. She must not shame herself or her family by letting all these prying eyes know that her dreams had been shattered, once and finally. Her parent also must play this game out to the end.

"Control yourself, Mother," she said, quietly but firmly.

Sir Lindsay came to dance with her and take her to supper. So occupied was he in pretending not to notice Kitty that, thankfully, he appeared oblivious to Sarah's distress.

The rest of the evening passed in a fog, and afterward she could recall none of it except the marquess making toasts with champagne, dancing every dance with Lady Mansfield, accepting congratulations, and completely ignoring Sarah.

At last it was time to leave. They must pay their respects to their host, and for once Sarah was grateful that the cluster of people prevented any intimate exchange.

"I hope you will both be very happy," she managed to blurt, and nearly tripped in her haste to make her exit. Then, thank goodness, she and her mother were out the door and back in their carriage.

"Well," said Lady Rowdon, "at least there is still the baronet."

This thought did nothing whatsoever to cheer Sarah. The moment she returned to her room, she burst into tears that even Jennie could not stem.

The abigail, much concerned, undressed her mistress and got her ready for bed. Sarah managed to stammer out a brief account of what had happened, ending with her mother's remark.

"Oh, Jennie, I do not see how I can marry him," she gasped. "I find his touch distasteful, and further, I know him to be in love with Kitty Williams, although he will never admit it."

"Perhaps there is some other way," said Jennie, and wished she could think of one. She had come to love her young lady in their weeks together, and would have given her Finley himself had she thought that would help matters.

"No, there is no hope for it." Sarah put aside a sodden handkerchief and accepted a replacement. "For myself, I would gladly find a post as a governess, or throw myself on the charity of my mother's family, from whom we are estranged. But I cannot leave my father to be taken off to debtor's prison."

"Surely it is unjust that you should be as good as sold off, for your father's sake," said Jennie. "It is not your fault all the money has been lost."

"But he did it trying to help me." Sarah found the tears abating at last. "It was to increase my inheritance that he made so many investments. How could he know they would all go bad? Even had it not been for my sake, we are a family. When misfortune strikes any one of us, we must all help each other."

Jennie chewed on her lip, as if making a difficult decision. "Would you really be so miserable, married to Sir Lindsay?"

"I would be wretched not only for my own sake, but for knowing that I have spoiled the happiness of two innocent people, my own husband and Kitty. But I must do it, Jennie, I must." She began weeping anew.

"I think there is something you should know first, my lady," said Jennie.

=== 23 ===

Lᴏʀᴅ Bʀᴏᴀᴅᴍᴏᴏʀ Cᴏᴜʟᴅ not discern how a revenge planned with such delicious anticipation could turn out to be so flavorless.

He had delayed the announcement until the last possible moment, and it was clear from Lady Sarah's responses to him throughout the evening that her hopes had been raised.

He could tell from the buzz of voices and the glances darting to and fro that his guests also were eagerly awaiting the announcement. With proper fanfare and preparation, he had sprung it on them.

Yet there was no thrill, no climax, only a half-hearted smattering of applause before the room filled up again with ordinary chatter.

The only ones in the crowd who appeared surprised were the Rowdons. The marquess caught a flash of shock on Lady Sarah's face, which was briefly satisfying, but it was quickly replaced by an unreadable blandness.

Within minutes, congratulations were offered, partners were chosen, and the supper dance began. Sir Lindsay claimed Lady Sarah, and Lord Broadmoor found himself squiring Lady Mansfield and wondering how the devil people could go so calmly back about their business.

He wasn't sure what he had expected, but certainly more than this tepid response by society, and this rapid recovery by Lady Sarah.

She should have cried out in horror, cursed his name, fallen to her knees . . . Good heavens, he was indulging in a flight of fancy that might rival any of hers.

Lord Broadmoor looked at Lady Mansfield, who wore a fixed smile and a veiled expression as she waltzed with him. He intended to start some sort of conversation, but what was there to say?

"Do you prefer a long betrothal or a short one?" he asked.

"As you wish, my lord."

Had the woman no spirit at all? "Quires has been out of sorts this evening, wouldn't you say?" he tried again.

This time she looked directly at the marquess, and he saw he had caught her attention. Her reply, however, proved a disappointment. "Do you think so?"

He hoped she was not going to go through life in this boring manner. "Yes, he's scarcely spoken a word to anyone, which is most unlike him. Perhaps the incident of Sir Lindsay and Miss Williams has discouraged him from gossiping."

"I do hope not," said Lady Mansfield. "He is so very good at it."

At last, a topic that stirred a tiny spark. Could it be fanned into a flame? "I am surprised to hear you say that." The marquess steered their way around the Lenhams, who might have been blindfolded for all the notice they were paying to anyone else. "It was my impression that you disapproved of idle chatter."

"Of course you are right." Stella frowned ever so slightly. "I cannot think what made me say that."

Broadmoor gave up and passed the rest of the waltz in silence.

The supper was consumed amid the well-wishings of numerous acquaintances, and the remainder of the evening somehow limped to a close. The ship of his triumph, which the marquess had expected to unfurl sails of exhilaration, instead sank without a ripple.

The only moment not shaded with tedium was when Lady Sarah said good-night. He half expected a glare or a lip curled in contempt, but she remained true to her pretense. With aching sincerity she wished him happy, and stumbled as she hurried away.

It occurred to him that, could she have kept up the simulation in private life, he might have almost enjoyed being married to her. What lively conversations they had, and how she diverted him with her silly dreams and passionate concerns!

Four years of bitterness came to his aid. He could never have forgiven her, nor overlooked the fact that her only interest in him was for his money and title.

Lady Mansfield stayed on until the end, near four o'clock in the morning. Faint lines about the eyes indicated weariness, but she stood ramrod straight as she bid him good night.

"When shall I call on you?" asked Broadmoor. "Will this afternoon serve?"

"Whatever you wish," said his fiancée.

"Until then." He bowed over her hand, and tried to tell himself he would be counting the hours.

Lord Quires was departing also, and he too looked tired.

"I understand that you intend quitting London next week," said the marquess. "May we hope to see you again before the end of the season?"

"Doubtful," said his guest dully.

"I am sure the ladies of Covent Garden will miss you greatly."

"The . . . ah, yes." The viscount nodded. "Not really satisfying in the end, though, that kind of business. Well, best wishes, old chap. You're the luckiest of fellows."

Indeed I am, thought the marquess as, alone at last, he went up to bed. Everything has gone exactly as I intended.

But what the deuce was he going to talk to Stella about for the rest of his life?

"Something I should know?" In her woebegone state, Sarah was not thinking very clearly. She stared at her abigail in bewilderment.

"Yes." Jennie swallowed hard and sat on the bed beside her mistress. "A bit of information I've learned from Finley. You remember him, Lord Quires's man?"

"I remember your speaking of him." Sarah was certain there must be a point to all this, and no doubt she'd have seen it at once if she had her wits about her. "Is there something wrong with Sir Lindsay, Jennie? Are you trying to tell me he's got a wife hidden away already?"

"Oh, no, nothing wrong with Sir Lindsay." Jennie searched for the right words. "It's . . . all those debts your father has."

"Yes?"

"They're gambling debts."

This was still not making sense. "He has some gambling debts? Well, that's not surprising, in a gentleman, you know, Jennie."

"Not *some* gambling debts," said the abigail. "Lots of them. Thousands and thousands of pounds."

"Don't be absurd. He couldn't possibly. He hasn't got that kind of money to gamble; he lost it all in the investments."

"He didn't lose it in the investments." Jennie spoke slowly, patiently. "There weren't any investments, my lady. It's gambling, all of it."

"Jennie, this is foolishness. Are you trying to tell me my father lost our home in the country and is about to lose this very house because he wagers?" Sarah felt odd, as though the floor beneath her had begun to shake for no apparent reason.

"Lost both houses, and your mother's dowry, and any hope of an inheritance for you," Jennie confirmed.

Sarah sat very still, trying to sort it all out. "You mean to say that this business of my marrying well, for his and my mother's sake, is all made necessary by his vices, and he has lied to me about them?"

"I'm afraid that's right, my lady," said Jennie.

Yet another ramification occurred to Sarah. "That would mean that when he forced me to turn down Kenneth four years ago, it was to cover for his own poor character and not because of genuine misfortune."

"Must have been."

"Oh, Jennie, what nonsense. How could you possibly know this?" demanded Sarah. "It cannot be anything but vicious gossip."

"Finley swears that it is true, and you know how on the mark Lord Quires is," said Jennie.

"He was wrong about Kitty Williams."

"Yes, but this is different." Jennie leaned forward earnestly. "Finley got it all himself, and he's certain it's true. He says all London knows about it, except you."

Sarah felt the blood draining from her cheeks. "Jennie, this can't be. How humiliating, that Lord Broadmoor should think I wanted to marry him only to pay off my father's wagers. Gambling debts! That would explain why Father is always at his club."

"You see, my lady, you don't have to marry Sir Lindsay if you don't want to," said Jennie. "You don't have to throw your life away to save a father who . . . well, I won't speak ill of his lordship, Lady Sarah, but you take my point."

"There is also my mother to consider," said Sarah.

"But surely she could go to live with her own family; don't you think they would take her in, without him? She only has to cast him off."

Cast him off. What a monstrous sound it had! Sarah thought of her father, of his worried, lined face as he bent over his books, of the gentleness with which he sometimes ruffled her hair in passing.

She remembered what delight he had taken in giving her Christmas gifts as a child, and how he had told her Christmas stories before the fire. She could not imagine this man to be a foul wretch who would throw away every penny his family possessed and try to sell off his daughter so that he could go on making bets.

"I know that Finley has looked into this matter, but there must be some explanation," said Sarah. "I will go to Father myself."

"He will only deny it." Jennie sighed. "I know I'm getting above myself, my lady, talking to you this way, but it's only because I do love you and I don't want to see you spend the rest of your life unhappy."

That, thought Sarah, is inevitable anyway, with Kenneth to marry Lady Mansfield.

She pictured him again, standing on that platform with his fiancée at his side. There was no joy or love between them; that much had been evident. But he had chosen to cast his lot that way, and how could she blame him, especially after what she had just been told?

"Perhaps your concern for me has overridden your better judgement." Feeling chilled, she climbed into bed and pulled up the covers about her chin. "What everyone knows to be true may not be so at all, Jennie. I am sure your Finley would tell you that I am myself concerned only with money and position. Do you not agree?"

"Possibly," Jennie conceded reluctantly. "But tomorrow Sir Lindsay comes, and you must promise yourself to him forever. Oh, Lady Sarah, please consider what I have said!"

"Very well," said her mistress. "I will think about it tonight and let you know my decision in the morning, Jennie."

The maid departed, taking with her the branch of candles and leaving an exhausted but sleepless young woman behind in the dark.

I half wish Jennie had not spoken at all, thought Sarah, burrowing deeper into the bedclothes. Now what am I to do?

Her mind whirled with images: Kitty's sorrowful expression at the ball, Sir Lindsay's distractedness, Lady Mansfield's eternal composure, and above all Lord Broadmoor, paying Sarah formal, meaningless compliments as they danced.

She could make no sense of his conduct. On Friday he had come there in anger, then appeared to be swayed by her explanations. He had even called once to see Father. Something must have happened in the interim to change his mind, but she could not guess what it might be.

I cannot think about that now, she told herself, forcing back the tears. I must make some decision about tomorrow.

If I reject Sir Lindsay and Jennie proves to be wrong, I will forever bear the guilt of having betrayed my true and loving parents. Yet if I marry Sir Lindsay and Jennie is right, the baronet and Kitty and I all face lives ruined to no purpose.

Indeed, if Father is so confirmed in his ways as Jennie believes, he would likely only continue to wager after my marriage until he and Mother find themselves once again in dire straits, and then they will be as badly off as ever.

I cannot believe he would destroy my life for his own pleasure, thought Sarah. Not Father. And Mother, why would she lie to me? Could she love me so little as to sacrifice me for his vices?

What an irony it was that had the marquess offered for her, Sarah might never have known the truth of the matter—if it *was* the truth—nor been forced to make such an agonising decision.

She tossed about in the bed, balancing one explanation against another, one future against the other.

What it came down to in the end was that she could not throw away her family's only hope of salvation on the word of a pair of servants.

But what Finley knew, Lord Quires also knew. And the word of a viscount was a different matter altogether.

Sarah stopped thrashing. Yes, of course. She would rise early, and she and Jennie would call upon Lord Quires. Surely he could confirm or deny these rumours, and settle matters for her.

She fell asleep at last, and dreamed of a hero who rode away from her on his white horse, never hearing her cries of distress.

24

FINLEY WAS UNABLE to disguise his look of astonishment when he saw the two women at his master's door Sunday morning at ten o'clock.

"I know it is early, and we all made a late night of it," Sarah told him. "But it is urgent that I see Lord Quires immediately."

"Please wait here, and I shall inquire." The valet ushered them into the entrance hallway to the viscount's rooms. Sarah caught a quick, hungry glance exchanged between him and Jennie before he vanished to seek his master. So that was why the girl had happened to talk at such length with him.

Sarah clutched nervously at the skirts of her green cambric walking dress. It was highly improper for a lady to call upon a gentleman at his quarters. Furthermore, while her parents had been fast asleep when she and Jennie crept downstairs this morning, they might awaken at any time and raise a hue and cry over her absence.

In the end, she was forced to wait a quarter of an hour before being admitted to his lordship's breakfast room where, clad in a long dressing gown, he offered her tea and an array of dishes.

"Tea will do for me, thank you, my lord," she said, taking a seat beside the small bay window through which sunshine streamed across the table. The two servants retreated to a nook at one side, maintaining propriety and privacy simultaneously.

The viscount poured out a cup of strong tea, his lusterless expression showing none of the curiosity she would have expected.

"I apologise for intruding upon you at such an early hour," she said, "but I must have some information and you are the only person I can rely on to supply it."

"Yes?" Quires nibbled at a bit of toast.

"I wish to know whether it is true that my father has enormous gambling debts, and whether it is these debts rather than unlucky investments that have led to our financial ruin." She found herself breathless at the end, having rushed through her statement before she could lose her courage.

Lord Quires sighed. "My dear young lady, this is a matter for you to put to your parents."

"If they have not told me the truth before, they will not tell it now," said Lady Sarah.

He eyed her with reluctant admiration. "You have more spark than I gave you credit for, Lady Sarah, but that is not to the point. I cannot in good conscience interfere between a daughter and her own parents. My honour simply does not permit it."

"Your honour?" she said. "I recall a certain promise you made to me, Lord Quires, concerning an incident in Covent Garden. Where was your honour when you told Lord Broadmoor of it?"

"My promise was not to make it idle gossip," he protested. "Informing a prospective bridegroom about a lady's indiscretions can scarcely be called idle chatter."

"Lord Quires . . ."

"My mind is made up, Lady Sarah," said the viscount. "I do not dispense information on demand. It is up to me when and in whom I choose to confide."

"Oh?" she returned. "I certainly think I have earned the right to a bit of your 'news,' as you call it, having provided you with plenty through my abigail these past few weeks."

Her host stared, momentarily nonplussed.

"Are you not aware that your underhanded method of paying people's servants to learn their doings has provided me—and others, I suspect—with means to further our own ends?" she demanded.

"Oh, really, now, Lady Sarah . . ."

"What about Kitty Williams?" She would not be stopped. "That is precisely what she did, and you fell into her trap. I believe this business of an announcement at Lord Broadmoor's ball was given you by him a-purpose. And I know I have instructed Jennie to inform you of certain matters also. So do not prate to me about the inviolability of your tittle-tattle."

The shocked expression on Lord Quires's face told her she had hit the mark.

"I cannot believe . . ." He continued to stare at her. "But it is true, isn't it? About Miss Williams . . . I shall never gossip again. Never."

"Oh, yes, you shall," said Sarah. "Having meddled about in my business as much as you pleased, you at least owe me the information I seek. I will not leave until I get it."

Lord Quires gazed out the window as if hoping someone would arrive to rescue him, then dropped his shoulders in a gesture of defeat. "I have no desire to cross swords with you further. Very well. Yes, it is true about your father's gambling."

Still Sarah could not quite believe it. "How much is true?" she demanded. "Are all of the debts due to his wagers?"

"As far as I am aware, yes."

"Perhaps he began gambling after losing most of our money to poor investments, in the hope of making some recovery," she said.

The viscount shook his head. "He has gambled as long as I have known him, Lady Sarah. He went through a considerable fortune of his own before starting on your mother's dowry, and then running up debts besides."

She had thought herself prepared to hear this, but now she could not believe ill of her father. "Nevertheless, perhaps his desire to marry me off well stems more from a wish to see me comfortably settled than from the intention of improving his own position."

"You have asked for the truth and you shall have it," said Lord Quires. "In my presence, he stated that he would marry you to a savage if it would settle his debts."

She felt suddenly dizzy, and caught at the edge of the table.

"Are you unwell?" The viscount sounded genuinely concerned. "I will have Finley fetch your coachman."

"We came in a hackney," said Sarah.

"Then my carriage is at your disposal."

"Very kind, but not necessary." She sipped at her tea. "I feel steadier now. It is difficult for me to accept, Lord Quires, that my parents have so little compassion for me."

"Do not expect me to hold you entirely blameless in this business," replied Lord Quires. "You are not so artless as you pretend. I did not see precisely how it happened, but I recall you tumbling Broadmoor to the floor at Almack's, rather neatly denying him the opportunity to snub you. I cannot think such a clever move was pure chance."

Sarah knew it made no difference now whether the rest of the *ton* thought her a low schemer, but for her own dignity she wished to clear herself before Lord Quires. "In all honesty, my mother had proposed I faint into his arms, but I could not. I was doing my best to avoid him, but I have this dreadful habit of daydreaming."

"Daydreaming?"

Hot with embarrassment, Sarah admitted, "I imagine myself to be the heroine of some novel, fighting off evildoers."

"So that's why you always have your head in the clouds."

"Yes, my lord, and sometimes I act upon my fancies without intending it. I was dodging a gang of cutthroats when I lost my footing and smashed into Lord Broadmoor. I was greatly surprised when he did not chastise me."

The viscount examined the backs of his hands and did not speak for several minutes. At last he looked up. "If you are really as ingenuous as you claim, Lady Sarah, then Broadmoor has greatly wronged you. He intended public humiliation last night, did he not?"

"I suppose he did," she agreed in a small voice. "But it was not the opinions of others that I cared for. Well, I shall say no more of my feelings toward Lord Broadmoor, except to assure you that were it not for my parents I should have gladly accepted him four years ago and shared his life as a poor officer."

"You must despise him, after last night."

"No, I could never do that," said Sarah. "You see, Lord Quires, I cannot blame him for his bitterness towards me, nor for not wishing to ally himself with the daughter of a gamester. Well, I thank you most earnestly for your help."

They both stood up. He looked as though he intended to ask her what she would do next, then stopped himself. Could the viscount truly be serious about relinquishing gossip as his hobby?

Jennie came away from her corner none too eagerly, but she was smiling as Lord Quires handed them up into his carriage, which he insisted on loaning them.

"You are looking very gleeful," said Sarah. "What is it, Jennie?"

The girl could scarcely contain herself. "It's Finley. He and I are to be married! If you'll give your consent, of course."

Sarah temporarily forgot all her troubles. "Oh, Jennie, of course I will! I was worried that you might find yourself out on the street again. What glad news!"

"He is going to ask Lord Quires for his permission, and then we hope to be wed before they leave for the country." Jennie hesitated. "You will not be angry, will you, my lady? I know I am leaving at a bad time."

"Not at all," said Sarah. "If things work out as I expect, I shall be going to my aunt's as a poor relation, and I shall certainly not require an abigail."

Only when the maid lapsed into silence and she was left alone with her thoughts could Sarah face the true impact of what had transpired. She now knew that her parents had betrayed her.

The father she trusted had thrown away their money, lied to her, and tried to marry her off with no care for her happiness. The mother she loved had exposed her to public humiliation and hidden the truth from her.

Yet none of those things mattered compared to the fact that her parents, from their own selfishness, had prevented her from marrying Kenneth when he offered for her. She did not think she would ever love another man the same way.

She could still see her mother clasping her bosom and pretending—for it must have been pretense—to be near collapse. She could hear her father's voice telling her how deeply he regretted her pain but that the future of her family depended upon her marrying well.

I believed them. I would have laid down my life for them, thought Sarah bitterly. Now I am alone in the world, utterly alone.

The orphaned child crept through the winter snows, shivering inside the thin shawl . . .

Oh, do be sensible! she ordered herself. Enough of this self-pity.

The day ahead of her promised to be a long and difficult one, but she would see it through with her head high, as she had endured the torment of the previous evening.

Luck seemed to be with her. Lord and Lady Rowdon did not arise until a half hour after their daughter returned, and she was able to avoid seeing them by pretending to sleep even later than they. Henderson frowned at such goings-on, but Sarah commanded him fiercely to say nothing of the morning expedition, and he reluctantly obeyed.

She was still at her breakfast at two o'clock when Sir Lindsay came to call. Bidding Henderson bring him to her, Sarah thought how oddly reminiscent this scene was of the one this morning, except that now it was she who sat buttering a bit of toast.

"Good afternoon," she greeted the baronet. "May I offer you a cup of tea?"

He accepted with a curt nod. "Well, you know why I'm here, Lady Sarah. No sense beating about the bushes, eh?"

She poured out the tea. "A month ago, you were kind enough to propose marriage to me, Sir Lindsay, and you have been patiently awaiting my answer since that time."

"Very patiently," he grumbled.

"If it is not too rude of me, Sir Lindsay, may I inquire why you should wish to marry me?" She noted with relief that her mother was leaving the two of them alone, for this matter would have been difficult to conclude in her presence. "I do not flatter myself that I possess any rare beauty, and I certainly do not possess fortune."

"Why?" repeated the baronet. "Why should I wish to marry you? Because you are a biddable lass, Lady Sarah, a quiet, meek sort of girl who will raise my children and not interfere with my life."

"I admire your frankness." She stirred her tea, although it needed no stirring, as she summoned up her courage. "But suppose I am not so sweet and retiring as you think."

"Eh? What's that?"

"Suppose that I confronted a villain at Vauxhall Gardens and drove him off to save the girl who is now my abigail. Suppose that, hearing her tales of misery, I sold my jewellery and went with her to an evil house in Covent Garden and rescued half a dozen other such girls, and was almost cast into slavery myself."

"What bosh is this?" snorted the baronet. "I cannot believe these things, and I cannot imagine why you should say them to me."

"As for their being true, I refer you to Lord Quires, who can attest to them. It was he who rescued me at Covent Garden." Lady Sarah felt calmer, now that the worst was done. "As for my reason in telling you, it is because I know what you are too stubborn to admit: that you love Kitty Williams and will never be happy unless you are married to her."

"This is outrageous!" The baronet glared at her. "You dare to tell me my own sentiments? You dare to suggest that I marry someone else, someone who has shown by her actions that she is dishonest and untrustworthy?"

"She is guilty only of folly and self-importance, characteristics found in some of England's greatest ladies," replied Sarah. "Do you know, Sir Lindsay, that only last night at the ball she confessed to me that she is heartbroken over what has happened, and most earnestly hoped that I would wed Lord Broadmoor so that she could have you."

He opened his mouth as if to contend further, then closed it again. A puzzled look crossed the baronet's broad face. "Heartbroken?"

"She was almost in tears," said Sarah.

The wall clock ticked off another minute. "Regrets her actions, does she?"

"With all her being."

"Won't work." Sir Lindsay nodded his head as if assuring himself he was right. "Too full of herself, that girl. Wouldn't go off quietly to the country. I've no doubt she'd stay right here in town and make my life wretched."

"I agree that she would never consent to being packed off," said Sarah. "But this idea of yours about wanting a tepid sort of wife, Sir Lindsay, this came before you knew Miss Williams, did it not? I have seen how you look at her, and how melancholy you have been since your estrangement from her. I cannot help thinking you would enjoy seeing her every morning, and going about with her every evening. Is that not true?"

"Dash it, Lady Sarah, it galls me to admit it, but there's some truth to what you say," muttered the baronet. "Though I cannot for the life of me think why you should want to give me up, in view of your situation."

"That, I think, is my affair, Sir Lindsay," she said. "But I do release you from any obligation to me, if you will agree to ask Kitty to be your wife."

He shot her a startled glance. "Where did I ever get the idea you were obedient? Such a high-handed young woman I never did meet! Well, it seems I will get nowhere with you, so if Miss Williams is breaking her heart over me, I suppose I must do the gentlemanly thing and offer for her."

"Indeed," said Lady Sarah.

He bowed over her hand and departed, a new jauntiness to his walk.

She rose from the table and started for her room. She must write to her aunt in Torquay to ask permission to come and live with her.

At the foot of the stairs, Sarah encountered her mother.

"What, has Sir Lindsay left?" asked Lady Rowdon. "He did not speak to your father about the arrangements."

"There will be no arrangements, Mother." Sarah faced her squarely. "Sir Lindsay is going to marry Kitty Williams."

Anna Rowdon sagged against the banister. "He came here to tell you that? Your father will call him out!"

"Nonsense," said Sarah sharply. "There will be no need for dueling. He came to renew his offer, and I refused him and pointed out that he is really in love with Kitty and she with him. And he agreed."

"You refused him?" A succession of colours, from white to red to green, infused her mother's face. "Refused him?"

"Yes." Sarah kept her chin up. "And now I am going to my room to write to my aunt, that I am coming to live with her, if she will permit it."

"You will do no such thing." The cold fury in her father's voice caught at Sarah's throat like a black-gloved hand.

She turned to see him standing in the door of his library. "If you have chased off Sir Lindsay, my gel, I will marry you to the first man who will have you, be he a sailor with the pox or an Ethiope with a ruby in his ear."

25

BEFORE SHE COULD speak, Sarah found herself seized by the arm and jerked into her father's library. Her mother stalked in behind them and closed the door.

"You will marry Sir Lindsay if you have to run after him in the street and throw yourself on your knees in the gutter!" snapped Lord Rowdon. "Do you know to what trouble I went, to secure him in the first place?"

His grip was hurting her arm, and she stared at him with dawning horror. She stood at last face to face with the villain of her imaginings, and it was her own father.

"And I, Father, will not be consigned to a loveless marriage because you are an inveterate gamester who has no thought for anyone's happiness but his own." Sarah wondered that the heavens did not open up and lightning strike her down for her boldness, but the sky outside the window continued clear and bright.

Anna gasped. "My heart! Oh, I cannot bear this shame, that my own daughter should speak thus."

"And I, Mother, cannot bear any more of this absurd and cruel pretense," said Sarah. "All my life I have done nothing but try to please the two of you. For you I gave up the only man I will ever care for. And then, also for you, I exposed myself to public ridicule to try to win him back. I have done enough, more than enough. You created your own troubles, and you shall not sell me to the highest bidder to solve them."

Both parents glared at her. "Who has been telling you these lies?" demanded the earl.

"You know perfectly well I'm right," replied his daughter. "If not, show me the books. Show me the bad investments, the ships that sank and the farms mismanaged. Present me to your agent, who conducted this business on your behalf."

"These are not affairs to concern a mere slip of a girl," muttered Lord Rowdon.

"Does my own future not concern me?" Her hands trembled at her own daring, and she tucked them behind her back. "Can you not think of my happiness, even once?"

"How dare you speak to your father in that manner!" Her indisposition forgotten, Lady Rowdon sprang to her husband's defense. "Go and gather your things, and get out of this house. We have done our best for you, and now we see how you repay us!"

"If you insist that I leave before I can make arrangements with my aunt," responded Sarah, "I am sure there are those who would take me in. Lady Jersey, perhaps, or Lady Lieven. No doubt they would be happy to shelter me for a few days in order to learn why I have been cast out of my home."

The threat hit its mark. Her mother took a step backward, and her father looked as if he had been physically struck.

"Your mother was not serious, of course," he said hoarsely. "Naturally we would not turn out our own child."

Her mother made as if to argue, but the earl gestured her to silence.

"I thought this day would never come," he said quietly. "But now that it has, Sarah, I will not try to hide the truth any longer. Yes, I am a gamester. It is in my blood, I suppose. Even when I saw that it was destroying my family, I could not stop making wagers—or drinking, either."

"Are you going to go on this way, Father?" she asked, his gentle self-reproach reminding her that this was, after all, the parent she had loved for twenty-three years. "I wish I knew some way to help you."

"I am the only one who can help myself." He turned away to gaze out the window. "Go now, and leave me alone."

She shot a worried look at her mother, but Anna had eyes only for her husband.

She does love him, in spite of everything, thought Sarah as she watched her mother move toward the figure in the window.

Sarah let herself out of the room and went upstairs to write the letter.

"Where is that nice Lord Quires?" asked Patience Buxton for the third time.

"Must I continue to tell you that he is not expected?" Stella Mansfield's voice sounded frayed at the edges.

Indeed, Lord Broadmoor felt a bit frayed at the edges himself as he stretched his stiff legs and shifted in the wing chair. He had been in Lady Mansfield's presence for only half an hour and already they had exhausted their stock of conversation.

He would, in fact, have welcomed a visit from Quires. It would relieve the tedium, and furthermore he surely could confirm what everyone expected, that Lady Sarah had become betrothed that same day to Sir Lindsay.

Blast the chit! All morning she had danced through his dreams, with the consequence that the marquess had awakened about noon still as weary as when he went to bed.

"I take it Lord Quires has been a frequent visitor here," he observed idly.

Stella brushed an almost invisible wisp of hair back from her face. "He has made it a habit to call frequently, no doubt in hopes of learning some news. Still, one does become accustomed to knowing what is going on. I can see how some people could find gossip interesting, if they had nothing else to occupy their time."

"By the bye, how *do* you occupy your time?" Lord Broadmoor was truly curious. He could never have imagined that they would set the wedding date and location and all other relevant details within fifteen minutes of his arrival and bore each other to death for the remainder of the visit.

"Reading, embroidery, running the household," said Stella. "All the things a lady is expected to do."

A deceiver Sarah might be, but at least she never did what was expected, the marquess thought.

"There he is," said Mrs. Buxton, who was seated by the window.

"Lord Quires?" Stella's face took on an animation Lord Broadmoor had not seen before as she hastily rose and crossed to the window. "Yes, it is. Whatever can he want?"

They were soon to learn, as the butler showed in the guest and greetings were exchanged all round.

"Pardon my coming here like this," said Quires when he was settled, his face still red with exertion. "Such extraordinary developments! I had meant to give up tittle-tattle entirely, but I am making an exception today, and I did not want to keep two of my dearest friends in the dark."

Broadmoor was not certain he wished to qualify as one of the viscount's dearest friends, but he made no comment. Furthermore, he had the nagging suspicion that it was Lady Mansfield whom Quires had really come to see.

"It concerns Lady Sarah," he began.

The marquess felt a tightening in his chest. "Yes?" he urged.

"She has refused Sir Lindsay."

A momentary pause. "Why on earth?" asked Stella. "I thought her situation was desperate."

"So it is, but she refused him just the same," Quires continued gleefully. "Sir Lindsay told me so himself, at the club. He was ordering champagne all round, to celebrate."

"How odd," said Mrs. Buxton. "Is it not uncommon to celebrate having one's offer of marriage rejected?"

"I have omitted to explain." Quires smiled broadly. "He went straightaway to propose to Miss Kitty Williams, and she accepted him."

"But you have not told us why Lady Sarah would do such a thing," protested Lady Mansfield.

"She does not love him," said the viscount. "And furthermore, she knew even before he did that it was Miss Williams he loved, and told him so."

Lord Broadmoor was not certain how to take all this. The devious wench he knew would scarcely have turned down her only hope out of high-mindedness. "This has an odd ring to it," he said. "Is there more?"

"Indeed there is." Quires was almost beside himself with the joy of telling such news. "Lady Sarah came to see me this morning. Said she'd learned that her family's misfortune was due entirely to her father's gambling, and wanted me to confirm it. She'd been told some yarn about bad investments."

"Was this before she refused Sir Lindsay?" asked the marquess.

"Oh, indeed. Am I getting it too twisted in the telling?" the viscount inquired anxiously.

"I think we are following it well enough." Lady Mansfield's tone made it clear the entire matter was of no great concern to her. "Is that all?"

"No, not quite." Quires wagged his head back and forth as he tried to remember what he might have left out. "I called on Lady Sarah myself just now, after learning she'd refused Sir Lindsay, to make sure her rogue of a father hadn't taken the whip to her."

Inexplicably, the marquess felt a black rage well up in his chest and his hands form themselves into fists. "And had he?"

"Not at all. She was writing to an aunt in Torquay, asking to go and live there, but she said that after his initial anger her father was quite reasonable. Saw him myself on the way out, and his words to me were, 'Quires, you old talebearer, go and tell everyone that I will never gamble again.' No one will credit it, of course."

"Strange goings-on," muttered Mrs. Buxton.

"Strange indeed." Broadmoor was having difficulty piecing his own thoughts together. The picture Quires painted was of an innocent girl manipulated by unscrupulous parents. But it did not fit the facts. "I cannot believe Lady Sarah is as blameless as you suggest, Quires."

"Oh, that business about Mrs. Shamford's?" The viscount flushed. "I think I was mistaken, Broadmoor."

"Who is Mrs. Shamford?" Stella was looking at them expectantly.

"An . . . innkeeper of our acquaintance," said Lord Broadmoor. "No one to concern yourself with, my dear. In fact, I was not referring to that, Quires, but to another incident. Do you recall at Almack's, how she knocked me down? It was all planned out in advance; nothing accidental about it."

"If she planned it, she might have done it less awkwardly." Stella sniffed. "Waving her arms about wildly and then crashing into you. She might have done you injury."

"Well, there's a bit of irony," said Quires. "Seems her mother did have some idea of her fainting into your arms, Broadmoor, to prevent your snubbing her, but she had no intention of doing it. Then she was having some daydream about fighting off villains or whatnot and wham! she acted it out, with you as the target."

"Do you mean that that is why she always goes about looking vague?" demanded Lady Mansfield. "She is imagining herself the heroine of one of those lending-library novels? What rubbish! The girl must have a weak mind."

At that precise moment it became clear to the marquess that he could never marry Lady Mansfield.

It also became clear to him that he loved Lady Sarah, that mad, maddening, contradictory little chit with her tangle of dark hair and mesmerising green eyes. Quires's remarks, and her refusal of Sir Lindsay, made it clear that all along it had been Lady Rowdon and not her daughter who plotted and schemed.

But . . . what about her refusal, four years before?

"It may be true that she is as guileless as you say, but she was not so when I first met her," said Broadmoor. "She pretended to love me with all her heart, but refused to marry me. I realise that her parents opposed the match, but I begged her to elope, and she would not. Her parents did not need my money then, but she scorned my poverty."

Quires shrugged. "Is that so unusual, Broadmoor? What young lady would willingly consign herself to a life of scraping and saving? I am sure you make too much of this."

"No, no, his lordship is right," reproved Mrs. Buxton, much to everyone's surprise. "If she truly loved, a dreamer like Sarah would give up everything. The only possible conclusion is that there was some explanation that she dared not confide in you, Lord Broadmoor."

This was an entirely new idea and one that filled the marquess with hope. Strange what a fresh light it shed on the past. But was it true?

Before he could find out, he must deal with another, more pressing matter. "Lady Mansfield," he said. "Could I speak with you privately?"

Stella accompanied him to the morning room. Amid the fresh daisies and daffodils set out in a blue china vase, her fair beauty struck him anew. Yes, she was lovely, but he felt only admiration, without any desire of possession.

"My dear Stella," he began. "I have something very difficult to say to you."

"Why not spare us both?" she returned tightly. "Do not think me blind, Lord Broadmoor. I am well aware of your feelings for Lady Sarah. If you like, I will end our engagement. The notices have not even been sent to the papers yet, for Patience has managed to mislay them, although I fear your announcement last night may make our positions awkward."

"I am certain Lord Quires would oblige us by spreading whatever story you prefer." The marquess regretted the pain he was undoubtedly causing, yet his spirits skipped lightly about the room on a sunbeam.

"I will tell him and Patience the news myself. It would be best, I think, if you were to leave directly." Difficult to tell, from her cold smoothness, how she truly felt.

"As you wish." He bowed over her hand and departed, leaping eagerly into the seat of his phaeton and heading for the house off Clarence Square.

As for Stella's reaction, she was finding the entire incident distasteful. If only he had not blurted it to the entire assembly last night!

Feeling distinctly out of sorts, she made her way back to the drawing-room. "I have ended the engagement," she informed her guest and her cousin. "It is evident to me that Lord Broadmoor and I should not suit."

The viscount stared at her. "My dear lady, is this the result of something I have said? I certainly did not intend . . ."

Stella had reached the end of her patience. "Yes, it most certainly is the result of something you said! One would think you planned it a-purpose, coming here with these tales of poor Lady Sarah, how very put-upon she is, and how you feared her father might whip her! One might suspect you wished to stir the marquess's sympathies, for your words certainly had that effect."

"Did they?" Lord Quires's expression cleared. "Well, then, my dearest Lady Mansfield, I must make amends, and I shall."

"I do not see how you can compensate me for having driven off the most eligible man in England."

"Perhaps not," agreed the viscount. "But would you consider the substitution, though humble, of another titled lord? One who possesses wealth, although not so great as Broadmoor's, and, further, loves and treasures you so that he would never leave you, no matter what tales he heard from some nodcock of a man who goes about meddling in other people's business?"

"I . . . I am not sure I take your meaning," said Stella.

"I am asking you to do me the honour of becoming my wife," said Lord Quires. "Would you like me to kneel?"

Stella could not repress a smile. "That will not be necessary. I accept your offer, my lord."

He stepped forward and took her hands in his. "And I promise you that I have learned my lesson, and will never waste my time on gossip again."

She pretended to frown at him. "What? Now that you have accustomed me to knowing what is going on? Nonsense. I must have the very latest news every morning with my breakfast, for you are better than the *Gazette*."

He was only too happy to consent.

== 26 ==

THE BRIGHT SPRING roses, rising long stemmed and perfectly formed into the clear sunlight, filled the garden with perfume. How petty we are, with our quarrels and our loves, compared to nature's grandeur, thought Sarah, but the notion held very little comfort.

What a bizarre day it had been. First the painful morning call on Lord Quires, then the interview with Sir Lindsay—at least that had gone well, and she was relieved to hear from the viscount of Kitty and Sir Lindsay's betrothal.

Then, after the tormented confrontation with her parents had come the reconciliation, only moments before, as she sat in this very spot.

She had looked up in surprise to see her parents coming toward her. Her astonishment deepened when they explained that they also planned to leave London.

In his desperation, the earl had identified one last asset: his title. If he were to relinquish it to the next in line, an ambitious and wealthy cousin, he had reason to believe the man would clear his debts and cede him a small house in some remote part of the country.

"I will never gamble again." Lord Rowdon spoke the words heavily, as if saying goodbye to a loved one. "I see how low I have brought myself and the two people I care for most, my wife and my daughter. You will live better in Torquay than with us, Sarah, but please know that we do love you."

"And I love you," she murmured. It was true, she thought, watching them walk back to the house arm in arm. How sad that it had taken so much pain to bring them to be honest with one another.

She sat staring after them, long after they disappeared from sight. Through those same doors—was it only two days before?—the marquess had gone also. It was the last time they had spoken in privacy.

If only he would return now. What a futile dream it was, but one that bid fair to replace all her other fancies.

Into the sweet fragrance of the afternoon strode Lord Broadmoor, unannounced, his eyes searching out Lady Sarah.

Into the sweet fragrance of the afternoon strode Lord Broadmoor, unannounced, his eyes searching out Lady Sarah.

Sarah shook her head, but the tall figure moving toward her gave no sign of vanishing.

"My lord?" She looked up at him wonderingly.

The marquess sat beside her on the stone bench. "Lord Quires tells me you have refused Sir Lindsay."

"Yes." Sarah's tongue refused to exert itself further.

"He has told me other things as well. It seems I have repeatedly misinterpreted your actions." Broadmoor was gazing at her with unnerving steadiness. "Can you forgive me?"

"Oh, yes." What a perfect ninnyhammer he will think me, if that is all I can say, she scolded herself, but it did no good. A rare trembling inside threatened to make itself apparent in her voice, and so she kept still.

"There is one matter even Quires could not explain," Lord Broadmoor continued. "I confess I meant to come and tax you upon it, but now I realise I was wrong."

"What matter is that?" Sarah managed to inquire.

"Your reason for refusing me, four years ago." She started to speak, but the marquess laid a finger to her lips. "Hush. I was unreasonable, Sarah, my dearest. In my selfishness, I was willing to consign you to a life of near-poverty that would have ground down one as delicate as you. Why did I not see it myself? You were right to refuse me."

"But that was not why!" Her voice quivered but Sarah pressed on. "My parents had already lost their money, but I was forbidden to make it public knowledge, for fear of frightening away any eligible suitors. I could not marry you, and leave them penniless, yet I could not explain to you either."

His large hands enclosed her small, smooth ones. "How much grief would we have been spared had you told me of this weeks ago, when we met again."

"That would have been presumptuous!" Sarah straightened, forgetting her nervousness. "Whatever would you have thought if I had come up to you at Almack's and said, 'My dearest Kenneth, now that you are rich and important, I confess that I only rejected you because my parents had already lost their money. And now that I have explained, I am sure you will forget all the misery I caused you and demand that I become your wife.'"

A slow grin spread over the marquess's face. "Do you know that you say the most delightful things, my sweet Sarah?"

"You mean the most outrageous things, do you not?"

"I mean that whatever you say is utterly captivating and I could not be bored with you in a thousand years." To her astonishment, Lord Broadmoor knelt before her on the garden path, heedless of the damage to his perfectly creased dark blue trousers. "Will you marry me, Sarah? And I will not accept any answer that is not 'yes.'"

"But you are betrothed to Lady Mansfield!" she protested.

"Oh." A sheepish look came upon his handsome features. "I have omitted that point, have I not? I—we—that is, she—terminated the engagement half an hour ago."

"Why?" said Sarah.

"Now, look," replied the marquess. "For the past month you have flirted with me scandalously, cast me to the floor in Almack's at great expense to my dignity, tried to seduce me at Vauxhall, won five shillings from me at cards, and otherwise done your devilish best to bring me up to scratch.

"Well, you have succeeded, and here I am, in this dashed uncomfortable position—I wish I could get my hands on the man who first thought of it—and instead of agreeing to become my wife, you are interrogating me as to why my previous engagement was broken."

"Of course I will marry you, and do get up, Kenneth," said Lady Sarah, "but I wish to know why Lady Mansfield wanted rid of you. Or did she do it at your request?"

"When I confessed that I loved another, naturally she . . . Did you say you would marry me?"

Before she could reply, the marquess had resumed his seat, folded her into his arms and was bestowing a shower of kisses on her cheeks, nose, eyelids, and lips.

After a moment he lifted his head and added, "However, I do not promise to provide your parents with unlimited funds."

Sarah told him then of her father's promise and his plans. "I think it is best this way," she said. "Were they to remain in London, it would be well nigh impossible for him to keep his word."

"Do you prefer that I give them no money at all?"

She considered. "I will stay in touch with them. If they have real need of funds, I can supply them, as a personal loan, telling them I must take the money from the allowance you give me. That way, they can expect no large sums and will make no demands directly of you. It will be best for them in the long run, to live within their means."

The marquess nodded. He kept his eyes upon Sarah's face, as if he could not bear to look away for fear she might vanish.

Then Lord Broadmoor took Sarah into his arms again and kissed her long and tenderly, and she nestled against him and knew she would be happy forever.

Then Lord Broadmoor took Lady Sarah into his arms again and kissed her long and tenderly, and she nestled against him and knew she would be happy forever.

If you have enjoyed this novel and would like to receive details of other Walker Regency romances, please write to:

Regency Editor
Walker and Company
720 Fifth Avenue
New York, New York 10019